* * * * * * *

"His blood pressure is dropping."

The tone of Barbara's voice was a clear indication of the severity of the situation.

"Get the blocks," Mark ordered.

This was no time to worry about who outranked who. A man's life was in the balance. Barbara did as she was told. She bent down and picked up the blocks. Mark moved to the foot of the treatment table and lifted it up so that Barbara could place the blocks under the wheels of the table. Then Mark set the table down on them.

Barbara quickly returned to the airman's side to check his vital signs. The drop in the naval airman's blood pressure seemed to stabilize.

Mark put an oxygen mask over the airman's face and turned on the oxygen. He adjusted the mask to give the airman the maximum amount of oxygen possible. His main concern at the moment was that the airman might go into shock.

* * * * * * *

Other titles by J.E. Terrall

Western Short Stories	Western Novels
The Old West	Conflict in Elkhorn Valley
The Frontier	Lazy A Ranch
Untamed Land	(A Modern Western)
Tales From The Territory	The Story of Joshua Higgins

Romance Novels	Mystery/Suspense/Thriller
Balboa Rendezvous	I Can See Clearly
Sing for Me	The Return Home
Return to Me	The Inheritance
Forever Your	

Nick McCord Mysteries
Vol – 1 Murder at Gill's Point
Vol – 2 Death of a Flower
Vol – 3 A Dead Man's Treasure
Vol – 4 Blackjack, A Game to Die For
Vol – 5 Death on the Lakes
Vol – 6 Secrets Can Get You Killed

Peter Blackstone Mysteries	Frank Tidsdale Mysteries
Murder in the Foothills	Death by Design
Murder on the Crystal Blue	Death by Assassination
Murder of My Love	

BALBOA RENDEZVOUS

by
J. E. Terrall

Printed in the United States of America
First & Second Printing / 2008   www.lulu.com
Third Printing / 2015   www.createspace.com

Cover: designed by J.E. Terrall

Book Layout/
Formatting: J.E. Terrall
                    Custer, South Dakota

BALBOA
RENDEZVOUS

In memory of my dear friend who shared
an important part of my life, and the one
person that I will never forget, ever:
Fr. Owen B. Klapperich

FORWARD

BALBOA RENDEZVOUS is a love story that takes place in San Diego, California in 1963. It was at a time when the Vietnam War was just really getting underway for the United States. Young men from all walks of life were being drafted while others were returning from the war to be cared for in an effort to make them whole again, both physically and mentally. It was an uncertain time for all.

In 1963 the main entrance to the U.S. Naval Hospital in San Diego was located on Park Boulevard across the street from Balboa Park and just up the hill from downtown San Diego. Balboa Naval Hospital as it was called was one of the largest and busiest military hospitals in the country. Its emergency room was one of the best equipped anywhere in the world.

When the phone in the emergency room begins to ring, almost anything could happen. The emergency room was located on one of the lower levels of the six story high medical building called "The Gray Ghost". It was called that because it was a concrete building and it was gray, the color of the concrete. Most of the other buildings on the hospital compound were a Spanish style with red tile roofs and stucco exteriors. There were several 'H' shaped barrack type buildings left over from WWII and the Korean War on the base. Most of those were used to house staff while some were used to house patients that were able to get around by themselves, but still needed some care and were not ready to return to duty or be released from service.

I was a Hospital Corpsman at Balboa Naval Hospital during the time of this story. I was stationed there for the better part of my four years and four months of active duty in the U.S. Navy. During my tour of duty at Balboa, I had the opportunity to work in several departments in the hospital including, Sick Officer's Quarters/Surgery, the Burn Ward, Intensive Care Unit/Medical, the Emergency/Receiving Ward and in other areas for short periods of time.

The background of *Balboa Rendezvous* is real, but the characters are fictional. Like most of the characters in fictional novels, they are often similar or based on real people. The story is fiction, but like so many fictional stories there are a few bits of reality woven through it, like the threads in a piece of fine cloth. While each piece of thread holds the cloth together, each piece of reality gives life to the story. I will leave it up to you to decide what is reality and what is fiction.

J. E. Terrall

PROLOGUE

HOSPITAL CORPSMAN MARK WALKER had been a hospital corpsman for a number of years. He had pulled duty aboard ships where he had to handle all types of medical situations alone because many of the Navy's smaller ships, like destroyers and frigates, didn't normally have a doctor on board. In those cases, the hospital corpsman is often the entire medical staff.

Of all the different types of duty that Mark had experienced, he preferred to work in the emergency room of the naval hospital. The emergency room offered him the greatest challenges. There, he had seen all kinds of injuries and illnesses. The situation he would face this afternoon would be nothing new to him. He had seen a number of young men die while he was trying to save them.

Barbara Sanders, on the other hand, was new to the military. She had graduated from nursing school in the spring of 1963 and entered the Navy a month after graduation as an Ensign. She was immediately assigned to duty in the emergency room of Balboa Naval Hospital. Her only experience working in an emergency room had been a couple of weeks during her last year of nursing school. She was new to the type of duty she was seeing here, but she had been handling her assignment very well, so far.

Today, Miss Sanders would learn the real meaning of "emergency room nurse". For the first time, she would work with patients that were severely burned.

10

CHAPTER ONE

IT WAS AN UNUSUALLY QUIET afternoon in the summer of 1963 when the emergency room telephone began to ring. Richard Sherman, one of the Hospital Corpsman on duty, immediately answered it. He scribbled a few notes on a pad, then hung up. The receiver had no more than settled into its cradle when the sound of sirens began to filter into the emergency room.

"We have two burn cases coming in from the Naval Air Station."

Richard's announcement set the staff into action. Mark Walker, the senior Corpsman on duty, put down the file he was working on and rushed out of the nurse's station. He went directly for the burn cart and immediately began preparing for the incoming patients. Three of the other hospital corpsmen and the duty nurse took gurneys and rushed to the emergency room entrance.

Lt. Commander Wilson, the duty doctor had been called and arrived just as the two burned naval airmen were being rolled into the treatment area. The airmen were quickly transferred from the gurneys to the treatment tables.

The first airman was severely burned on the upper chest, neck and lower part of his face. He also had burns to his left shoulder and upper left arm. As Lt. Commander Wilson examined him, he began issuing orders for treatment.

"Walker, start another IV of normal saline. Keep a close watch on his vital signs. Get his clothes off and wash him down with normal saline. Cut away any charred tissue. Use moist packs where the skin has been burned away. Try to keep him from going into shock."

"Yes, sir," Mark replied and immediately began searching the airman for a good place to start the second IV.

As Lt. Commander Wilson turned his attention to the other treatment table and began examining the second airman, Barbara Sanders moved closer to the treatment table to assist Mark. Another corpsman began washing the soot and dirt from the airman's face, chin and neck while Mark cut away the airman's badly burned uniform. Barbara assisted by closely monitoring the airman's vital signs.

As Barbara watched the airman's burned uniform being cut away, she began to realize just how severely the airman was injured. She could not help but watch Mark work. The skill and efficiency Mark showed in an emergency situation impressed her. In the short time she had been working in the emergency room, she learned first hand that Mark was easier to work with if you simply let him do his job.

Mark removed the dead and contaminated tissue from the airman, then cleaned and packed the burned areas with moist sterile packs designed for burns. Miss Sanders continuously monitored the airman's vital signs, keeping Mark advised.

"His blood pressure is dropping."

The tone of Barbara's voice was a clear indication of the severity of the situation.

"Get the blocks," Mark ordered.

This was no time to worry about who outranked who. A man's life was in the balance. Barbara did as she was told. She bent down and picked up the blocks. Mark moved to the foot of the treatment table and lifted it up so that Barbara could place the blocks under the wheels of the table. Then Mark set the table down on them.

Barbara quickly returned to the airman's side to check his vital signs. The drop in the naval airman's blood pressure seemed to stabilize.

Mark put an oxygen mask over the airman's face and turned on the oxygen. He adjusted the mask to give the airman the maximum amount of oxygen possible. His main concern at the moment was that the airman might go into shock.

Mark looked over at Miss Sanders as she continued to check and recheck to make sure the airman's vital signs were remaining stable. He could see the stress and worry on her face. It was apparent to Mark that she had not had many experiences like this in her short career as a nurse.

"He seems to be stabilizing," she said, as she looked up at Mark.

There was a hint of relief in her voice, but it was clear she was still very concerned. Without any comment, Mark returned to packing the areas around the airman's neck, shoulder, arm and especially his chest where the skin had been burned away. It was important to pack the damaged areas well to prevent the airman from losing any more of his vital body fluids. If the airman continued to lose body fluids, nothing they could do would save him.

"Everything okay over there?" Lt. Commander Wilson asked without looking up from his patient.

"For the moment, sir," Barbara replied.

The tone of her voice indicated that she was not really sure of the situation, or herself. Mark looked at Miss Sanders again. The look on her face told him that things might not be going so well for the patient, or for her. He could not figure out if something was wrong with the airman's vital signs, or if she was having trouble coping with the situation. Maybe, it was a little of both.

"Everything okay?" Mark asked quietly as he looked into Miss Sanders' eyes.

She said nothing, but simply looked at Mark. Her eyes told him that she had come to the realization that the airman might not survive, something experience had already taught Mark.

The young airman opened his eyes and looked up at Ensign Sanders. It was clear that he was in a great deal of pain, even though he had been given a strong pain medication. He turned his head slightly to get a better look at her. He spoke to her, but she could not hear him.

Barbara looked from the airman to Mark, then back at the airman. Slowly, she leaned down closer to him to listen. His breathing was labored and difficult. She could hear a distinct rattling sound with each shallow breath the airman took. She held his hand in an attempt to provide him with some small measure of comfort.

"Thank - - - you," the airman whispered.

Barbara straightened up to look down at the face of the young airman. His eyebrows were singed, his face was red from the burns and most of the area about his chin and neck were covered with third degree burns. Even with the severe pain, the airman's eyes seemed to be smiling up at her.

He gently squeezed her hand. Then, slowly, the airman's grip on her hand loosened and his eyes closed. The airman gave out a long, slow exhale. With hardly a sound, the airman was gone.

Barbara couldn't move. Her eyes filled with tears as she watched the young airman slip away. As if in shock, she forgot her training and made no effort to try to revive him.

"Oh, God," she cried in an almost inaudible whisper.

"We're losing him. I need help," Mark called out.

Mark moved to the head of the treatment table, across from Miss Sanders. Lt. Commander Wilson quickly moved around to help Mark. Lt. Commander Wilson gently, but firmly, pushed Ensign Sanders aside as another hospital corpsman joined them. Mark immediately began to give external cardiac massage while the other corpsman, using an air bag, began pumping oxygen into the airman's lungs.

Lt. Commander Wilson prepared an injection of sodium bicarbonate. When the injection was ready, Mark stepped back to give him room. Lt. Commander Wilson injected the solution directly into the airman's heart.

While they worked to save the young airman's life, Barbara stood in the corner, watching. Her hands were over her mouth as tears rolled down her cheeks. She watched the frantic movements of the doctor and the hospital corpsmen as they tried to put life back into the young airman.

It soon became clear that there was nothing anyone could do to save him. He was gone. All attempts to revive him were stopped. Lt. Commander Wilson simply turned away and went back to work on the other airman.

Mark looked at Miss Sanders. She was standing against the wall. She looked pale. Her eyes were red and filled with tears. Mark had seen this happen before. Many new corpsmen and nurses were not able to deal with situations like this. Most of them learned to deal with it, but those who could not were assigned to other jobs. Miss Sanders was no different. She would have to learn to deal with it or find another job.

Mark knew what had to be done. He shut off the oxygen, removed the mask from the airman's face, then pulled the IV's out of his arms. There was nothing left for Mark to do now except to wrap the body in a sheet and take it to the morgue.

"I want her out of here," Lt. Commander Wilson said calmly, without looking up from his patient or even giving Ensign Sanders a glance.

Mark looked at her as he pulled the sheet up over the airman's face. He felt sorry for Miss Sanders as she just stood there looking at the dead airman.

"Mark, give the operating room a call. We're going to have to do emergency surgery on this one," Lt. Commander Wilson said.

Mark moved around to the other side of the treatment table. He gently took Miss Sanders by the arm and led her to the nurse's station. She gave him no resistance. He led her to a chair, and she sat down.

"You sit here for awhile, Miss Sanders. We'll talk a little later," Mark said calmly.

Barbara wanted to say something to Mark, but did not know what to say. She had failed to do her job. She felt it might help if she could explain her actions to him, but she couldn't even explain them to herself.

Mark picked up the phone and dialed the operating room. When the phone was answered, he calmly said, "We have a burned naval airman who is being prepared for emergency surgery. We will be transporting him to surgery within the next fifteen minutes, as soon as we can get him stable. Doctor Wilson will need a complete surgical staff with burn specialists."

Mark listened for a minute, then hung up the phone. After glancing over at Miss Sanders, he returned to the emergency room floor. Mark could understand what was going on inside Miss Sanders' head. He had had that same feeling of helplessness the first time he lost a patient. In fact, he still had it; but he had learned to keep it under control, and certainly not let it get in the way of what he had to do.

Mark thought Lt. Commander Wilson was a little hard on Miss Sanders. He understood as well as the Lt. Commander that no one on the emergency room staff should fall apart when they were needed the most. It was not an easy job. Not everyone was cut out for that type of work.

After all this was over, Mark would try to talk to Miss Sanders about what had happened. He would let her know that she was not the first, nor would she be the last, to give into the stress. Right now, he had to let Lt. Commander Wilson know the operating room was on alert and gearing up for the surgery.

Barbara sat in the nurse's station. She was sure that she would not be allowed to continue to work in the emergency room. As soon as her nursing supervisor found out, she would be reassigned to another ward that did not have the pressures found in the emergency room.

She looked over at the phone. Barbara knew that she should call her supervisor before Lt. Commander Wilson had the chance to report her. She reached out to pick up the phone just as Mark walked back into the nurse's station. Barbara looked up at him, tears still in her eyes. She liked Mark, liked him very much. It hurt her to know that she had disappointed him. His respect for her meant more than just about anything.

Mark could see the hurt and disappointment on her face. He was sure she felt she had let him and everyone else down. All she needed was a little more experience, a little more confidence in herself and a little more time. Mark decided that he would have a talk with Lt. Commander Wilson and see if he would give her a second chance. Maybe, bend the rules just a little and let her stay.

"Don't make any calls right now, Miss Sanders. Give me a chance to talk to Lt. Commander Wilson. He's firm, but he's also fair," Mark said.

"I don't think he will let me stay. Not now."

The depression she was feeling came across clearly in her voice. She hung up the phone to listen to Mark.

"Don't judge him too hard, and don't judge yourself too hard, either. You are not the first one to take the loss of a patient hard, and it won't be the last patient you lose. He has had others in here that did the same thing you did. He has given others a second chance. Let me talk to him."

"What makes you think he will listen to you?"

"I've worked with Lt. Commander Wilson for almost two years. He has been known to listen to me from time to time. Let me talk to him. What can it possibly hurt?"

"I don't know."

"The worst thing that can happen is you will be reassigned to another ward, and that will probably happen anyway. So what have you got to lose?"

Mark smiled in an effort to lighten things up and make everything look a little less depressing. She didn't really think he could help, but it certainly wouldn't hurt to let him try. He was right, she didn't have anything to lose.

"Nothing, I guess," she replied with just a hint of a smile.

Barbara always liked to see Mark smile, especially in the morning. His smile seemed to brighten her day and get it started off right.

"That settles it. I'll talk to him as soon as I can get a minute alone with him."

"Thank you."

Barbara did not hold any real hope that Mark could get Lt. Commander Wilson to let her stay, but she did appreciate the fact that he was willing to try. Somehow, Mark made everything seem a little brighter. She wondered if he made others feel the same way.

Mark left the nurse's station. He met Lt. Commander Wilson halfway between the treatment tables and the nurse's station, and stopped him.

"Sir, I would like to talk to you for a minute, either now, or when you get out of surgery."

"Okay, but I only have a minute. What is it?" Lt. Commander Wilson asked.

"It's about Miss Sanders."

"What about her?"

"This is the first time she has seen someone die like this. I think she will make a good emergency room nurse if she is given the chance."

"You don't waste words, do you?"

"We don't have time for that, sir."

"I guess you're right. You're pretty sure she will make a good nurse?"

"Yes, Sir. There are very few of us who have not felt the same way she does at one time or another. I would rather have someone who really cares about human life than to have some cold fish who thinks of a patient as just an object with little or no value. An object you try to fix and if you can't, the hell with it."

"I agree with you on that, but I can't have someone here who falls apart every time things turn a little sour."

"I understand that, sir. I don't think she will fall apart again. She has a good head on her shoulders. I think if you give her another chance she will do it right."

"And what makes you so sure it won't happen again?"

"I'm not sure, but my gut feeling is she will make a good emergency room nurse, given the chance."

"I like you, and you're a good corpsman; but I don't know about this. I should report her to her supervisor."

"I know you should, sir. In fact, she was just about to call her supervisor herself, but I asked her to wait until I had a chance to talk to you."

Lt. Commander Wilson looked over at the nurse's station. He could see Ensign Sanders sitting behind the desk. He realized that he had not worked with her as much as Mark. He also remembered the first patient he lost in medical school and how it had affected him. He looked back at Mark.

"Mark, I probably shouldn't do this, but I'm not going to report this incident to her supervisor. She can stay, but let me warn you. If it happens again, she will be out of here so fast she won't know what the hell happened. Do I make myself clear?" Lt. Commander Wilson asked.

"Yes, sir. Very clear, sir."

"Now call the operating room and tell them we are on our way down."

"I've already called them, sir. They are waiting for you with burn specialists on hand."

Lt. Commander Wilson just shook his head.

"That's why I like you, Mark. You're always on top of things."

Mark simply smiled, then returned to the nurse's station to tell Miss Sanders she could stay. When he walked in, he noticed she was gone. His first thought was she had gone to report the incident to her supervisor. He heard a door close and turned around to see Miss Sanders returning from the hall.

"I hope you didn't talk to your supervisor yet."

Her eyes were red and it was clear that she had been very hard on herself, probably harder on herself than anyone else. He could understand that, she wanted to work in the emergency room more than any place else.

"No, not yet," she replied softly.

"Well, don't. I had a talk with Lt. Commander Wilson. He said he would not say anything this time. He did say if it happens again, he will get you out of here so fast you won't know what happened," Mark warned her.

Barbara sat down and looked up at him.

"It won't happen again," she said with a sigh of relief.

"If you don't say anything about this, no one will ever know."

"What about the other hospital corpsmen? What will keep them from saying something?"

"They won't say anything. They're all friends of mine, and they know how much pressure this place can put on a person. I'll talk to them," Mark reassured her.

"Thank you," she said smiling up at him.

"Don't thank me too much. It's up to you to prove you should be working here. It won't be easy. Lt. Commander Wilson will be watching every move you make. One little mistake and you're gone. I'm not all that sure I did you any favors," Mark said knowing Lt. Commander Wilson meant what he said.

"Thank you anyway, Mark."

"Well, we better get back to work. We have a lot of cleaning up to do," Mark reminded her.

They returned to the floor and began helping the other hospital corpsmen clean up the treatment areas. Barbara watched Mark as he pulled each of the other hospital corpsmen, one at a time, aside and talked them. She noticed that they seemed to agree with whatever it was Mark was telling them. Mark had gone out on a limb for her, and she would not let him down.

Barbara restocked and replaced the medical supplies that had been used. She realized she not only had to prove herself to Lt. Commander Wilson, but she would have to prove herself to Mark and the others as well. It would take some time before they would all feel like they could depend on her again.

THE NEXT FEW DAYS were rather uneventful. Mark found it difficult not to be watching Miss Sanders as the routine emergencies came and went. He knew it might make her nervous if she felt he was always watching her, but after all, he had stuck his neck out for her.

The thought passed through his head that if she did well, they would be able to continue to work together. He liked being around her very much, something he had not given much thought to until recently.

Mark had just finished checking one of the supply cabinets and was walking back to the nurse's station when he noticed a young woman, about Miss Sanders' age, in the nurse's station talking with Miss Sanders. He stopped at the door.

"Excuse me, but here are the keys to the cabinet."

"Mark, come in. I would like you to meet Carol Jackson. She is one of the nurses who lives with me," Barbara said as she reached out and took the keys.

"Hi," Mark said, sort of shyly.

Because Carol was not in any kind of nurse's uniform, Mark was not sure if she was an officer or if she worked in one of the local civilian hospitals.

"Hi, Mark. Mark, we are having a little party Friday evening at our place. Would you like to come?" Carol asked.

Mark looked from Carol to Miss Sanders, then back to Carol. He didn't know just what to say. He didn't know the woman at all.

"Say you will come, please," Barbara said, hoping that he would accept the invitation.

"Well, I'm kind of busy this weekend, but I'll drop over for a little while," he replied.

"Great!" Barbara replied with a grin.

"Please excuse me, but I have some blood to run over to the lab," Mark said.

Carol and Barbara watched as Mark left for the lab.

"Nice looking guy. You Like him?" Carol asked.

"Yes," Barbara admitted shyly.

Barbara liked being around Mark. She liked talking to him and she had to admit that she did like him.

CHAPTER TWO

IT HAD BEEN HOT all Friday afternoon, but as the sun began to set a cool breeze blew in off the ocean making it more comfortable. The evening looked as if it would be pleasant.

Mark drove along the coast highway toward the beach house where the party was to be held. His little green '55 MG roadster purred along smoothly.

Mark was thinking about Miss Sanders. She seemed to be on his mind quite often lately. The past few days in the emergency room had been slow, and it had given him the opportunity to get to know her a little better. She had been working hard to prove herself, and that worried him. He wondered if maybe she was trying a little too hard.

His thoughts were interrupted when he realized that he had missed the turn. He quickly checked the traffic and made a U-turn. When he reached the beach road, he turned and started looking for the house number on the mailboxes. After driving a short distance, he saw the house number he had been given and pulled over to the curb. He shut off the motor and looked at the house.

The house was big, but it had a kind of pleasant charm, an almost welcome look to it. Although they called it a beach house, it was really a year-round home. The Spanish style gave it an elegant look. The front yard showed great care had been taken to keep it neat and well groomed.

Mark swung out of his car and walked up to the house. As he approached the door, he could hear music coming from inside. It sounded as if the party was already in full swing. He reached out and took hold of the large brass doorknocker and gave it a couple of raps. Almost immediately the door swung open.

"Hi, Mark," the tall blond said as she opened the door wide and motioned for him to enter.

"Good evening, Miss Sanders."

"None of that here. We are not on the base, nor are we in uniform. Please, call me Barbara," she said with a smile.

Mark nodded that he agreed, although he was not sure it was a good idea to start calling her by her first name since she was an officer.

"Good. You will find the bar in the kitchen and a keg down on the beach, if you prefer a beer. Feel free to help yourself to anything you like. They're about to start the fire on the beach, so it will be a little while before we eat."

"Thank you," Mark said politely.

Mark looked around as he walked past her and started toward the large glass windows at the back of the house. He looked out over the beach where a couple of men were building a fire. He could see the sun would be setting before much longer. He was sure that it would be a beautiful sunset tonight.

Mark was not ready for a drink and decided that he would look around first. If he had a chance to relax a little, he might get in the spirit of things and enjoy himself.

Barbara watched him as he walked away from her. Like many of the other nurses, she found Mark handsome with his dark brown hair and dark eyes. He stood about six foot two inches tall. He was not really muscular, but he did have broad shoulders and a narrow waist. She smiled as she thought to herself, "he has a nice rear, too".

Barbara was reasonably sure that he did not have a girlfriend. She had heard rumors that he had dated several of the nurses, but that he never developed a serious relationship with any of them. She wondered why he had not asked her for a date. Could it be because they had not known each other very long? Possibly, it was because they worked so closely together. Maybe, it was because he felt she did not know her job. After all, he had stepped in and saved it for her.

Mark stood on the deck leaning against the rail. The sun was still warm, but the breeze felt good and made him feel a little more comfortable. Although he was looking out at the great vastness of the ocean, he was thinking of Barbara.

He was not used to seeing her in civilian clothes. The light blue slacks she was wearing fit her well and accented her narrow waist and the smooth curve of her hips. The matching pullover top showed off her round firm breasts. Her short blond hair and blue eyes were the perfect match for the silky smoothness of her skin.

She was a beautiful woman. Mark had seen many beautiful women in California, but Barbara was different. She was from the mid-west, Iowa, if he remembered correctly. For some reason, that seemed to make a difference to him.

Although she was as beautiful as any woman, she still maintained that "girl next door" type of personality. She was open and friendly, yet with a touch of shyness. Mark had thought several times of asking her out, but he could not seem to bring himself around to it.

Returning from the kitchen with a tray of snacks for the table, Barbara noticed Mark was still standing at the rail on the deck looking out at the ocean. For some reason, he had not gone down to the beach with some of the others.

She set the tray down on the table and watched him. He was usually more open around others, but today he seemed distant and unusually quiet. He seemed to be somewhere else. She was sure that something must be troubling him.

"He sure is a good looking guy, isn't he?"

Barbara was startled by the question and turned to look at the woman who had come up behind her. Carol was well known for saying what was on her mind. The rather short, cute, redhead with the bouncy personality was one of

Barbara's best friends. All though they were as different as night and day, they could talk to each other about almost anything. They often discussed their most personal thoughts and feelings with each other.

"Yes. Yes, he is," Barbara replied as she looked back toward Mark.

"You know, all you have to do is walk up to him and talk to him."

"Yes. I know, but he seems so distant tonight, so far away. It's like he doesn't want to be here."

Barbara's obvious concern for Mark showed in her voice. Carol realized Barbara was more than just a little concerned. Barbara really cared about Mark, and he didn't appear to be showing any sign of interest in her. Carol wondered if Mark had eyes in his head. How could he not notice someone as beautiful as Barbara?

"Well, you'll never get to know him if you don't spend some time with him. I mean away from work and away from other people," Carol advised.

"What am I supposed to do, walk up to him and ask him for a date?" Barbara asked sarcastically.

"Well, that would be one way to break the ice," Carol admitted.

Barbara looked at Carol with a look of disgust on her face. Carol knew Barbara would never ask a guy for a date.

"Okay. It was only a suggestion. Why don't you go over and stand next to him. See if he will talk to you."

"But what happens if he doesn't say a word to me. What do I do then?"

"You could try talking to him."

It suddenly dawned on Barbara how silly she was being. She was a grown woman. How hard could it be to talk to another adult, for crying out loud?

Barbara could not figure out why it was so difficult to talk to Mark. Did she have feelings for him that she did not fully understand? Maybe she had feelings for him that she could not handle, yet. Was it possible that she more than 'liked' him? Her mind filled with questions she could not, or would not answer, at least not now.

"For God's sake, go talk to him," Carol said in disgust as she gave Barbara a gentle push toward the patio door.

As Barbara approached the doors, she set her mind. She was going to talk with Mark, even if she made a fool of herself. She would take the first step, if that was what it was going to take to get to know him.

Barbara walked through the open patio doors just as Mark turned around. He watched her walk toward him.

"Hi," Mark said softly.

The tone of his voice and his pleasant smile told her that he was glad she had come out on the patio. All her doubts and worries seemed to have been for nothing.

"Hi," she replied.

Barbara returned his smile. Mark's smile had relieved her apprehension and made her feel more at ease. She moved up next to him along the patio railing. As she leaned against the railing and looked out at the ocean, he turned back around and looked out toward the water with her. Mark was the first to break what seemed to be a very long silence between them.

"The sun setting in the ocean like this is very pretty."

"Yes, it is," she replied without even turning to look at him. "You never see a sunset like this at home."

"Where is home?" he asked as he turned and looked at her.

The gentle breeze ruffled her soft blond hair. The light from the setting sun sparkled in her hair and in the corners of her beautiful blue eyes.

She turned to look at him. His eyes told her that he really was interested in her.

"I grew up in Des Moines, Iowa. Where are you from?"

"I'm from Lincoln, Nebraska. Well, near Lincoln anyway. I grew up on a small farm outside of Lincoln. What about your family?"

"Both of my folks work for the state of Iowa. I have one brother who is going to college at the University of Iowa."

"I hate to interrupt this conversation, but the fire is ready," Carol announced. "If you don't get down there, the food will be all gone,"

"Well, I guess we better go if we want to eat," Barbara suggested.

Without even thinking, she reached out and took Mark by the hand. Mark did not resist, not even a little, but walked with her down the stairs to the beach. Her hand was small and soft, yet it seemed to have a certain strength to it.

Not far from the fire, a table had been set up. The table had all kinds of fixings on it. There was potato salad, cole-slaw, a couple of Jell-O salads setting in ice and several kinds of potato chips.

Barbara led Mark over to the table and handed him a plate. She then took one for herself.

"Help yourself to anything you would like," she said as she watched him look over all the food on the table.

"Tell you what, why don't you fill up a plate for yourself and one for me. I'll cook us a couple of hot dogs. Are hot dogs all right with you?" he asked.

"Sure."

Barbara had not expected this. She did not know him well enough to know what he liked or didn't like.

He smiled at her, picked up a couple of hot dogs, a stick to cook them on and walked over to the fire. She looked at him, then at the table and thought for a minute. Thinking that he was probably a pretty good eater, she filled a plate for him with a little of everything.

Mark sat down on a log near the fire next to a man he did not know. He put the hot dogs on the stick and held them out over the fire.

"Hi. I don't believe we've met. I'm Bill Fischer."

"Hi, Mark Walker," Mark said as he stuck out his free hand.

"What do you do? You work at Balboa Naval Hospital?" Bill asked while shaking Mark's hand.

"Yes. I work in the emergency room," Mark answered but offered no additional information.

"You work with Barbara?"

"Yes."

Bill sensed Mark's apparent uncomfortable feeling. He could understand that. After all, Mark had been asked a bunch of questions by a complete stranger.

"I've been dating Carol Jackson for about six months. I first met Barbara when she moved in with Carol."

"How many nurses live here?"

"Four in all. Janice, the tall gal over there with that big ape, Jim something or other. I can never remember his last name. Maybe that's because I don't like him."

Mark looked over in the direction Bill had indicated. The "big ape" was standing next to a rather tall, slim, very nice looking young woman. The woman seemed too young to have such a worried look on her face. Jim appeared to be very angry and was talking directly into Janice's face. She looked as if she was about to cry.

It was apparent to Bill that Mark could see that trouble was brewing between those two.

"It's a shame she is so hung up on that creep. She would be better off to dump him. One of these days I think he might hurt her."

"What makes you think that?"

Mark felt the same way, though he had no reason to believe Jim would hurt anyone. He didn't know either of them, but his gut feeling was in agreement with Bill.

"I don't know. It's just the way he acts. Even the other girls wish she would dump him. I think they're all afraid of him. He thinks that all problems can be settled with his fists.

As far as I know he has never hit any of the girls, but I heard that he beat up some girl down on the strip."

Bill was not the type to put up with a bully. And Mark had an instant dislike for Jim, too.

"I know the type. Settles everything with a fight. His kind will end up meeting someone who will not be afraid of him. Fighting is usually the only thing his kind understand," Mark said.

It bothered Mark to know there was someone like that around Barbara.

"You might be right. Anyway, Laurey's the dark-haired one over there with Lieutenant Holland A. Bishop. Holland is a hell of a nice guy. He's a fly-boy from the Naval Air Station. I think they are pretty close to tying the knot, but I don't think they have set a date, yet. She works in the maternity ward at Balboa Naval Hospital.

"I believe you know Carol. I would guess she met you at Balboa Naval hospital since you both work there."

"Yes. I met her at the hospital, but when I saw her she was not in uniform. I didn't know if she was an officer or not," Mark said with a grin.

"That's just like her. She doesn't take being an officer very serious, but she is one hell of a good nurse. I met her in the hospital. I was one of her patients for a little while."

Carol and Barbara came up behind them. They both had a plate in each hand filled with food.

"Bill, what lies have you been telling him?" Carol asked as she knelt down next to him.

"No lies," he said as he smiled at her.

"You have to watch these two every minute. They tell each other everything, and I mean everything," Bill said as he turned and looked at Mark.

Mark looked up at Barbara and smiled.

"I don't mind watching them at all," Mark said.

"I like this guy of yours, he has taste," Bill said as he winked at Barbara.

Barbara wondered if Mark really meant that he liked looking at her. It embarrassed her a little. It wasn't the fact that Mark liked to look at her that embarrassed her, but that she liked to have him look at her.

Mark interrupted her thoughts when he said, "These hot dogs are ready, shall we eat?"

"Sure," Barbara replied.

"You bet," Bill agreed.

"I'm starved," Carol said.

Mark moved over to make room on the log for Barbara to sit down next to him. She stepped over the log and sat down while Mark placed the hot dogs in buns, then put a hot dog on each plate.

"What would you like to drink?" Mark asked Barbara as he stood up.

"A beer would be fine."

"Be right back. Don't eat it all before I get back," Mark said as he smiled down at her.

"I might save you something," Barbara answered as she watched him walk toward the beer keg.

"See, I told you all you had to do was to talk to him," Carol said with a grin.

"Are you playing matchmaker again?" Bill asked.

"No, I'm not. I simply told her if she wanted to get to know Mark, all she had to do was to go up to him and talk to him. Now if that is playing matchmaker, than I guess I'm a matchmaker. Besides, she has the hots for him," Carol said with her devilish grin.

"Carol! I do not have the 'hots' for him. I - - I just like him," Barbara said a little embarrassed to admit it.

"Well, he seems like a nice guy to me."

Bill said nothing else. He didn't want to embarrass Barbara any more.

Mark returned with a beer in each hand. He stepped over the log and sat down beside Barbara. Balancing a beer on the log, he reached out for the plate Barbara held out to him. Taking the plate, he handed her the other beer. He could see that Barbara looked a little embarrassed about something.

"Say, did I miss something?" Mark asked.

"You didn't miss a thing," Barbara quickly replied.

It was obvious they were not going to let him in on it so he decided that it might be best if he just let it drop.

There was very little talk while the four of them ate their dinners. After they finished, Bill and Carol took their empty plates and glasses and walked up to the house. When Mark and Barbara had finished their meal, Barbara stacked the plates together and picked up the glasses.

"I'll take these up to the house and be right back," Barbara said as she stood up.

"I'll help the others clear the table and clean up out here," Mark replied.

"That would be nice. I'll join you back here after we get things put away."

Mark watched her as she walked to the house. As she started up the stairs, Mark joined the others in clearing the table and cleaning up. After everything was cleaned up, Mark went over to one of the logs and sat down to wait for Barbara to return.

CHAPTER THREE

THE FIRE HAD BURNED down by the time Mark had returned. There were a few bright yellow flames dancing on a few of the remaining pieces of wood, but most of the fire had reduced itself to a bright reddish-yellow glow. Every now and then a few bright yellow sparks would fly up and float up into the sky, then disappear.

Although he was looking into the fire, he was thinking about Barbara. She had a very special quality about her that made her fun to be around. She was different from the other women he had dated.

Mark was so deep in his thoughts that he did not hear Bill come up behind him. He was startled by Bill's sudden appearance.

"What are you thinking about?" Bill asked.

"Nothing special," Mark answered as casually as he could.

"Let me guess. I'll bet you were thinking about Barbara." Bill was grinning like a Cheshire cat.

Mark looked over at Bill. A smile came over his face.

"Is it that obvious?"

"Sure as hell is. I don't blame you. She's a very nice gal, and pretty, too."

"Yeah. By the way, where are the girls?"

"They're cleaning up the kitchen. The party has kind of broken up. Laurey and Janice left already. They left Carol and Barbara to clean up and put things away."

"Maybe I should go, too."

Mark didn't really want to go, but if the party was breaking up, he didn't want to wear out his welcome.

"If you go, Carol will kill me. They threw me out of the kitchen and gave me instructions to keep you here until they could join us. Don't you dare say anything to the girls, but it seems Barbara is very much interested in you and doesn't want you to go. Well, not yet, anyway. Barbara is kind of shy and a little old fashioned. She doesn't believe that the girl should chase the guy. Now Carol is not at all old fashioned," Bill said with a grin.

"Well, I guess I had better stay then."

"If you don't stay, it will be a long lonely night for me." Bill made it sound like a joke, but he was only half kidding.

"We can't have that, now, can we?"

"No. We certainly can't."

They heard the girls approaching and stood up to greet them. Carol went right up to Bill, put her arms around him and kissed him lightly on the lips.

Barbara looked from Mark to Bill and Carol, then back to Mark. She would have liked to kiss Mark like that, but she was too shy. She was not sure what Mark would think.

"Would you like to take a walk down the beach?" Mark asked.

"Sure," Barbara replied as she reached out her hand to him.

Mark took hold of her hand. They started down toward the water's edge where they turned and walked along the shore. The moon was almost full and its light sparkled on the water. The waves gently washed up on the shore with a quiet, almost subtle, little splash. It was as if the waves were trying not to disturb them.

Mark didn't say anything. He felt comfortable and relaxed walking along the shore with her hand in his. He didn't seem to know how to tell her that he liked being with her, or if he should.

Barbara was thinking about Mark. She wondered if he was really as shy as he seemed to be tonight. She could feel the strength in his hand, not that his hand was rough or that he was holding her hand too tightly, it was just a feeling she had about him.

The cool salt water of the ocean gently washed up on their feet as they walked. Suddenly, Mark stopped and looked at Barbara. She turned and stepped around in front of him. Mark reached out and put his free hand on the side of her face and gently touched the soft skin of her cheek. She looked up him.

"May I kiss you?" Mark asked nervously.

It was not like Mark to be so nervous around women. He could not remember the last time he asked a woman if he could kiss her, but it seemed to be the right thing to do.

"Yes," Barbara replied softly.

Barbara felt like a schoolgirl who was about to be kissed for the first time. A rush of feelings ran through her that she could not understand.

Slowly, Mark leaned forward. As he moved closer to her, she tipped her face up to meet him and tilted her head to one side. She closed her eyes as their lips met in a warm gentle kiss.

As their kiss ended, Barbara slowly opened her eyes. She could not explain the feelings that were deep within her. The feel of his fingers touching her on the cheek and the gentleness of his kiss made her feel strange inside. The rest of the world seemed so far away. She had often thought his kiss would be nice, but she had no idea it would have this kind of an effect on her. It seemed to take her breath away and leave her weak in the knees.

Mark looked into her eyes. Her lips had been soft and warm, and her cheek was smooth to the touch. The simple kiss and gentle touch had stirred feelings within him that he had not felt before. He had not expected a simple kiss to affect him so deeply. It brought to mind the realization that he cared very much for her, and that fact scared him a little. He had never felt this way about any woman before.

He continued to look into her eyes. It was too dark to see the deep blue of them, yet he could see the love in her eyes. He took his hand from her cheek and gently turned her around. Sliding his arm around behind her, he gently guided her to his side. She put her arm around behind him and leaned against him as they slowly walked along the shore.

They had gone some distance down the beach when they came to some rocks that jutted out into the ocean. The waves splashed against the rocks in a slow methodical rhythm. The moisture on the rocks sparkled in the moonlight making it look like a thousand little stars landing in the darkness of night. Farther away from the water, the almost black rock seemed to fade away into the weeds and on into the vast nothingness of sand and ice plants.

Walking along the rocks, Mark found a small outcropping that was dry. Turning in front of Barbara, he reached out and put his hands on her narrow waist. She put her hands on his shoulders as he gently lifted her up so she could sit on the ledge. He then jumped up on the ledge and sat down beside her, taking her hand is his. Barbara looked up at the stars in the sky as she leaned against his shoulder.

"It's pretty out tonight. It's so clear, and the stars are so bright. It reminds me of home. I used to lay on the back lawn at home and watch the stars," Barbara said thoughtfully.

"It's not much different in Nebraska. I remember what it was like to lay in my sleeping bag down by the river and watch the stars."

It was so peaceful and quiet. The only sounds were those of the waves washing against the rocks. Barbara was feeling very comfortable next to Mark. She did not have to prove anything to him here. He liked her, she could feel it, and that was all that was important.

Their peaceful moment was disturbed by a soft, almost inaudible sound that did not seem to fit in with the rest of the sounds of the night. It caught Mark's attention.

"Did you hear that?" Mark asked as he tried to listen more carefully.

"I didn't hear anything."

"Listen carefully. It seems to be coming from over there, near where the rocks and the weeds come together."

They both listened very carefully for almost a full minute before the sound was heard again.

"It sounds a little like a puppy that might be lost," Barbara suggested.

Barbara thought it sounded kind of like a puppy, but yet it didn't. Mark was not sure.

"I don't think so. It sounds more like a human crying. Come on, we better check it out. Someone might be hurt."

Mark jumped down off the rock, turned and helped Barbara down. He took her hand and they started moving toward the place where the sound seemed to be coming from. Even with the full moon, it was very hard to see anything in the darkness. They moved closer, straining their eyes to see what was there. Suddenly, Mark spotted a white tennis shoe.

"Over here," he said as he let go of Barbara's hand and ran on ahead of her.

There, in the weeds, lay a woman face down. He knelt down beside the woman. She was sobbing uncontrollably. Mark immediately noticed the woman's blouse was torn nearly off. Even in the darkness, he could see the dark stains of blood on the side of her head. He noticed dark stains on her side and on her left leg.

"Oh, my God, it's Janice!" Barbara cried out as she put her hands over her mouth in shock.

Mark had seen Barbara act this way once before, in the emergency room, but this time Barbara quickly got control of herself. She knelt down beside her friend and started checking her friend's pulse.

"Barbara, go call for an ambulance and the police," Mark instructed her.

Mark made every effort to keep a calm tone to his voice. He needed Barbara's help right now and needed her to remain calm, too. He had to ask himself if he was still afraid that she would do the same thing she had done in the emergency room a couple of days ago. Why did he think of that now? After all, she was right beside him, trying to help her friend.

Barbara looked at Mark. His instructions seemed like military orders. Was he dismissing her to do the only job he felt she could do, or was it just the way he acted in an emergency? She felt that he was still afraid she might fall apart. It hurt her to even think that he might still feel that way about her. She had been trying so hard to prove herself to him that it did not cross her mind that it was the only thing they could do for her friend right now.

As Mark took off his shirt to cover Janice, he looked up at Barbara and saw the hurt in her eyes. He wanted to say something to make her understand, but before he could say anything she turned and began running back toward the house.

"Damn," he thought to himself. He had been afraid that the first time he told her what to do, she would take it as a lack of trust in her ability. There was no time to worry about it now. He had to do what he could for Janice, which was very little. He had no equipment and very little light to see the extent of her injuries.

Mark carefully laid his shirt over her. He checked her pulse and counted her respirations. Her pulse seemed a little rapid, but under the circumstances it was to be expected. Her respirations were labored. She was taking short shallow breaths, which seemed to hurt her. There was a very strong possibility she has some broken or bruised ribs.

"Janice, it's me, Mark, Mark Walker. Can you talk to me?" he asked.

"Yes," she said between sobs and shallow breaths.

"Where do you hurt?"

"My chest, - - - arm - - and leg. I - - may - - have - - some ribs - broken. I think - - my - - left- - arm is - - broken. My - - left - - leg - - hurts - - real bad, too."

"Relax as best you can, help is on the way," Mark said.

It was unwise to move her for fear of causing more injury to her, like puncturing a lung if her ribs were broken. There was little he could do except keep her as calm and as comfortable as possible until the ambulance arrived.

BILL AND CAROL WERE sitting by the fire when they saw Barbara running toward the house. At first, they didn't think anything of it. When they realized that Mark was not with her, Carol became concerned.

"Something's wrong. I better go see what happened," Carol said as she stood up and started running toward the house.

"I'll go down the beach and see if I can find Mark," Bill called out to her.

Bill stood up and watched Carol run toward the house. He then turned and ran down the beach in the direction Barbara had come. He had no idea what he would find, but he felt that he might be needed.

Carol entered the house and saw Barbara was already on the phone. She overheard only a part of the conversation.

"We are unsure of the injuries at this time, but we will need an ambulance, and please send the police," Barbara was saying into the receiver.

She hung up the phone and looked up at Carol.

"What's going on?" Carol asked.

Her first thought was something had happened to Mark.

"Janice has been hurt. She's down at the end of the beach by the rocks. Mark is with her now."

"What happened? Did she fall in the rocks?"

"No. I don't think so. We don't know what happened, but she didn't fall. I think Jim is responsible for this."

The tone of her voice showed the anger she was feeling.

"What makes you think so?" Carol asked even though she felt that Jim was capable of hurting someone, even a woman.

"Janice's injuries are too severe to have been caused by a fall on the rocks," Barbara explained.

"What do you want me to do to help?"

"One of us had better wait here for the ambulance," Barbara said as she stood up and started for the door, but she stopped suddenly and turned toward Carol.

"Go ahead," Carol said. "I'll wait for the ambulance. You go help Mark."

"No, I better wait. I know right where Janice is. You go on ahead and see if Mark needs any help."

Barbara's suggestion made some small measure of sense, but how difficult could it be to find the end of the beach where the rocks run out into the ocean? They had all been out there numerous times. Carol quickly realized this was not the time to argue about who was going to help Mark. Mark might need some help and it was clear that Barbara was not going to be the one to help him.

Carol turned and went out the door, down the stairs and out onto the beach. As soon as she was on the beach, she began running toward the rocks.

Barbara went out the front door toward the street to wait for the ambulance. What Barbara saw as Mark's dismissal of her from the scene began to consume her thoughts. It was clear in her mind that he still didn't trust her to respond professionally in an emergency. She could not keep the tears from welling up in her eyes. It didn't matter that going for help was the only thing that could be done. Barbara couldn't see it that way.

Barbara could hear the sound of the ambulance as it came closer. She wiped the tears from her eyes and stepped out into the street to flag the ambulance to a stop. When the ambulance stopped, she jumped in and directed them to a place on the road that was as close as the ambulance could get to where Janice lay.

"Stop here," Barbara insisted.

As the ambulance came to a stop, Barbara jumped out and began running toward the rocks. The ambulance attendants grabbed their bags and followed her.

Mark had seen the lights of the ambulance as it came down the road toward them.

"The ambulance is here. You're going to be fine. Just relax as best you can," Mark said to Janice.

As the ambulance attendants approached, Mark stood up and backed out of the way. One of the attendants asked Mark what happened.

"We don't know what happened. I do know she apparently has some broken ribs, a broken left arm and possibly a broken leg. I'm a hospital corpsman from Balboa Naval Hospital. She's a nurse at Balboa Naval Hospital."

"The police will be along in a minute. They will want to talk to each one of you," the attendant said.

"Okay," Bill replied.

Bill had walked up alongside Mark and had been listening to everything.

As the attendants prepared Janice for transport to the hospital, Mark looked over at Barbara. She was standing off away from the others with her arms folded in front of her. Barbara did not take her eyes off Janice or the attendants as they worked.

Mark knew that he had hurt her by taking charge of the situation without so much as a thought to anything or anyone else. He was afraid that he had shown her that he still did not trust her under pressure, even though he did not mean it to turn out that way.

As the ambulance attendants placed Janice on the gurney and began moving her toward the ambulance, the police arrived. The police officer stopped and talked briefly to one of the attendants. He looked toward the woman the attendant had pointed out, nodded his head, then walked up to Barbara.

"I understand that you are the one who called for help?"

"Yes," Barbara replied.

"Can you tell me what happened here?"

"Not really. We had been walking down the beach. When we got to the rocks, we heard Janice crying and found her lying in the weeds. I ran back to the house and called for the ambulance."

"You said 'we'. Who was with you?"

"Mark Walker," Barbara replied pointing toward Mark.

The policeman looked over at Mark. Mark acknowledged the policeman with a slight nod.

"I take it you know the woman, is that correct?"

"Yes. She is Ensign Janice Miller, a nurse at Balboa Naval Hospital. We live in a house just down the beach. Do you mind if I go to the hospital to be with her?"

"Do you need a ride?"

"No. I can drive myself."

As the sound of the ambulance's siren faded into the distance, Barbara started toward the house to get her car. She walked right past Mark, without even a hint of stopping. She glanced up at him, then quickly turned and looked away. After passing him, she began to walk faster, almost running toward the house.

The look in her eyes told Mark what he already knew. He had hurt her. He also knew there was nothing he could do about it and simply watched her as she ran away.

The policeman immediately went to talk to Mark. He asked him almost the same questions he had asked of Barbara.

"There is one other thing. I think she was beaten and I think I know who did it," Mark added.

"What makes you think she was beaten?"

"The kind of injuries that she has could not have occurred in a fall here. She could not have crawled here if she fell somewhere else, especially with the injuries she has."

"If what you say is true, who do you think might have done this to her?"

"I would start looking for her boyfriend," Mark stated flatly.

"Why?'

"I met him tonight, or at least saw him. He was arguing with Janice just before dinner. They left the party early, and I did not see either of them until we found Janice lying here."

After the policeman had finished, Mark started toward the house to get his car. He walked rather slowly as he tried to think. Mark was afraid that whatever Barbara and he might have had was most likely over.

"Mark," Bill called out.

Mark stopped and turned to see Bill coming toward him with Carol right behind him. Mark waited for them to catch up to him even though he did not feel like talking to anyone right now.

"What happened back there?" Bill asked.

"Barbara and I were out by the rocks when we heard Janice crying. We found her lying in the weeds and called for an ambulance," Mark explained simply.

He did not feel like a long report was necessary, he just wanted to leave.

"No, that's not what I'm talking about. What happened between you and Barbara?"

Mark looked at Bill. His first thought was to tell Bill to mind his own business, but thought better of it. He liked Bill and did not wish to alienate him.

"Nothing," he replied flatly.

"What do you mean 'nothing'? Didn't you see the look she gave you? Man, if looks could kill, you would be dead. What did you do to her?" Carol asked angrily, demanding an answer.

Mark looked Carol right in the eye. She was giving him the third degree. She had no right to do that to him. What had happened between Barbara and him was none of her business. It made him very angry that she thought she could talk to him as if he was some raw recruit, and she was a superior officer. She may be an officer, but she had no right to interfere in his personal life.

Mark looked back at Bill. Bill seemed to understand what was going on in Mark's mind. Mark said nothing more. He simply turned around and walked away.

Bill stood there watching Mark walk toward the house. Carol did not like the fact Mark did not answer her. She started to follow Mark, but Bill grabbed her by the arm. Stopping suddenly, she turned toward Bill and gave him a sharp look.

"Let him go," Bill said quietly, but firmly.

Carol looked at Bill. His expression was telling her that she had no right to talk to Mark that way. Carol realized he was right. It was not her place to interfere in other people's lives, even if one of them was a very close friend. She turned away from Bill and looked up toward the house just as Mark was going around the corner.

Mark walked up to his car and got in. He sat there for a couple of minutes looking out over the hood. He couldn't decide what to do next. Should he go to the hospital and wait to see how Janice was doing? Maybe, he would get a chance to talk to Barbara and explain. Maybe, he should just go back to the barracks and forget it for tonight. He could check on Janice first thing in the morning.

Mark decided it would be best to return to the barracks for tonight. He was sure that Barbara would not want to talk to him tonight. The thought crossed his mind that she might not want to talk to him again, ever.

Mark reached up to the dash and turned the key. His little green MG's engine jumped to life. He shifted it into first gear and pulled away from the curb. After making a quick U-turn, he drove back the way he had come. When he reached the highway, he ran the little car through its gears until he was cruising down the highway.

It felt refreshing to have the wind in his hair. Whenever he had something on his mind and he needed time to think, he would go for a drive. The fresh air and the purr of the MG's little engine seemed to help clear his mind and help him think.

CHAPTER FOUR

BARBARA DROVE DIRECTLY to the hospital. She parked her car in the staff parking lot behind the emergency entrance and ran across the parking lot. Upon entering the emergency room, she looked around. There was no sign of Janice anywhere. Her first thought was that Janice had been taken to another hospital. Barbara turned around quickly and almost ran into Lieutenant Marlene Halston.

"Slow down Ensign Sanders," Lieutenant Halston said slowly and patiently with a forced smile. "What is your big hurry?"

"I thought Ensign Miller had been brought here, but I guess she was taken somewhere else. I was going to start calling around to find out where she was taken," Barbara explained.

The urgency in her voice was apparent to Lieutenant Halston.

"Ensign Miller was brought in. She is in X-ray at the moment. It looks like she will be going to surgery shortly."

"How is she doing?" Barbara's eyes were pleading for information on the condition of her friend and roommate.

"She is doing well, considering. The doctor thinks she will heal just fine. They will take her to surgery to set her arm, but otherwise she seems to be doing well. Do you know what happened to her?"

"No. I really don't know what happened. Mark and I found her near some rocks down the beach from our house."

"Would that be Mark Walker?"

The tone of Lieutenant Halston's voice showed her disapproval of an officer dating an enlisted person.

Lieutenant Halston was from the old school where that sort of thing was just not allowed.

"Yes," Barbara replied reluctantly.

Lieutenant Halston was a busy body and a gossip. It was impossible for Lieutenant Halston to keep her mouth shut, especially if she thought she had something on one of the staff, even one of her nurses. She usually tried to hold it over them.

Barbara also knew that it might not set too well if Captain Jessica Hunt, the Head Nurse, found out that one of the nurses was dating an enlisted man. Captain Hunt was kind of a stickler for rules. Even though there was no clear-cut rule against officers dating enlisted personnel, it was not looked upon favorably by some of the older officers.

"I see."

Again, the tone of Lieutenant Halston's voice was making her message of disapproval clearer than the words she had spoken.

"Mark was at a party at our beach house. We had just gone for a walk along the beach when we found Janice," Barbara tried to explain.

It made Barbara angry to think that she had to defend herself to Lieutenant Halston. It made her even angrier because she tried.

"Where is Walker now?"

"I don't know. Please excuse me."

Barbara turned sharply to leave.

"Wait! Just one minute, Ensign," Lieutenant Halston said with a very demanding tone in her voice.

"Yes, Lieutenant," Barbara replied after she turned back around.

The look in Barbara's eyes and the tone of her voice came across to Lieutenant Halston as almost a dare. Her first thought was to pull rank on Ensign Sanders in an attempt to find out more about Barbara's relationship with Mark.

However, Barbara's sharp response made her decide not to press the issue.

"Ah, that will be all, Ensign," Lieutenant Halston said in an effort to keep herself from looking like a fool.

Barbara turned and walked down the hall toward the door to the parking lot. The Lieutenant was always trying to use her position to get information on anyone and everyone. It upset Barbara that she had told her as much as she had, since it was none of the Lieutenant's business who she was with when she was not on duty.

Barbara walked out the door and went across the parking lot to her car. She opened the door and got in. Leaning over the steering wheel, she let out a heavy sigh.

"Damn that woman," she said out loud.

Barbara was feeling the pressures of the day. It seemed the whole day had gone down the drain. She had let Lieutenant Halston get to her, Janice was in the hospital and for how long was anyone's guess; and Mark had hurt her by not trusting her under pressure. It seemed everything had gone wrong just when things were starting to look up.

Mark's touch on her cheek had been so soft and gentle. His kiss had been light on her lips, yet warm and deep with feeling. She could not believe that he could be so gentle and kind one minute, and the next minute he would put her in her place.

Barbara laid her head down on her hands. She was feeling so tired and hurt that she began to cry. She could not help herself. Deep down she knew she was being very hard on Mark, but what she didn't realize was how hard she was being on herself. Everything had piled up on her in such a short time that she was having difficulty handling it. Lt. Commander Wilson may have been right. Maybe she didn't have the right stuff to work under pressure. Maybe, she shouldn't be working in the emergency room at all, especially if Mark was working there.

Slowly, reality began to take hold of her. She began to realize that she was depressed because of all the pressure she had put on herself in her effort to prove herself. Today had just been the last straw. She was feeling exhausted and what she needed was a good night's sleep.

This was not the time to make any important decisions about her future. All decisions could wait until she was better prepared to cope with things. It was time to go home and get some sleep. In the morning, she might see things a little differently. Janice was in good hands, and Mark had probably gone back to the barracks. She should go home and get some well-needed rest. Carol would be the only one at the house.

She straightened up in the seat and wiped the tears from her face. As soon as she had pulled herself together enough to drive, she started her car.

On her way to the main gate, she drove past the men's barracks. Almost unconsciously, she scanned the row of cars parked in front of the building. She did not see Mark's little MG. It crossed her mind that he had either parked around back or he had not come back to the barracks. She wondered where he might be.

"What do I care where he is," she blurted out loud.

Hearing herself say that she didn't care made her realize just how much she did care. The thought came to mind that this was not the first time someone she had really cared about had hurt her. A guy in college whom she loved very much had dumped her for one of her friends.

She left the hospital compound and started down the highway toward the beach house. Her mind was so muddled that she did not see the little green MG go by, headed toward Balboa Naval Hospital.

When she arrived back at the house, she noticed all the lights were off except the lights in the kitchen. Parking her car in the driveway, she sat behind the wheel for a minute in an effort to prepare herself to face Carol.

Barbara took a deep breath and got out of her car. As she went into the house, she hoped she could get to bed without having to see or talk to Carol. She knew there was little chance of that happening.

"Barbara, is that you?" Carol called from the kitchen.

"Yes," Barbara replied.

She was already feeling the pressure of having to talk to Carol. Barbara reluctantly went to the kitchen. Carol was sitting at the small breakfast table in the corner.

"How is Janice?" Carol asked as Barbara flopped down in a chair.

"When I left the hospital, she was in X-ray. She will have surgery to have her arm set in a little while. She may already be in surgery."

"Do you think one of us should be there when she comes out of surgery?"

"I don't think so. It will be a long time before she would even know we were there. She will need someone in the morning more than she needs someone now."

"Will there be any long term effects?"

"They don't think so, but it's still too early to tell."

"You know, you look like hell," Carol stated bluntly.

"Gee, thanks a lot. That's just what I needed to hear," she said sarcastically.

Barbara was tired and did not need anyone telling her how she looked. She knew her eyes were red from crying, and she was sure that she had dark circles under her eyes.

"What happened between you and Mark?"

Barbara looked across the table at Carol. Carol was really concerned about her. No matter how concerned Carol was, Barbara was not willing to talk about it.

"I don't want to talk about it now."

"Hey, this is Carol you're talking to, not some stranger."

"I'm sorry. It's just that I need to think things out for myself first. I'm just too tired to talk about it now."

"Okay, but we will discuss it tomorrow."

Carol made it quite clear she was not going to drop the subject.

"Okay, tomorrow. I'm going to bed."

Carol watched Barbara as she stood up, turned and walked out of the kitchen toward the bedrooms. Carol could understand what Barbara was going through. She had had her share of doubts about her job, her abilities and her relationships, until she met Bill. Bill had helped Carol pull her life together simply by being there when she needed him.

Somehow, somewhere in the back of her mind she felt Mark could do the same for Barbara if they could just talk. It was clear that Barbara liked Mark very much. She was sure that Mark liked Barbara, too.

Barbara walked into her bedroom and sat down on the foot of the bed. Bending down, she untied her white sneakers and slipped them off her feet. She dropped them on the floor at the end of the bed. She stood up, took off her pullover top and her slacks. She tossed them on the chair as she went into the bathroom.

Once in the bathroom, she reached into the shower and turned on the water. She finished undressing and stepped into the shower. The spray of warm water on the back of her neck felt very relaxing. Slowly, the tension in her body seemed to be washed down the drain with the water.

She just stood in the shower, letting the warm water wash over her. She tried to forget about all that had happened today. But even with the soothing water running over her skin, she could not forget the hurt she felt inside.

Barbara turned the water off and stepped out of the shower. Taking a large towel from the towel rack, she wrapped it around her. It soaked up the droplets of water from her skin as she patted herself dry. After returning the towel to the towel rack, she slipped into her terry cloth robe that had been hanging on the back of the door.

With a smaller towel, she began drying her hair. When it was as dry as she could get it with the towel, she wrapped the towel around her head, returned to her bedroom and sat down in front of her dresser. Looking into the mirror, the reflection that came back to her was that of a young woman who was very tired and very confused.

She unwrapped the towel from around her head and began combing her hair. She avoided looking at her reflection as much as possible. It was too depressing for her to see herself like this.

After a short time, she simply gave up and decided she could fix her hair in the morning. She put the comb down on the dresser, then stood up. Turning off the light, she slipped out of her robe. She pulled back the covers on the bed and slid in between the sheets. The sheets felt cool against her bare skin.

She lay on her back looking up at the ceiling. All she could think of was Mark. The more she thought about him, the more confused she became. She was too tired to sort out her feelings and to put things in their proper perspective. Barbara closed her eyes in the hope that sleep would make things better.

Her last thoughts before sleep finally came were of Mark. The gentle touch of his fingers on her cheek and the way his lips met hers. She could remember the way her heart pounded when he kissed her. They were good thoughts, the kind that allowed her to sink into a deep, restful sleep.

MARK TURNED AT THE main gate of the hospital. He went directly to the men's barracks and drove around behind the building to park. He sat in his car for a minute to think about the evening's events. Usually Mark's head would be clear after a long evening drive alone, but not tonight. He had hurt Barbara, even though he had not meant to.

Mark knew Barbara was off duty for the weekend. He needed to talk to her, to explain to her that he did not mean things the way they sounded. Janice's need for help was all he had thought about.

He decided to call her late in the morning so he would not wake her from her rest in case she wanted to sleep in. It was important for Mark to let her know that he wanted to see her again. He did not want things to end between them before they even had a chance.

Mark looked up at the barracks. All the rooms looked dark. He got out of his car and snapped the tonneau cover over the seats to protect the interior from the early morning dew, then went inside.

Mark shared a room with another Second Class Petty Officer, James Dalton. James was one of Mark's friends. Mark figured he would be in bed and asleep. Being as quiet as possible, Mark slipped his key into the lock, opened the door and entered the room.

"Mark?"

It was apparent from the sound of James' voice that he had either just fallen asleep, or that he was just about to doze off.

"Yeah. Sorry, I didn't mean to wake you."

"That's all right. I have a message for you from the Master-at-Arms," James said as he sat up in bed and turned a light on.

"What's the message?"

"They want you over at the Master-at-Arms office as soon as you come in. They said it didn't matter what time."

"You know what it's about?"

"No. They didn't tell me anything."

"I better get over there and see what's going on."

"I'll come with you," James said as he swung his feet off the bed and stood up.

"Okay. I have a call to make while you get dressed."

Mark sat down at the desk, picked up the phone and dialed the emergency room. The phone rang only twice before it was answered.

"Emergency room, Hospital Corpsman Anderson speaking."

"Jeff, this is Mark."

"Hi, Mark. What's up?"

"I need to know how Ensign Miller is doing. She was brought in earlier this evening.

"Sure. She's in the recovery room now. The last word we had was that she will be admitted to Officer's Sick Quarters on the sixth floor when she wakes up from the surgery."

"Thanks, Jeff. I have to go, talk to you later," Mark said then hung up the phone.

While Mark was on the phone, James had slipped into some street clothes. Together they walked over to the Master-at-Arms office.

"Sir, I'm Second Class Hospital Corpsman Mark Walker. I understand you wanted to see me?"

"Yes. Walker, we got a call from the California State Police. They would like you to come in and see a Sergeant Mortimer sometime tomorrow. Something about an assault?"

"Okay. Thanks for the message, sir," Mark said.

"You know what this is all about?"

The duty officer was surprised that Mark seemed to know what the police wanted from him.

"Yes, sir," Mark replied.

"You mind letting me in on it?" the duty officer insisted.

It irritated him a little that Mark did not offer more information.

"It happened off base. One of our nurses was apparently beaten up by her boyfriend, a civilian. The police are investigating it."

"And just what is your part in this?"

"I found her," Mark replied simply.

Mark was getting a little annoyed with all the questions.

"Is that all, Sir?"

"Yes, that will be all for now."

"Thank you, sir."

Mark turned and walked toward the door with James hot on his heels. As they walked back to the barracks, Mark explained about finding Ensign Miller and what he believed happened to her.

"What are you going to do about it?" James asked.

"What do you mean?"

"I mean, are you going to let this bum get away with beating up one of our officers?"

"I'm going to let the police handle it."

As they continued walking back to the barracks, Mark's mind was running over the possibilities. Mark knew Janice was afraid of her boyfriend and that she might not press charges against him. If she did not press charges, something would have to be done to keep him away from her; or he might hurt her again, even kill her next time. Mark knew he could not stand by and let Jim beat up on a woman.

When James and Mark reached the barracks, it was getting very late. Mark had not forgotten about Janice, but his thoughts had turned to Barbara. In the morning, he would decide how he would approach Barbara and explain his actions to her. He hoped she would give him the chance to explain.

Mark undressed and crawled into bed. He wanted so much to tell Barbara he was sorry. The thought passed through his mind that he could call her now, but it was very late and she was probably in bed. This was probably not the best time to talk to her anyway. He decided it would be best to stick to his original decision to wait and call her in the morning.

He lay on his back with his hands behind his head. Mark had to force himself to close his eyes and force himself to seek the sleep he needed.

His last thoughts, before he finally got to sleep, were of Barbara. He could almost feel the warmth of her kiss and the softness of her lips. He could picture her in those blue slacks and pullover top. She was a beautiful woman. He just hoped he had not spoiled any chance he might have had to see her again.

CHAPTER FIVE

BARBARA BEGAN TO STIR from a deep restful sleep. Her mind told her it was time to get up, but she had no reason to get up this morning. It was her day off, and she had the house all to herself.

Barbara rolled onto her back and reluctantly opened her eyes. She raised her arms above her head and stretched. The sheet clung to her body as every muscle stretched in an effort to wake up. It felt good to be rested.

For several minutes, she lay just staring at the ceiling. Barbara's thoughts turned to Mark and what had happened last evening. She realized she had not been fair to him and had taken things far too personally. After all, he had gotten to Janice first, had seen her injuries first and he knew what was needed. He had only told her what she could do to help, and it was the same thing he would have told anyone else. She just happened to be the only other person there.

Barbara began to think that she had been very childish in the way she had treated Mark. It had been stupid of her to let her own insecurities come before what was best for Janice. She had been selfish and unfair, and she would have to do something about it.

Barbara decided she would get up, fix her hair and get dressed. She would then call Mark and tell him she was sorry for the way she had treated him. Maybe, he would come over and spend at least some of the day with her on the beach.

It sounded so easy on the surface. She desperately hoped she had not ruined everything between them. If she could talk to him, just for a couple of minutes, maybe she could make things right again.

Barbara rolled over and sat up on the edge of the bed. The sheet slid down off the smooth lines of her body as she stood up. She picked up her robe and slipped into it as she went into the bathroom.

When she came out of the bathroom, she had a towel wrapped around her head. She had washed her hair, only now she felt like fixing it. Sitting down in front of the mirror, she began to comb her hair. She remembered how she had looked last night before going to bed. The person looking back at her in the mirror looked much more refreshed and rested.

Barbara also remembered the way she had felt when Mark had touched her cheek, and the way his lips had felt against hers. She realized that she missed him very much.

After fixing her hair, she went to her closet. She picked out a blouse and shorts outfit that would show off her figure nicely. "Mark would like this," she said to herself as she took off her robe and tossed in over a chair. Looking nice for Mark seemed to give her the courage she needed to call him.

As soon as she was finished dressing, Barbara went to the phone. She picked up the receiver, but hesitated for a second.

"What if he won't talk to me? I'd feel like a fool," she said out loud.

She knew that she had to take the risk if there was going to be any hope of building a relationship with him. She forced her fears aside and dialed the number for the men's barracks. Each ring of the phone made her wonder if she was doing the right thing. The phone rang just four times before someone answered it, but to her it seemed like forever.

"Men's barracks, may I help you?" the voice asked.

"Ah, yes. Could you see if Mark, ah, Corpsman Walker is in, please?" Barbara asked nervously.

She was afraid that even if he were in, he would not come to the phone.

"Sure. Hold on a minute while I check."

Barbara waited for the man to return to the phone. She hoped Mark would not be upset with her for calling. It was too late to worry about it now. Maybe Mark didn't want to have anything to do with her anymore.

"Hello. You still there?" the voice asked.

"Yes."

"I'm sorry, but Walker isn't in right now."

"Do you know when he might be back?"

"No. I did see his car out in the parking lot, so I would guess he is on the base somewhere. Most likely he has gone over to the mess hall for something to eat. Would you like me to leave a message on his door?"

"No. No thank you. I'll call back later," she replied, then hung up the phone.

Barbara sat in the chair and wondered whether he was really at the Mess Hall, or if he just didn't want to talk to her. She let out a sigh of disappointment and went into the kitchen. After fixing a pot of coffee, she poured herself a cup and sat down at the table. A feeling of loneliness came over her like she had never experienced before.

She decided that if anything were to come of her relationship with Mark, it would simply happen. She would talk to Mark as soon as possible. If he did not want to talk to her, she would accept it as the end.

"Damn," she said out loud.

She knew it would not be as simple as she made it sound. It would not be that easy for her to get him out of her mind.

After finishing her coffee, she put the cup on the counter. She decided she would spend the day relaxing. Maybe read a good book and try to call Mark in the evening.

After picking out a romance novel, she went out on the covered deck, sat down and began to read. Time passed rather slowly and she found it hard to concentrate on the book. Every time she stopped reading for even a second or two, thoughts of Mark would fill her mind.

She stopped reading, laid her book on the table next to the chair, and looked out over the beach. The sun was bright in a clear blue sky. There was a gentle breeze coming in off the water. The surf was gently rolling in onto the sandy beach. It was a perfect day for a swim in the ocean.

It was the type of day that should be shared by two people who care about each other. It would be a perfect day for Mark to come out and go swimming with her, but she felt the day was being wasted without Mark to share it with her.

She looked at her watch. It was just a few minutes past ten. She realized she had not been up all that long. The day seemed to be dragging along at a snail's pace. She knew there were things she could be doing around the house, but she just didn't have the ambition to do them.

She wondered what Mark was doing now or where he had gone. Barbara thought about calling him again, but decided it would be best if she just stuck to her resolve to call him later.

Barbara went back inside the house, sat down next to the phone and called the hospital. The phone rang only twice before it was answered. She told the operator who she wanted and was immediately transferred to Janice's room in Officer's Sick Quarters.

"Hello," the rather weak voice on the other end said.

"Hi. This is Barbara, is this Janice?"

"Oh, hi. Yes, it's me." Janice replied sounding a little more chipper.

"How are you doing?"

"Not too bad, I guess. I'm still a little groggy."

"I didn't figure you would be awake much earlier, so I didn't call sooner. Is there anything you need? I'm planning on coming up in a little while to see you."

"No. I don't think so, at least not for now. I've been sleeping on and off most of the morning."

"I'm sure you have," Barbara replied. "Have the police been by to see you?"

"No, not yet. I guess the doctor has told them that they can not visit with me until tomorrow. I don't really want to talk to them."

"You are going to file a complaint against Jim, aren't you?" Barbara asked.

She was upset that Janice might let Jim get away with beating her.

"I don't know," Janice said with a long sigh.

"What do you mean 'I don't know'?" Barbara blurted out.

"I really don't want to cause any trouble," Janice replied weakly in her own defense.

"You can't let him get away with this. He will only do it to someone else or he will do it to you again."

Barbara was angry.

"I don't feel like talking about this now," Janice said knowing very well Barbara was right.

"I'm sorry. I didn't mean to upset you. I'll see you after lunch," Barbara said apologetically.

"Why don't you come up tomorrow morning? I'm really tired. I'll probably sleep most of today anyway." Janice was sure she would not be able to handle another tongue lashing without completely breaking down.

"Okay," Barbara agreed reluctantly. "I'll see you in the morning."

Barbara waited until she heard Janice hang up the phone before hanging up. She sat and stared at the phone.

"Damn it," she said, realizing she should have tried to be more understanding and more sympathetic toward Janice's feelings. It was hard for her to understand how anyone as intelligent and nice as Janice could let some creep like Jim beat her up and do nothing about it. Barbara wished she could do something about it, but she realized there was nothing she could do. It was up to Janice, and she was sure that Janice was afraid of Jim.

Barbara decided it was time to get busy around the house or she would get nothing done. There was nothing she could do about Janice, and there was nothing she could do about Mark. She might as well do something to get her mind free of those things.

Barbara sat down at the table, took a sip of her coffee, then picked up the pen. She began to write herself a to-do list. It read, "Have lunch, clean up kitchen, wash a load of clothes, clean bathroom, call Mark." She paused for a minute and looked at the last item on her list, 'Call Mark'. She knew she did not need a reminder to call him.

She took a deep breath and let out a long sigh. She had to mentally shake herself. She stood up, went to the refrigerator and began fixing herself some lunch.

MARK WOKE UP WITH the sun creeping in around the edges of the shade on the window above his bed. He lay there for several minutes with his hands under the back of his head, just looking up at the ceiling, but not really seeing it.

"You going to get up?" James asked.

Mark turned his head and looked across the room to see James sitting on the edge of his bed. James was already dressed for the beach.

"Yeah," Mark replied.

"Several of us are going to Ocean Beach today, you want to come along?"

"No. I don't think so."

"Why not? It's a beautiful day to go to the beach and several of the corps waves are going."

James was ready to spend the day at the beach.

"I'm sure it is a beautiful day to go to the beach, but I have other things to do, okay?" Mark said with a sharp tone in his voice.

"Okay. Okay."

James held his hands up as if to protect himself from the onslaught of words from Mark.

"I'm sorry. I didn't mean to bite your head off."

"That's okay. You're still welcome to come along. Pam is going. You know how she looks in those skimpy bikinis she wears all the time," James said with a devilish grin.

Mark smiled because he knew what Pam looked like in her bikini. He had seen her in it many times.

"One of the girls, who lives on the same floor of the women's barracks as Pam, said that Pam would go skinny dipping with you anytime you want."

"I'm not interested in Pam. I like her and she is very nice. She's just not my type."

"I understand."

"You go to the beach and watch her run up and down the beach with her big boobs bouncing up and down. I have other things to do."

"Okay, I will. It sounds like a great way to spend the afternoon, especially the watching part."

"Maybe you can get her to go skinny dipping with you," Mark suggested.

"I wouldn't turn down that kind of an offer."

"I've heard that she likes you, too."

"Not as much as she likes you."

"That may or may not be true, but you are available, I'm not."

Mark had made it clear that Pam was fair game. If James wanted to pursue her, he would not be stepping on Mark's toes.

"Just who does interest you, anyway? Is it Ensign Sanders?" James asked.

Mark looked at him. He was not sure he wanted to answer that question, but he felt he could trust James.

"Between you and me, and no one else, the answer is yes."

"You do have good taste. I'll say that much for you."

"Thank you."

"Well, I have to get going. Good luck on your quest of Ensign Sanders. By the way, don't worry about me, I won't say a word." James turned and started out the door.

"Thanks. And good luck with Pam," Mark called out as James disappeared into the hall.

Mark sat up on the edge of his bed. "Good luck, indeed," he said quietly to himself. He was sure he was going to need a lot more than luck to get Barbara to even talk to him.

Soon after James left the room, Mark gathered up his shaving kit and a clean towel. He walked down the hall to the showers. After cleaning up, he put on a clean uniform. Satisfied that he was in the proper uniform of the day, he walked out into the hall.

It was quiet around the barracks, but that was not unusual for mid-morning on a Saturday. On a day like today, most of those who did not have the duty had already headed out to enjoy the day. Or they were sleeping in late, most likely after a late night in the downtown bars or at the base EM Club. Mark rarely went to any of the downtown bars. There were too many heavy drinkers and too many fights.

As Mark passed the phone, he thought about calling Barbara, but felt it might be a little early to call. He thought that she might have been up late, if she stayed at the hospital to see how Janice was getting along.

Mark decided he would stop in and see how Janice was doing after he got something to eat. She might even be able to give him some kind of a clue as to how Barbara felt about him. As Mark stepped out the main entrance of the barracks, the phone in the front lobby began to ring. The ringing of the phone only slightly registered in his mind as the door closed behind him.

In the two and a half blocks to the mess hall, Mark mulled over in his mind what he should say to Barbara. He thought about going out to the house and confronting her face to face, telling her that he was sorry he had upset her and hoped she would forgive him for his 'take charge' way of doing things.

Mark entered the mess hall and went directly to the serving line. After filling his plate and getting a cup of coffee, he picked out a deserted table in the corner, sat down and began to eat.

"Excuse me," a voice said from behind him.

The sudden sound from behind him startled Mark, causing him to spill a little of his coffee. Mark turned around to see who it was. Looking up at the young corpsman, Mark could tell that the young corpsman knew he was going to get reprimanded.

"I'm sorry, sir," the corpsman said.

"What is it?" Mark asked not really wanting to be disturbed.

"Are you Mark Walker?"

"Yes. What do you want?" Mark replied sharply.

"I just wanted to let you know that you had a call this morning at the barracks," the corpsman explained nervously.

"Who was it?"

"I don't know. She didn't leave her name. She called for you, but you had already left. She said she would call back later."

"Did she say when?"

The sharpness of his voice had mellowed. He could only think of one woman who might try to call him. Mark was sorry he had been so sharp, after all the young corpsman was only delivering a message.

"No, sir."

"Thank you."

"I'm sorry about the coffee."

"Forget it."

The corpsman turned around and went back to his table. Mark was sure he knew who had called. Just the thought that it was Barbara lifted his spirits considerably.

Mark finished his meal, dropped off his tray on his way out of the mess hall and went to the elevator. Arriving at the sixth floor, he went directly to the nurse's station of Officer's Sick Quarters to inquire about Janice's condition. The senior corpsman was the only one at the nurse's station when he arrived.

Mark knew the senior corpsman, but not very well. He had seen him around and they had even talked briefly from time to time.

"Hi. I was wondering if you could tell me how Ensign Miller is doing?" Mark asked.

"She is doing pretty well. It does look like she will be here for awhile. Are you aware of her injuries?"

"Yes. What I want to know is how is she doing now?" Mark asked.

"She has been sleeping most of the morning."

"Can I see her if she's awake?"

"Sure. The doctors have been keeping non-medical visitors out."

The senior corpsman led the way down the hall to Janice's room. He slowly pushed the door open and looked in. Janice was awake.

"Excuse me. Do you feel up to talking to someone?"

"Who is it?"

"Mark Walker."

"Sure."

The senior corpsman pushed the door open to allow Mark to enter. He closed the door after Mark entered the room.

"Hi. How are you doing?"

"Pretty good, I guess."

"That's good. Is there anything you need?"

"No. They're taking pretty good care of me. I want to thank you for helping me last night."

"You're welcome," Mark replied with a smile.

"Barbara is lucky to have you as her friend."

The smile on Mark's face quickly faded away. Janice noticed Mark's reaction to her comment. It was apparent that she may have hit on a tender spot.

"Are you and Barbara not getting along?"

The concern in her voice disturbed Mark. He had come here to cheer her up, not upset her. She had enough problems without concerning herself with his.

"No. Everything is fine," he replied, but there was an unmistakable tone in his voice that told her there was a problem between them.

"Come on. Don't lie to me, Mark. What happened?"

"Maybe I should just go and let you get your rest," Mark said trying hard not to have her worrying about him and Barbara.

"I don't know you very well, Mark, but I have heard a lot about you. You seem like a very intelligent man and you are very concerned about others. I also understand that you are more than willing to help anyone you can. I know what you did for Barbara. I know what you did for me, and I am very grateful.

"I don't want to be pushy, but I want you to know that if you want, you can talk to me anytime. I consider you a friend, a very dear friend, and anything you tell me will remain between us," she explained.

"Thank you, but I don't think it's a good idea for me to talk to you about Barbara and me for two reasons. One, you don't need the additional worries right now; and two, it would put you in the middle since you are a friend to both of us."

"I understand. Let me tell you this then. Barbara is a little insecure right now. She has not been a nurse very long, and she has not been in the Navy very long. All this is fairly new to her. She will adjust once she has a little more experience and gets used to the Military life style.

"She also had a very bad experience with a boyfriend back in Iowa. She fell very hard for this guy, and then he dumped her for one of her close friends.

"Barbara likes you very much. Everyone at the party could easily see that. But, she is afraid of getting hurt again," Janice explained.

"I don't want to hurt her."

"I know you don't, but you should be aware that she can be easily hurt. I wouldn't have said anything if I thought you would hurt her."

"I need to talk to her, but I don't know if she will even answer the phone," Mark said in frustration.

"Don't call her. Go out to the house and see her. Maybe you two can work things out. I believe she will be alone at the house today," Janice said with a smile.

"I don't know."

"Listen, Mark, Barbara likes you, and I think she knows it. But, she is afraid to like you too much. Go see her. Try to get things worked out. Now, why don't you go so I can get some rest. I'm very tired," Janice said.

"Okay. I'll stop up and see you later. And, thanks."

Mark understood he was being dismissed, but he didn't mind. He walked out of the room toward the elevator. He wondered why anyone as nice as Janice would get involved with some jerk as mean as Jim.

As he got on the elevator, his thoughts turned back to Barbara. Maybe Janice was right. Maybe he should just go out to the house and see her face to face. If he did, he would know right away where he stood with her.

Getting off the elevator, he went directly to the barracks and changed into civilian clothes. Since he was going out to the beach, he decided to wear shorts and a nice sport shirt.

He started out the door, but stopped. He turned around and picked up his swimsuit and a towel. He thought that he might just want it along. The idea hit him that if things didn't go well with Barbara, he would join the others at Ocean Beach. Deep down he knew that if things didn't work out he would not go to the beach to join the others. He would want to go somewhere he could be alone.

Mark left the barracks, got into his car and drove out the main gate, turning onto Park Boulevard. He glanced at his watch, it was a little before noon when he turned down the ramp onto the freeway and headed out toward Mission Beach.

By the time he reached the turn off to go to the beach house, it was a little past noon. He pulled up to the curb in front of the house. Mark had his doubts about talking with Barbara face to face. He would not like it very much if she decided to slam the door in his face. If she slammed the door in his face, there would be no doubt in his mind that it was over between them.

Mark kind of smiled to himself. "I must be really hung up on this woman if I have to have her slam a door in my face for me to get the message that she doesn't want to see me any more," he said to himself.

"Hell, listen to me, I'm even talking to myself," he said as he shook his head.

He got out of his car and walked up to the door. He rapped on the door, then waited.

CHAPTER SIX

WITHIN A MINUTE, two at the most, the door opened. Barbara looked beautiful in her pale blue blouse, white shorts and bare feet. Mark wanted to grab her, take her in his arms and tell that her he was sorry. Not being sure how she might feel about being grabbed and kissed, he decided against it.

"Hi," Mark said softly.

"Hi. Would you like to come in?"

"Yes. I would like to talk to you."

Barbara stepped back from the door, allowing Mark to enter. He walked past her then turned around to face her.

"Have you had lunch yet?" she asked.

"No, I mean yes. I mean I had a late breakfast and I'm not hungry. But if you are eating lunch, I'll wait."

"I've finished. Would you like something to drink, a cup of coffee or pop?"

"Sure. Coffee would be fine."

She walked past him and into the kitchen. He followed her.

"Why don't you sit down," she said.

Mark sat down and was feeling a little uneasy. He was not sure how to get the conversation started.

"We don't have to sit here."

"No, this is fine. Back home where I grew up, we had our more serious discussions around the kitchen table," Mark explained.

"Is this going to be a serious discussion?" Barbara asked.

"Sort of, I guess."

"Okay."

Barbara pulled a chair up next to him and sat down. She didn't say anything. She just looked at him and waited for him to start talking. She knew he was going to tell her that it was over between them. Serious talks never seemed to have happy endings for her.

"I came over today to tell you that I'm sorry about the way I treated you last night. I really enjoyed being with you. I was hoping that we could see each other again."

Mark was nervous and was trying to pick his words very carefully. Tears started to come to her eyes. Mark looked at her as a tear started to roll down her cheek.

"Damn. I knew I wasn't going to say it right. Maybe I should just go," Mark said, feeling frustrated and angry with himself.

"No. Please don't go." Barbara said softly. "I tried to call you at the barracks this morning to tell you I was sorry for the way I treated you."

"I'm sorry, too. Do you think we can start over?" Mark asked softly.

"I would rather pick up from where we left off to help Janice," Barbara said looking into his eyes.

"You mean here," Mark said as he leaned over and kissed her gently on the lips.

Barbara felt the same feeling run through her that she had felt the previous night when he kissed her. She squeezed his hand as they kissed and was glad she was sitting down.

Mark drew back and smiled at her.

"We've wasted enough of the day, what do you say we go somewhere?"

"We could stay right here. We have the house to ourselves all day. There's a nice beach right out in front that's not crowded," she suggested.

"Okay, but later you have to let me take you out for something to eat," he said as he squeezed her hand.

"Okay. Do you have your swimming suit with you?"

"Yes. I'll go get it."

Mark stood up and was about to go to his car, but he stopped. Instead, he leaned down and kissed Barbara lightly on the forehead. He slipped his hand out of her hand as he left the kitchen.

Barbara watched him as he walked away from her. All her worries had been for nothing. She was feeling so relieved that she felt bubbly inside. It was going to be a good day after all.

When Mark returned to the house, Barbara stood up and took hold of his hand.

"You can change in here," she said as she led him to the bathroom down the hall.

Mark smiled at her and went into the bathroom. He slipped out of his clothes and into his swimsuit.

Barbara went into her bedroom to change. She slipped out of her blouse and shorts, then went into her bathroom to wash her face. Right now, she could not have been happier. There was hope that things could work out between them after all.

Barbara removed the rest of her clothing and picked out a blue one-piece swimming suit. As soon as she was ready, she looked herself over in the full-length mirror. She was satisfied that she looked good for him. On her way out of her room, she picked up a large bath towel and flung it over her shoulder.

Mark was standing on the deck waiting for her. As she approached him, he turned and looked her over. Her swimming suit accented the smooth curved lines of her body.

She didn't mind having him look at her at all. The expression on his face and the look in his eyes told her all she needed to know. Mark approved of how she looked, and that made her feel desirable.

She also looked Mark over. She noticed he had a very nice build. He was trim, with broad shoulders and narrow waist. His arms were not massive hunks of muscle, but they were obviously strong arms. She thought how nice it would be to be held in those arms.

"Are you ready?" Mark asked with a smile.

"We will want that blanket," she said pointing at a large bright yellow blanket neatly folded on a chair.

"Oh. I should take some suntan lotion, too," she added.

Mark smiled as he watched her turn and go back into the house. He noticed how nice her swimsuit fit her as he watched her walking away from him. The low cut back of her swimsuit showed off the smooth lightly tanned skin of her back, all the way down to the small of her back. Her long shapely legs accented her narrow waist and the smooth curving lines of her hips.

Mark picked up the blanket and draped it over his arm. He leaned against the deck's railing while he waited for Barbara to return. Before long she reappeared with a tube of suntan lotion in her hand.

"We ready now?" he asked with a smile.

"Yes."

Barbara took his hand and they walked down the steps to the beach. It was going to be one of those days when it would be easy to get sunburned. The sun was bright and hot, but a cool breeze off the ocean didn't make it feel very hot.

They spread the large yellow blanket out on the warm sand. Barbara laid down on the blanket, with Mark beside her. Lying on her stomach with her head resting on her arms, she looked over at Mark. She felt relaxed and comfortable.

They lay quietly for several minutes. It seemed so natural to be together. The only sounds were those of the waves gently rolling up onto the beach, and the squawk of a few distant sea gulls.

"Where are you taking me for dinner?" she asked breaking the silence.

"I don't know yet. I haven't decided."

"I have a suggestion, if you don't mind."

"Where would you like to go?"

"Well, I was thinking that, maybe we could go to the amusement park at Ocean Beach and get something to eat there."

"For dinner?"

He was surprised she would pick a place like that for a dinner date.

"Sure, why not?"

"Well, no reason, I guess. I thought you would like to go some place that was, well, fancier. You know, some place you could sit down to eat."

"If you don't want to go, that's all right. I just thought it would be kind of fun to get a couple of hot dogs and maybe ride a couple of the rides."

Here was a woman who liked the simple things in life. He was not going to have to impress her.

"When was the last time you were on a Ferris wheel?" he asked.

She could see the gleam in his eyes. It excited her that he had accepted her suggestion.

"It has been a long time. I think it was at the State Fair in Iowa several years ago," she replied after giving it some thought.

"Okay. We will go to the amusement park for dinner. I know a vendor over by the amusement park who makes the best chili dogs in the world."

Mark found himself excited about going to the amusement park with her. It had been a long time since he had ridden on a Ferris wheel or a merry-go-round.

"Would you rub some suntan lotion on my back?" Barbara asked softly.

"Sure."

Mark sat up and knelt down beside her. He picked up the lotion and squeezed a little in his hands, then rubbed the lotion over her back. Her back felt warm to the touch and her skin was smooth and soft.

Barbara could feel the tightness in her neck and shoulders slowly disappear.

"Mmmmm. That feels good," she sighed.

Mark rubbed some of the lotion on the back of her legs. He could feel the firm smoothness of her legs as he gently let his hands slide over them.

"Do my shoulders again, please." she said as she rose up a little and slipped the shoulder straps of her swimsuit down her arms.

Rubbing the lotion on her neck and shoulders, he noticed there were no tan lines on her shoulders. She must sunbathe without a top on. Knowing that she was shy, he guessed that she usually sunbathed on the deck where no one could see her.

"That feels good."

Though his fingers were strong, he had a gentle touch and smooth hands.

"Don't get to liking it too much, or I might insist you do it for me," he teased.

"Well, I guess fair is fair."

"Yes, it is," he said as he sat back on his heels.

Barbara was indeed a beautiful woman. Her blond hair was soft and moved gently in the breeze, and her shoulders and back were smooth and nicely tanned. Barbara's narrow waist and shapely curved hips were accented by the curve from the small of her back to her firm, smooth behind. Her legs were shapely, yet appeared to be strong. Mark felt very lucky to have found such a beautiful woman who liked him.

Barbara rose up and pulled the straps of her swimsuit back up over her shoulders, then rolled over and sat up. Pulling her legs up and leaning against them, she wrapped her arms around her legs.

"Would you like me to put some lotion on you?" she asked.

"No. I'm okay"

"Would you like to go swimming?"

"Sure."

She smiled at him, then reached out to him. Mark stood up, took hold of her hands and pulled her up in front of him. He let go of her hands and reached out, putting his hands on top of her hips. She reached up and put her hands on his shoulders. He leaned forward and kissed her gently. As he straightened up, he looked into her deep blue eyes and saw them sparkling in the sun light.

"Are you ready to get wet?" he asked with a devilish grin.

Mark did not wait for an answer. He scooped her up in his arms. She wrapped her arms around his neck as he carried her toward the water.

"You're not going to throw me in, are you?" she asked as she squirmed in his arms, but still hung onto him tightly.

"No. I wouldn't do that. I'm going to carry you out until we are beyond the breakers and it's deep enough for us to swim."

Reassured, she snuggled up against him and laid her head on his shoulder. She felt as if she could stay wrapped in his arms for the rest of the day.

Mark carried her out into the water. The gentle waves washed against his legs as he moved further out into deeper water. Once past the small breaking waves, the rolling waves began to wash up against her. The water felt cold against her skin causing her to shiver.

"Is it too cold?"

"No. It's just that I have to get adjusted to the change."

Once Mark had reached a point where the water was up to his chest, he carefully put her down. She did not take her arms from around his neck, but held onto him. He took her in his arms and held her tightly against him.

Barbara could feel the warmth of his body and the strength of his arms around her. It made her feel safe. It also made her feel loved.

Mark could feel the firmness of Barbara's breasts pressing against his chest. He looked down at her. She tipped her head back to look up at him. Slowly, Mark leaned down until their lips met.

The slow rolling waves washed against them as they kissed. Gradually, their kiss deepened as they pressed their lips and bodies together. It soon turned into a long, passionate kiss.

When their kiss ended, Barbara knew in her heart that he was the man she wanted to be with for the rest of her life. At least that is what her heart told her.

Laying her head on his broad shoulder, her mind raced in confusion. She knew he was the one for her, but a thought came from deep down in her mind to remind her that someone else had been the one for her, but he had ended up hurting her deeply. Yet, this time was different. She did not understand why she felt it was different, she just knew it was.

Mark's gentle stroking of her back and the touch of his hands eased some of the confusion in her mind. He was so gentle with her. He didn't seem to want more from her than she was ready and willing to share with him.

Mark seemed to sense that something was wrong, but it certainly felt right having her in his arms. Mark slipped his hands off her back and down to her waist. He gently pushed her back a few inches, and she looked up at him.

"I thought we came out here to swim. We can neck anytime."

Mark tried to lighten things up with a little kidding. He needed to give her time to put her feelings in order. He also thought it would be a good idea if he did the same.

"You're right," she agreed.

"Ah. Which one am I right about?" he asked grinning down at her.

"Well, I think you are probably right on both counts," she replied teasingly.

"In that case, what do you say to swimming over to that point and back," Mark suggested.

She turned and looked toward the rocky point. "Okay."

"It's not too far, is it?"

"No, I don't think so. We used to swim across lakes that looked farther."

She turned around to face the point, and Mark moved up beside her. Together they pushed off the bottom and began leisurely swimming toward the point. They swam side by side, never being more than a few feet from each other. It gave each of them time to think as well as enjoy being together.

As they approached the point and Mark was able to stand on the bottom again, he reached out and pulled Barbara up to him. He wrapped his arms around her and held her close. She wrapped her arms around his neck and held onto him. She laid her head on his shoulder while she caught her breath.

"Would you rather walk back along the shore?" Mark asked.

"I think it would be a good idea. I didn't realize it was so far."

"It might be a little harder to swim in a rolling ocean than in a lake. I used to swim in the river. The current was not very fast, but it was not easy to swim up stream."

"It was beginning to feel like we were swimming up stream," she said with a grin.

"You ready to head back?"

She smiled up at him and slid her arms from around his neck. The rolling waves broke against the back of their legs as they walked through the surf toward the sandy beach.

When they reached the beach, they turned and started back to where they had left the blanket, letting the surf wash over their feet. They didn't talk. It was enough for them just to be together, holding hands and walking in the sand.

CHAPTER SEVEN

MARK AND BARBARA returned to where they had left the blanket. Mark turned her in front of him and reached out, putting his arms around her again. She reached up and put her arms around his neck. He leaned down and kissed her. It was the kind of kiss that lets a person know you really care. Barbara then laid her head on his shoulder. She could feel the warmth of his body against her making her feel loved.

As Mark held her in his arms, he caught a glimpse of something out of the corner of his eye. He looked up toward the house. There was some movement in a large window in the bedroom overlooking the beach.

Barbara noticed that Mark's body seemed to become tense. His attention was no longer on her, but on something else. Something had caused him to be alert to his surroundings.

"What's the matter?" she asked as she looked up at him.

"Don't turn around. Should there be anyone in the house?"

The tone of Mark's voice caused a shiver to run through her. She started to turn around to look, but he held her tightly in his arms.

"Don't turn around. Just answer me," he commanded.

"No, I don't think so. Everyone should be gone."

Mark's question frightened her. What was it he saw that made him so tense?

"I thought I saw someone in the window, the large window to the right of the deck."

"That's Janice's bedroom."

"You stay here. I'm going to find out who it is."

"Be careful," Barbara pleaded as she let go of him.

Mark turned and ran toward the house. It did not take him long to cover the distance from the blanket to the steps leading up to the deck.

At first, Barbara watched Mark, but then she looked up at the house and saw the curtain in Janice's bedroom window move. She looked back at Mark just as he was entering the house. She wanted to yell at him to be careful, to warn him, but it was too late. He was already in the house.

Without even thinking, she ran toward the house. When she entered the house from the deck, she didn't see or hear anything. It was dead quiet. She looked around, but there was no one there. Fear for Mark took hold of her and made her heart race. What could have happened to him, she thought as her eyes quickly scanned the room.

"Mark," she called out, but there was no answer.

She moved toward Janice's bedroom and found the door closed. Reaching out, she turned the doorknob and slowly pushed the door open. She was shocked to see that the room had been completely trashed.

The bed had been torn apart with the sheets and blankets pulled off and dumped on the floor. The pillows had been cut open and the stuffing pulled out of them. The dresser drawers had been pulled out and everything that had been in them was now scattered around the room. The pictures that had been on the dresser laid smashed on the floor. The closet doors were open and Janice's clothes had been tossed about the room.

Barbara looked for Mark, but did not see him. It gave her heart a bit of a relief not to find him among the scattered belongings.

She turned and looked down the hall toward the living room. Where could he be, she wondered as she went to the front window and looked out toward the street. She could see Mark standing near the end of the driveway. He was standing with his hands on his hips and looking down the street. He seemed to be trying to catch his breath. She felt relieved that no harm had come to him.

Barbara turned away from the window and looked toward the hall. She wondered if any of the other rooms had been trashed. Barbara started down the hall toward her bedroom. She was reluctant to open the door. Turning the doorknob, she pushed the door open and looked inside. Her bed was still neatly made and her blouse and shorts were still where she had left them, on the foot of the bed.

She heard the front door close and turned around at the sound of footsteps behind her. It was a relief to see Mark coming down the hall toward her.

"Did you see who it was?" Barbara asked.

"No, not really. I heard the front door slam shut just as I came in from the deck. I ran out the front. Just as I got out to the driveway, I saw someone jumping into a red Chevy convertible. They burned rubber to get out of here," Mark explained.

"Did you see Janice's room?"

"No. Why?"

"Come with me," she said as she took his hand and led him down the hall to Janice's bedroom.

Mark noticed how tightly she held his hand. He could sense that she was scared, but she had every right to be scared. After all, someone had come into the house without anyone knowing it. Barbara pushed the door to Janice's bedroom open and Mark looked inside.

"My God! It looks as if it has been hit by a tornado. Are any of the other rooms like this?"

"I haven't check any, expect mine. My room is okay."

"I think we better call the police. We shouldn't touch anything."

Mark and Barbara walked back down the hall and into the kitchen. Mark picked up the phone and called the police. After hanging up, Mark looked over at Barbara. She seemed to be shaking a little. This had really upset her. He walked up to her and put his arms around her.

"The police will be here soon. They are sending a detective to look around."

"What's going on?"

She almost pleaded with Mark for an answer. She was obviously confused by it all. She had never seen anything like it before.

"I don't know."

Mark was feeling a bit helpless. He could not answer her questions, nor calm her fears.

"Why would someone just come in and destroy her things like that?"

"I don't know," he replied softly.

Mark's mind was working hard to try to make some sense out of this. Why would someone come in and destroy just the one room and why that room? Was this whole thing directed at Janice? Was it possibly a message to Janice? Mark's mind was filled with questions he could not answer.

"Why don't you sit down? I'll get you a cup of coffee," Mark suggested as he let go of her and pulled one of the kitchen chairs out.

"I would like my beach robe before the police get here."

"You just sit there. I'll get it for you. Where is it?"

"It's hanging on the back of my bathroom door."

Mark poured two cups of coffee and set them on the table. He then went to Barbara's bedroom. Entering the bathroom, he took her robe off the back of the bathroom door and returned to the kitchen.

Just as Mark returned to the kitchen, the doorbell ran. Barbara stood up. Mark held the robe while she slipped her arms into the sleeves. Barbara wrapped herself up in the robe and tied the belt tightly.

"I'll get it," Mark said.

Barbara followed Mark as far as the living room. She stood back and watched as Mark answered the door.

Standing on the porch was a rather tall slim man in a suit. Just behind him was another man, a little shorter, dressed in slacks and a sport coat. The taller of the two was holding out an identification card and a police badge.

"I'm Detective Sinclair of the San Diego Police Department and this is Sergeant Stanford. We got a call saying your house had been broken into."

"Yes, sir," Mark replied after looking at the identification card. "Come in, Please."

"Would you identify yourselves, please?" Detective Sinclair asked.

"Sure. I'm Mark Walker and this is Barbara Sanders. She lives here."

"What happened?" Detective Sinclair asked.

"We're not really sure. We were down on the beach when we saw someone in one of the windows. When I came up, he left out the front door and jumped into a red Chevy and took off," Mark explained.

"Did you get the license number of the car?"

"No. I couldn't see the lower part of the car because of the hedge out in front. By the time I got out into the street, it was too far away."

Barbara moved up along side Mark and took hold of his arm. She was still frightened and felt a little more secure holding onto him.

"Was anything stolen?"

"We're not sure. It looks like all he did was trash Ensign Janice Miller's bedroom," Mark replied.

"Ensign Miller?"

"Yes. She lives here with three other Navy nurses," Mark replied.

"Who are the others?"

"Well, myself, Laurey Michaels, Carol Jackson and Janice Miller," Barbara said.

"Where are the other nurses?"

"Laurey, Miss Michaels, is somewhere in the mountains with her boyfriend, and Carol Jackson is at Balboa Naval Hospital on duty. Janice Miller is a patient at the hospital."

Barbara noticed the look on Detective Sinclair's face when she mentioned Janice was a patient.

"Janice was beaten up last night, just down the beach," Barbara explained.

"I would like to see, ah, Miller's bedroom."

"Sure." Mark pointed down the hall toward Janice's bedroom.

Detective Sinclair pushed the door open and looked inside. He had seen worse, but at the moment he could not remember when. He turned around and looked at Sergeant Stanford.

"We better get a Crime Unit out here."

Sergeant Stanford simply nodded his head and went out to the car.

"Are there any other rooms ransacked like this?"

"We really haven't checked all the rooms. My room seems to have been left alone. Maybe, he didn't have time to go through the other rooms," Barbara suggested.

"Let's check out the other bedrooms," Detective Sinclair suggested.

Barbara led the detective from one room to the next. The only room that had been destroyed was Janice's. The rest of the house had been left untouched.

"The Crime Unit will be here shortly. I don't want you to touch anything until they are finished," Detective Sinclair said.

Mark could see that Barbara seemed to be uncomfortable. He was sure she might feel a little more at ease if she could get out of her swimming suit and into something more comfortable. He knew he would feel more comfortable in some street clothes.

"Would you mind if Miss Sanders goes into her bedroom and changes?" Mark asked.

"No, not at all. You can change too, if you like," Detective Sinclair replied.

Mark walked Barbara to her bedroom.

"Everything will be all right," Mark assured her as he put his arms around her while she put her hands on his shoulders.

She smiled up at him as he leaned down and gave her a light kiss on the lips. She was glad he was there. It helped her cope with everything.

Barbara slid her hands off his shoulders, turned and went through her bedroom into the bathroom. After taking off her robe, she took off her swimming suit, rinsed out the salt from the ocean, hung it up in the shower and returned to her bedroom. She decided not to wear the shorts and blouse she had laid out, but would put on a pair of slacks and a blouse.

Mark went into the main bathroom, took off his swimsuit and laid it on the edge of the sink. He would have preferred to take a shower, but decided to simply get dressed and get back out in the living room where the police were waiting.

"Do you live here?" Sergeant Stanford asked Mark when he returned to the living room.

"No!" Mark replied, wondering what that had to do with the break-in.

"What's your relationship to Miss Sanders?" Sergeant Stanford asked.

Barbara came into the living room and stood beside Mark. She took hold of his arm. It was clear that she was still a little shaken by the experience.

"We are very close friends," Mark replied.

"Just what does our relationship have to do with someone breaking into my house?" Barbara asked angrily.

"Well, if he doesn't live here, we want to know what he is doing here."

"He is here because I invited him to come over for the afternoon to go swimming."

Just then the doorbell rang.

"I'll get it if you don't mind," Detective Sinclair said.

Mark and Barbara watched as the detective went to the door. Two men came into the house carrying black cases. Detective Sinclair led them directly to Janice's bedroom without introducing them.

"It will probably take them a while," Mark explained to her.

Barbara squeezed Mark's hand. She was glad she did not have to go through all this alone. It just seemed to her that the police were treating them as if they were the criminals, rather than the victims.

After about fifteen minutes or so, Detective Sinclair returned to the living room. He had a picture in his hand and held it out to Mark. The picture was of Janice and Jim standing in front of a red Chevy convertible.

"Is this the car you saw?" Detective Sinclair asked.

Mark looked at the picture. "I think so. Yes, that looks like the car."

"Who are the people in this picture?"

"The woman is Ensign Janice Miller and the guy is Jim. I don't know his last name," Mark replied.

"His name is Jim Thorne," Barbara added.

It was obvious from the tone of her voice she did not like him.

"It sounds as if you don't care much for this Thorne fellow," Detective Sinclair said.

"I don't," Barbara replied flatly.

"Why is that?"

"Because he's mean. He beat up Janice last night and put her in the hospital."

"Did you see him do it?"

"Well, no. But I talked to her this morning and she indicated he was the one who beat her up, at least she did not deny it."

"Did she come right out and say he was the one?"

"No, not really."

"Has she pressed charges?"

"No, not yet, anyway. The doctors will not let the police talk to her until tomorrow."

Just then the two men who had been in Janice's room came out into the living room. Detective Sinclair excused himself and walked to the door with the men. They talked for a couple of minutes. Mark and Barbara could not hear what they were saying, but it was clear by the look on Detective Sinclair's face that he was not very happy. He returned to the living room.

"The Crime Unit is done in the bedroom. They found a message on the bathroom mirror. It was written with pink lipstick. The message read 'Don't say anything'. Do you have any idea what it might mean?" Detective Sinclair asked looking right at Barbara.

"I can probably make a pretty good guess," Mark offered. "It's a message from Jim to Janice not to file charges against him for beating her up."

Detective Sinclair thought for a minute.

"You may be right. Do you know when Miss Miller will be released from the hospital?"

"No, but my best guess would be not for some time. She was beaten up pretty bad. She had to have surgery to set a broken arm," Mark explained.

"She also has a broken leg and a couple of broken ribs," Barbara added.

"I think I would like to talk to this guy. He sounds like a real winner. Do you have any idea where he lives or where he might be found?" Detective Sinclair was sure he had a good suspect.

"I don't know where he lives, other than he lives some where near Muscle Beach. Janice's phone book should have his phone number. Maybe, it has his address, too. It should be in her room, somewhere," Barbara explained.

"If you should happen to find it, will you give me a call?" Detective Sinclair said as he reached into his pocket and pulled out a business card.

"Sure," Mark replied as he took the card.

"I have to be going. I will be in touch with you later."

Detective Sinclair turned and started toward the door. Mark and Barbara followed him. As he started to open the door, he stopped and turned around to Mark and Barbara.

Speaking directly to Barbara, he said, "By the way, I don't want to scare you, but might I suggest that you not stay here alone tonight. I don't think he will come back, his type usually doesn't if they know the police have been called. My guess is he already knows.

"Just to be on the safe side, you might have someone stay with you. I'll also have a black and white roll by here regularly to keep an eye on the place. At least until we get a better idea of who did this," Detective Sinclair said in an effort to reassure them.

Barbara looked over at Mark and squeezed his hand.

"Don't worry, she will not be alone," Mark said.

Detective Sinclair looked at Mark. He gave a little nod of approval and smiled. He turned and walked out to his car.

Mark shut the door and locked it. He turned around and moved up in front of Barbara. He put his hands on her hips and gently pulled her toward him.

Barbara reached up, put her hands on his broad shoulders and looked up into his dark brown eyes. She knew nothing was going to happen as long as he was with her.

"I guess I will have to stay here and protect you," he said with a devilish grin.

"Yes, I'm sure you will, but just one thing."

"What's that?"

"Who is going to protect me from you?"

"No one, my dear. No one," he said as he wrapped his arms around her, pulled her tightly against him and kissed her.

CHAPTER EIGHT

BARBARA HELD ONTO MARK and rested her head on his shoulder. Even as secure as she felt right now, she could not get the sight of Janice's bedroom out of her mind. It was not only the sight of her bedroom that caused her to shiver in his arms, but the thought that someone had simply walked into the house.

"You okay?" Mark asked feeling her shiver.

It was clear to Mark that she was frightened. He did not like the idea of her being here alone.

"Yes," she replied in a whisper.

"Would you like to get out of here for a little while?"

Barbara raised her head from his shoulder and looked up at him. She wanted to leave more than anything she could think of, but she felt that she should stay and clean up Janice's bedroom.

"I better stay here until Carol gets home," she said reluctantly. "If Carol gets home before we get back, she would not know what to do and would worry about me."

"Okay. I'll tell you what. Janice is not going to be able to clean up her own bedroom by herself, so why don't we do as much as we can while we wait for Carol? I'll help you."

Barbara was hoping he would help her. She was not sure she could stand to be in Janice's room by herself.

"Come on. Let's get at it," Mark said.

She gave him a quick kiss, took her arms from around his neck and took hold of his hand as they went to Janice's bedroom. Entering the bedroom, she just stopped. The task of cleaning the room seemed too much for them to do.

"Why don't you hang up the clothes and put them back in the closet, unless they are going to need to be put into the wash. I'll clean up this broken glass from the pictures and the stuffing from the pillows. We can kind of go from there," Mark suggested.

Barbara nodded in agreement. This time, she didn't mind Mark taking charge of things. She began sorting through Janice's clothes.

Mark picked up the dresser draws and put them back in the dresser. He knelt down on the floor near the dresser and gathered up the picture frames, removed the broken glass from the frames and set the pictures back on the dresser. Picking up all the pieces of glass and pillow stuffing he could find, he put them into the wastebasket. It was impossible for him to get all the glass out of the carpet without vacuuming it up. He gathered up the blankets and piled them on the bed. The sheets and pillowcases he put in a pile next to the door to be washed.

Barbara was still busy hanging up Janice's clothes when Mark was ready to vacuum. He looked at her as she worked. The task of cleaning up was hard on her and the whole incident had scared her. He could not imagine what was going through her mind, but he had to admire her for her determination.

"Where do you keep the vacuum cleaner?" he asked.

"It's in the hall closet."

Mark went into the living room and placed a quick call to the Hospital Master-at-arms. After completing the call, Mark went into the hall to get the vacuum cleaner. Just as he was about to open the closet door, he heard the front door open. He stopped and turned toward the door just as Carol came in.

Carol walked in the door and saw Mark.

"Hi."

"Hi," he replied.

"I knew you were here. I saw your little sports car in the driveway. Where's Barbara?"

"She's in Janice's bedroom. We need to talk to you. Let me get her," Mark said.

Carol had a feeling something was wrong. Why were they in Janice's bedroom? What was going on? Carol's mind suddenly filled with all sorts of questions.

Mark returned from the bedroom with Barbara.

"You two look very serious. It's too nice a day for that, so what's going on here."

"Carol, please sit down, we have to talk," Barbara said.

"Okay."

Carol's smile faded away rapidly. She walked over to the sofa and sat down. She had no idea what was coming, but she felt it must have something to do with Janice.

"Earlier today, someone broke into the house and trashed Janice's bedroom. We don't know for sure who it was, but we think it was Jim Thorne," Barbara explained.

"What?" Carol replied. "Why would he do such a thing?"

"We think the whole thing was to scare Janice enough so she won't press charges against him for beating her. The police have been here. They are looking for him," Mark explained.

Carol thought for a minute, trying to understand what she had been told. She did not know Jim any better than the others, but she was convinced that Thorne could destroy something belonging to someone else just to make a point.

"I talked to Janice just before I left the hospital. She said she was not going to press charges against Jim. She is afraid of him, and now I understand why," Carol said.

"What?" Barbara almost yelled out in anger. "She's going to let him get away with this? There must be something we can do."

"Whoa. Hold on a minute," Mark said in an effort to calm Barbara down. "He's not going to get away with anything."

"If she won't press charges, he will get away with it," Carol insisted.

"No, he won't," Mark insisted.

"What makes you so sure?"

It suddenly occurred to Barbara that Mark must have thought of something they had overlooked.

"It's really quite simple. Jim made his second big mistake when he entered this house without permission and his third when he trashed Janice's bedroom."

Barbara and Carol looked at each other, then back at Mark. In their anger they had overlooked the obvious.

"Janice doesn't have to press charges," Carol said as she began to understand what Mark was getting at.

"That's right. The two of you can press charges of breaking and entering, a felony, as well as destruction of private property," Mark explained. "When he trashed Janice's room, he damaged the wall in a couple of places."

"That's terrific. Why didn't we think of that?" Barbara said.

"That's good, real good. We can get him for the damage he did to the house and get him out of Janice's life all in one big swoop," Carol said with a note of excitement in her voice.

"Not so fast. There is one problem, though," Mark reminded them.

"What's that?" Barbara asked.

"We have seen just a sample of what he will do. It will not be as easy as it sounds. Things could get messy. I think he will do just about anything to keep from going to jail," Mark warned them.

"What do we do?" Carol asked. "We have to get this creep put away where he can't hurt anyone else."

"We finish cleaning up the mess in Janice's bedroom. The police already have pictures of it. We wait until the police have some kind of proof that Jim was in the room and did the damage.

"We also have a talk with Janice. We should try to convince her to press charges for the beating she got. It would be a lot easier for the police to protect her if she files the charges. If Janice files charges, she can get him put away for a very long time. If she won't file charges, then you can, at least for breaking and entering, and destruction of private property. It would be harder for the police to try to protect all of you, though," Mark explained.

"That makes sense. Janice will be in the hospital for at least a week, maybe more. She should be safe from him there," Carol agreed.

"I have already seen to that. I talked to the Master-at-Arms last night, and I called them again a little while ago. They have agreed not to let Thorne on the base. The ward personnel have also been instructed to call the Master-at-Arms if he should get on the base and finds out what ward she is on. If he comes on the base, they have assured me that he will be arrested for trespassing. On a military base, that's a federal offense."

"It sounds like you have everything taken care of," Carol said smiling up at him.

"That's why I love him so much," Barbara blurted out with pride.

It was the first time that Barbara had said she loved him. It took him by surprise.

It took Barbara by surprise, too. She had not even admitted to herself that she was in love with him. She had thought about it, but never really admitted it.

"If you girls file charges for breaking and entering and destruction of private property before Janice files charges, it could be a little dangerous around here for you. We have already seen how violent Jim can be," Mark warned.

"I, for one, don't care. I want to see that bastard in jail before he kills someone, maybe Janice," Carol said.

"I agree," Barbara responded.

"Okay, but I think we should talk this over with Bill. We will need his help in keeping an eye on the two of you," Mark said.

"I'm sure Bill won't mind that at all. He likes keeping an eye on me. In fact, both eyes," Carol laughed. "He will be over later. We can talk to him then."

Mark and Barbara returned to the bedroom to finish the cleaning. Carol changed out of her uniform and joined them. It only took them about an hour or so to have the room in pretty good order.

They had no more than finished cleaning the room when the doorbell rang. Carol rushed to the door. She opened the door and greeted Bill with a big hug and a kiss.

Carol led Bill into the living room where Mark and Barbara were sitting. Looking at the others, he sensed that something was not right.

"What's going on?" Bill asked.

Carol explained what had happened and what they had planned to do about it. Bill agreed with the plan, but the whole thing made him very concerned for Carol's safety.

"Bill, are you going to be around for awhile?" Mark asked.

"Sure."

"I need to go back to the base and take a shower. I told Barbara I would take her out to dinner. I would like someone here with the girls while I'm gone."

"Are we still going out?" Barbara was a little surprised that Mark still wanted to go.

"Sure. Why not? I have no intention of letting someone like Thorne have any control over my life," Mark said forcefully.

"I agree. If we let him control what we do or where we go, he will have won. I will not let him win," Bill replied angrily.

"We made plans to go to the amusement park for dinner and that is what we are going to do," Mark said firmly.

In her heart, she agreed with what Mark and Bill were saying, but her mind was not so sure. It seemed to her that too many things had happened. It just didn't seem right to still go out.

"How about if Bill and I go with you?" Carol suggested to Barbara.

"Sure. The four of us could go and have a good time. You need to get away from here for a little while anyway," Bill injected.

"Honey, it will do you good to get away from here. Besides there is nothing more we can do now. Sitting here and worrying about what might happen next isn't going to help," Mark said softly to Barbara.

"I guess you're right," she agreed reluctantly.

"Good. Mark, you go ahead and get cleaned up. I'll stay with the girls. When you get back, we'll go to the amusement park," Bill said.

Mark stood up and reached a hand out to Barbara. She looked up at him for a second, then reached up and took his hand. He gently, but firmly pulled her up in front of him. Slipping his hand around behind her, they walked to the door.

He turned in front of her and took her in his arms. Barbara laid her head on his shoulder. She wanted him to just stay with her, right here, right now. Barbara knew she was being foolish and probably a little childish, but she was afraid and he made her feel safe.

"Everything will be okay. There is nothing to worry about," he whispered. "I'll be back in about an hour."

Barbara looked up at him and forced herself to smile. She knew she was not very convincing, but it was the best she could do.

"You be careful," she whispered.

"I will."

He leaned down and kissed her. She opened the door for him and watched as he walked out to his car. He was in his car and pulling out of the driveway before she closed the door and went back into the living room.

Bill and Carol were still sitting on the sofa when Barbara returned to the living room. Bill looked up at Barbara and gently nudged Carol to look.

"Barbara, everything will be all right," Carol said in an effort to make Barbara feel better.

"I know," Barbara replied with a sigh. She said it, but deep down she wasn't so sure.

"I'm going to take a shower."

Carol nodded and watched her as she disappeared down the hall toward the bedroom. Carol was worried about Barbara, it showed on her face.

"She has really fallen for Mark, hasn't she?" Bill asked.

"Yes. That's what bothers me."

"Why? He seems like a nice guy."

"He is, I guess, but she has been hurt before by a so called 'nice guy'."

"I think you ought to take a look at Mark. It's easy to see that he has fallen for her, too."

"I suppose you're right, but I still can't help worrying about her."

"Worry about them if you must, but give them time. You might remember that we got off to a bit of a rocky start."

Carol looked at him and smiled. He was right. They had gotten off to a rocky start, but no one would know it to look at them now.

Bill put his arm around her and pulled her up against him. She nestled her head on his shoulder, but she could not stop worrying about Barbara.

Barbara went into her bedroom and sat down on the edge of her bed. Her thoughts were of Mark and whether she had made a fool of herself. She had told him, in front of Carol no less, that she loved him. She did love him, at least that is what her heart said. Her mind was still telling her something else. Her mind wanted her to be careful, don't go too fast, don't push him or she might lose him. There was nothing she could do now except hope that her spontaneous outburst would not cause him to shy away from her.

She stood up and undressed. As she took off her clothes, she threw them into the hamper. She went into the bathroom and turned on the shower. As soon as the water was at a comfortable temperature, she stepped into the shower.

The warm water flowed over the smooth curves of her body, washing the salt from their ocean swim off her soft silky skin. She took the soap and rubbed it over herself, washing away the lotion Mark had rubbed on her. The combination of the fragrant soap, the warm water and the feel of the soap on her skin helped to relax her.

The day had been an emotional roller coaster ride for Barbara. In fact, it had started last night with the walk along the beach. She needed to relax and enjoy Mark's company.

Barbara's mind filled with all sorts of thoughts. She knew she did not want to go through the same kind of hurt and disappointment she had experienced when her college boyfriend had dumped her.

In her heart, she knew Mark was different. He was mature and had a good sense of values. In the back of her mind she wondered if it might bother him, just a bit anyway, that she was an officer and he was enlisted. At work, she was in charge.

She had to stop and smile a little at that thought. At work, in an emergency, Mark seemed to take charge of things no matter who was there.

Although there was no written rule against it, Barbara knew the Navy discouraged officers from dating enlisted personnel. In her heart, she knew it would not be a problem for her, but her mind told her it might be a problem for Mark.

After rinsing off, she stepped out of the shower and wrapped a towel around herself. Slowly, she patted the droplets of water from her skin. After drying off, she went into her bedroom to pick out clean clothes that would be appropriate for the amusement park. She decided on a pullover blouse of bright red with little yellow flowers above the small pocket over her left breast and a pair of black slacks she knew Mark would like and were comfortable for her.

As Barbara turned around, she caught sight of herself in the mirror. She stopped and looked at herself for a minute. What does Mark see in me, she asked herself. There was no question she had a very beautiful figure, but was that all that Mark was interested in? She didn't think so. If he was only interested in a great figure there were plenty of girls who could fill that need better than she could.

Mark wasn't the kind of a man who would like someone just for their body or the way they looked. Barbara knew that much. She was just feeling a little insecure and some of her past fears had come back to haunt her.

"I think he likes you just the way you are," Barbara said to her reflection in the mirror. "Just who are you to question his good taste?"

Barbara made up her mind that she was going to have a good time with Mark for as long as he wanted to spend time with her. If more came of it, it would not be because she pushed him into anything, but because he wanted it that way. She hoped he felt the same about her as she felt about him.

AS MARK DROVE BACK to the barracks, he wondered if Barbara's spontaneous comment had been just that, or had she really meant it. In the past, all the girls that he had dated had their faults and their faults seemed to matter, just as his faults seemed to matter to them. With Barbara, it was different. She had her faults, but they somehow seemed to make her more interesting and more special. She seemed to be able to accept his faults even though it was not always easy for her.

Mark was sure Barbara loved him, but he was not sure how to proceed from here. Barbara had been hurt once before. He could not let himself hurt her again. He would have to play it cool. He decided that he would date her as long as she would accept a date with him. He would not push her into anything she was not ready for, nor would he push himself on her. He was just going to have to let nature take its course, so to speak.

Mark turned into the main gate of Balboa Naval Hospital. He drove directly to the rear of the Men's Barracks, parked his car and went immediately to his room. As he was opening the door to his room, James came around the corner from the front entrance.

"Hey, Mark. How's it going?"

"Not bad. How are you making out with Pam?"

Mark didn't wait for and answer. He opened the door and walked into the room.

"Not bad, my friend, not bad. I just came back to get cleaned up. I'm taking Pam out to dinner, and then I think I will take her dancing," James said proudly. "How about you? How are you doing with Miss Sanders?"

"I'm doing just fine. I came back to get cleaned up, too. It seems that I have a dinner date, too," Mark replied as they headed for the showers. "Where are you taking Pam for dinner?"

"I was thinking I would take her to the 'Top of the Tower' downtown. What do you think?"

"Sounds like money to me and a lot of it. That place is kind of expensive, but the food is real good."

"You think it's a little too much, maybe? I've never been there."

"That depends. If you're trying to impress the hell out of her, it's a good way to start. But, if you are trying to get her to like you for yourself, I don't think I would start there."

"Yeah. I see what you mean. It might be just a little bit overkill."

"Overkill would be the word I would use. Keep it simple until you find out how you feel about her and she feels about you."

Mark smiled as he washed up. He could see James was thinking over what he had been told.

"Say, where are you taking Miss Sanders?"

Mark smiled.

"You wouldn't believe me."

"Come on now. Where are you taking her?"

"Okay," Mark said as seriously as he could. "I'm taking her to the amusement park at Ocean Beach for chili dogs."

"You're kidding, aren't you?"

"No, I'm not. I said you wouldn't believe me. We are going to the amusement park to have chili dogs with another couple."

"You're really not kidding, are you?"

"No. I'm not kidding."

"You know, that doesn't sound all that bad an idea, but I think I will still take Pam to some place where we can sit down and have a good meal. I'm really hoping to get to know her. She seems like a nice person."

"She is nice and her reputation is not deserved," Mark said as he stepped out of the shower and began to dry off.

He took a glance at the clock above the row of sinks. He needed to get a move on if he was going to get back in an hour.

"Listen, I have to get going. Let me know how your date goes."

Mark shaved and combed his hair while James still stood in the shower. He returned to his room and quickly dressed in a pair of slacks and a knit pullover shirt. He put on a pair of tennis shoes and headed out the door to his car.

CHAPTER NINE

MARK TURNED OFF La Jolla Boulevard onto the beach road. As he swung around the corner, he got a glimpse of a red Chevy convertible. He slammed on his brakes and came to a stop in the middle of the street. He shifted into reverse and backed up to get a better look.

The red Chevy convertible was parked in a driveway partially hidden behind some bushes. He reached into the glove compartment for a pencil and paper and wrote down the license number and the address of the house.

He wondered if it was the same car, or if it was a different one that simply looked like it. There was nothing outstanding about the car that would help him identify it. If it was the same car, why had it been parked across the street from the house where Barbara lives?

A gray-haired man stepped out from behind the hedge with a pair of hedge shears in his hands. The man was in his late fifties, maybe early sixties. By the look on his face, it was apparent that he was wondering why Mark was sitting in a car in the middle of the street.

"Excuse me, sir. Is that your red Chevy?" Mark called out to him.

"Yes," the man replied.

It was obvious that the man was curious as to why Mark would want to know, but he was not interested enough to ask.

"Thank you," Mark replied as he reached down to shift his car into gear.

Mark decided that it must not be the same car. As he pulled away, he glanced in his rear-view mirror and saw a younger man step out from behind the hedge. Mark could not be sure, but he looked like he could be the man he had chased from the house. Maybe it wasn't Thorne who had wrecked Janice's bedroom after all. Maybe, Thorne got someone else to do his dirty work for him. Many such thoughts ran through Mark's mind, but no matter what his thoughts, they always seemed to come back to Thorne being behind it.

As Mark pulled into the driveway at Barbara's house, he decided not to discuss what he had seen until later. He did not want to cause any unnecessary worry for the girls.

As Mark approached the door, it swung open. Barbara was standing there waiting for him. He looked her over and smiled.

"You look very nice."

"Thank you. You look pretty good yourself."

"Hey you two, knock it off. Are we going or not? I'm getting hungry," Bill called out from the living room.

"Relax Bill. I don't think you will starve to death in the very near future, certainly not in the next hour," Mark replied.

Mark slipped his arm around behind Barbara and pulled her up against him. She slipped her arm around behind him and rested her hand on his hip. Together, they walked into the living room to join Bill and Carol.

"Well, are you ready to go or are you just going to sit there and wait for dinner to come to you," Mark said.

"If there is a chance of it coming to me, I might just sit here," Bill replied with a grin.

"There's no chance at all. If you want to eat, you will have to get up. I'm not fixing you dinner," Carol informed him as she got up from the sofa.

"In that case, I guess I'm ready," Bill said as he stood up.

Bill took Carol's hand and they followed Mark and Barbara to the front door. Mark stopped and turned to Bill.

"Bill, I think it would be a good idea if we went through the house and made sure that all the doors and windows are closed and locked."

"Good thinking," Bill replied.

"Why don't you girls wait in the car," Mark suggested.

Barbara and Carol walked out the front door while Bill and Mark went back into the house. As they reached the hall, Mark took hold of Bill's arm and stopped him.

"I need to talk to you. On my way back here from the base, I think I saw the red convertible and the guy I chased out of the house."

"Are you sure?"

"No. At least not one hundred percent sure."

"Where?"

"The red convertible was in a driveway just down the street. I got the license number and the address. I don't think the car belongs to the guy I chased. I think the car belongs to an older man, possibly his father. Well, it's a little hard to explain, but I think we should not leave the girls here alone."

"I definitely agree with that. I think we can work something out. Let's get the place locked up and join the girls before they come looking for us."

Mark nodded his head in agreement. They went quickly from room to room to make sure all the doors and windows were closed and locked, then went out and joined the girls.

Barbara and Carol were waiting next to Bill's car. They all got into the car. As Bill drove toward the amusement park at the end of Mission Boulevard, Mark pulled Barbara up against him. He put his arm behind her neck and over her shoulder. She laid her head on his shoulder leaning up against him.

Bill drove past several little shops along Mission Boulevard near the Ocean Beach Amusement Park before he found a parking space. He parked the car, shut off the engine, then turned and looked back over his shoulder to the lovers in the back seat.

"We're here. Time to break it up."

"Bill, quit teasing them." Carol said.

They got out of the car and stood on the curb. Bill looked up and down the sidewalk.

"Well, this was your idea. Which way do we go to get these fantastic chili dogs?"

"First of all, this was Barbara's idea, but I know where to get the very best chili dogs. There's a little hot dog cart with a bright yellow umbrella with red letters on it that spells HECTOR'S. Hector makes the greatest chili dogs in the world."

"You mean we have to find Hector before we can eat?"

"Oh, Bill, quit your complaining," Carol said grinning at Bill's continual kidding around.

"Follow us. We'll lead you right to Hector's."

Mark took Barbara's hand and started toward the entrance of the amusement park. Bill and Carol followed along behind. Just before they got to the entrance, Mark turned down toward the beach. They walked about another half a block, then turned again along the seawall. Just about one hundred feet in front of them was a hot dog cart with a bright yellow umbrella.

"At last we have found Hector. The dying man will at last be saved by the great and famous chili dogs of Hector, ah, what's-his-name," Bill spouted with a dramatic flare as they approached the vendor.

"Bill, would you cut it out."

Carol was unable to hide the grin that crept over her face.

"May I order dinner for you, Ma'am?" Mark asked.

"You may, kind sir," Barbara replied enjoying herself.

"Hector, how are you doing?"

"Mr. Walker! It is good to see you again. It has been a long time."

"Yes, it has. I would like you to meet some friends of mine. This is Miss Sanders, Barbara. I work with her at the hospital. This is Carol and her friend Bill."

"Nice to meet all of you. How can I help you?"

"Well, for starters, we would all like to have a chili dog and a Pepsi," Mark said as he reached for his wallet.

"Coming right up," Hector said with a grin. Hector went to work making the chili dogs and passing them out as each one was ready.

Mark paid for the dinner and thanked Hector. He pointed toward a couple of benches along the seawall as a place where they all could sit down and eat. Mark and Barbara sat down on a bench and began to consume the chili dogs.

No one talked much. It seems they were all very hungry, hungrier than they had realized until they started eating. Mark got seconds for Barbara and himself. He noticed Bill had gone for seconds, too.

After finishing their meal, they just sat for awhile to let their dinners settle. Mark and Barbara watched the people walking up and down along the seawall. It was a perfect evening for a walk along the seawall or along the warm sandy beach.

"Would you like to take a walk?" Mark asked.

"Sure. Would it be all right if we look around in some of the shops?"

Barbara always had enjoyed walking through the quaint little shops, especially the antique shops.

"Guys, we're going for a walk," Mark announced.

"Okay. Why don't we meet you back here in about, say, an hour and a half," Bill suggested.

"Sounds good," Mark replied after looking at Barbara to see if she agreed.

Mark stood up and reached a hand out to Barbara. She took his hand and stood up. They turned and began walking, hand in hand, along the row of shops.

Most of the shops were open front stores with a lot of their wares out on the sidewalk. They walked past surf shops with their surfboards and surfing things on display. They looked at the many different T-shirts and caps that were on display in a couple of T-shirt shops. They even watched an owner of one of the shops as he printed a T-shirt for a customer.

When they came to a little import shop, they decided to go inside and look around. The little shop was filled to the brim with all kinds of items that had been imported from such places as China, Japan, Taiwan, Hong Kong and even India. There were reed baskets, little dolls, toys, glass bowls, cups, dishes and all kinds of things including hand-made glass trinkets.

Barbara stopped at a case of hand blown glass and looked at some of the pieces. She found one that really fascinated her. It was a small hand blown glass angel.

"Isn't this pretty?" she asked as she held it up for Mark to see.

"Yes, it's very pretty. Would you like it?"

"No. I can't let you spend your money on this."

"Why not? If you would like to have it, I would like to get it for you."

"It's too much."

"It's eight dollars. Now is that too much for something for you?"

"Well, no," she said with a sheepish smile.

She really did like it and it would be nice to add to her collection of glass figurines.

"Then that settles it. I'll get it for you, but there is a catch."

"What's the catch?"

She wondered what kind of a "catch" he would put on such an item.

"Every time you look at it, you must think of me," Mark said playfully.

Barbara examined the figurine carefully, then looked at Mark and smiled.

"I hate to hurt your feelings, but I'm afraid looking at this beautiful glass angel just doesn't remind me of you."

"Cute, very cute."

"I love you," she said as she leaned over and kissed him on the cheek.

"Now that will get you the angel," Mark said grinning at her.

Holding the figurine in her hand, they went up to the counter. Barbara handed the angel to the clerk.

"Could you wrap this up so it won't get broken?"

"Sure," the clerk replied as she took the figurine.

Barbara watched the clerk as she wrapped the angel in several layers of tissue paper and placed it carefully in a small box. Barbara looked over at Mark. She knew every time she would look at the glass angel, she would think of this evening with him.

Mark paid the clerk and gave the small box to Barbara. As the clerk gave Mark his change, she thanked him. Mark simply smiled and nodded to the clerk. He again took Barbara's hand as they continued to look at things on their way out of the shop.

They had not gone far before they came to an antique shop. Barbara casually turned and dragged Mark in the front door. Once inside, Barbara let go of his hand and went straight toward an old grandfather clock standing near the door.

"Isn't this lovely?" Barbara said admiring the clock.

"Yes," Mark agreed.

Mark wandered off a little looking at some of the other antiques. He was looking over an old roll-top desk when Barbara caught up with him. Barbara walked up beside him and took his hand.

"Some day I would like to have a desk like this one," Mark said.

They left the shop and started down the sidewalk toward the amusement park. Barbara glanced up at him out of the corner of her eye. She had never felt so close to any other man as she felt to Mark. It seemed a little strange that she felt so deeply for him. Their first date had been just last night, yet it seemed as if they had been dating for years. How could she feel so strongly for him when she had known him for such a short time? The more she thought about him, the more she was sure she loved him.

"You want to go for a ride on the Ferris wheel?" Mark asked.

"What? I'm sorry. I was thinking about something."

"I hope it was about me."

Mark smiled at her. She seemed to be blushing.

"I'm sorry. I didn't mean to embarrass you."

"That's all right. As a matter of fact I was thinking about you," she said with a grin.

"You mind telling what you were thinking?"

"Well, yes, I do mind."

"Oh. In that case, back to my original question. Would you like to go for a ride on the Ferris wheel?"

"Yes."

Her response had been very firm, positive and upbeat. Walking hand in hand, they worked their way through the crowd toward the Ferris wheel. The noise of the crowd in the amusement park was loud and jumbled. Above the continual noise of the people were the sounds of music from several different rides. It really couldn't be called music. By the time all the sounds got mixed together, it became just noise.

They arrived at the Ferris wheel where Mark bought two tickets for the ride. They stood in line to wait their turn.

"How much longer before we have to meet Bill and Carol?" Barbara asked.

Mark looked at his watch.

"About fifteen or twenty minutes."

"Do we have time to take this ride?"

"Sure. Besides, they know where we are."

"How do you know that?"

Mark simply smiled and pointed up toward the top of the Ferris wheel. Looking down were Bill and Carol. Barbara waved up at them. They waved back.

Barbara put her arm around behind Mark's waist and he slipped his arm around behind her. She leaned against him. Somehow it just felt right for her to be here with him.

Mark was looking around at the people. He was very relaxed with her at his side. Suddenly, Mark straightened up and became tense, just like he had on the beach when he saw someone in the house.

"Take a look over there," Mark said as he pointed toward one of the penny pitch booths.

Leaning over the rail at the penny pitch booth, trying to pitch pennies into tiny little cups was Jim Thorne. Attached to his arm was a tall blond in skin-tight purple slacks and a bright yellow blouse.

Barbara held onto Mark tightly. She was not sure if she held onto him to keep him from going after Thorne, or if she held onto him to keep him close to her. She could feel the tension and the dislike build up inside Mark at the sight of that bully.

Mark wanted very much to go over and give him just a little sample of what he had given Janice. But, with Barbara at his side, he was not about to start any trouble. It was not the time or the place to get into a fight.

Thorne threw a penny toward the cup, but missed. He grabbed the woman's arm, squeezed it hard and jerked himself free of her. He pushed her away, almost knocking her down. Mark and Barbara could not hear what he was saying to the woman, but it was clear that whatever it was, it upset and frightened the woman.

"There he goes again. I wouldn't be surprised if she is the next woman he beats up," Mark said angrily.

"Do you think he will hurt her?" Barbara asked.

Mark didn't answer right away. He continued to watch to see if the woman would leave Thorne or hang around.

The woman was rubbing her arm. She yelled something at him and stomped her foot. He raised his arm as if he were going to strike her. She cowered and stepped back away from him. She looked at him for a couple of seconds, then stormed off into the crowd.

Thorne had frightened her enough to make her leave, which was probably the best thing she could have done. After she had disappeared into the crowd, Thorne turned back to the game he had been playing as if nothing had happened.

"I don't think he will hurt that woman tonight," Mark said.

"At least she was smart enough to get away from him."

"That remains to be seen. She was tonight, but what about tomorrow night or the night after that?"

"Hey, you people going to ride or not?"

Mark had been so absorbed in watching what Thorne had been doing that he did not notice it was their turn to get on the Ferris wheel. He didn't bother to answer the ride operator's question. He simply handed him their tickets, helped Barbara into the seat and sat down beside her. The operator grumbled something as he locked the safety bar in place.

The Ferris wheel began to move. Mark looked over at Barbara and smiled. He was not going to let someone like Thorne ruin his evening. He was going to shut him out of his mind for now. He wanted Barbara to do the same.

"What do you say we forget about Thorne for the rest of tonight and enjoy ourselves?" Mark suggested.

"That sounds like a fine idea to me," Barbara agreed with a smile.

"Then I think you should kiss me just as we go over the top."

"You do."

"Yes, I do."

Barbara smiled and leaned toward him. Mark put his arm behind her and leaned toward her. Just as the Ferris wheel was coming up toward the top of its circle, Barbara's lips meet Mark's. They held their kiss until they started back down the other side.

Mark held her close. The Ferris wheel kept going around and around. At the top of the circle they could see lights way up the coast to La Jolla. Up at the top, the view was very pretty with all the colored lights below and the lights off in the distance.

It seemed the ride had just begun when it was over. Once again they were left to mingle with the noisy crowd. They worked their way back to the benches where they had eaten dinner. Bill and Carol were waiting for them.

"Did you two have fun?" Carol asked.

"We did. We went for a walk and went into some of the shops, then went for a ride on the Ferris wheel. Mark bought me a glass angel to go with my collection," Barbara said as she held out her box for them to see.

"Well, we rode a couple of the rides, tossed some darts at balloons and took a few shots at some ducks as they swam by," Bill said.

"Yes, and we also saw Thorne with some painted woman hung on his arm. He sure looked concerned about Janice," Carol said sarcastically.

"We saw him, too. He got mad at the woman and almost hit her, but she was smart enough to leave before she got hurt," Mark added.

"What do you say we head for home? I have to get up in the morning. I have duty tomorrow," Carol explained.

"Sounds all right with me." Barbara agreed.

Bill and Carol started hand in hand down the street toward the car with Mark and Barbara following along. No one seemed to have anything to say, or they were thinking very hard about something.

"I think we should tell Janice what kind of an ass she is so hung up on," Carol blurted out.

Mark looked over at Bill. They were not only surprised by the suddenness of Carol's comment, but by the fact that they had all been thinking the same thing. They started to laugh.

"What's so funny? Have you all gone nuts?" Carol asked.

"No, honey. You see, we were all thinking the same thing. It's just that you were the first one to express it, and express it, you did," Bill explained.

"I, for one, think it's a great idea. The sooner Janice finds out he doesn't give a damn about her, the sooner she will get rid of him," Barbara added.

"What do you think, Mark?" Carol asked.

"I think you might be right. We need to put a wedge between Thorne and Janice," Mark replied.

"Well, I have a stronger word for him, but there are ladies present," Bill added.

"I'll tell Janice tomorrow when I go up to see her," Carol said. "But right now I need to get home and get some sleep. I have to work tomorrow."

The four of them got into the car and went back to the house. Bill and Mark went into the house first to make sure there was no one inside waiting for the girls. After they were sure it was all clear, the girls went into the house. Mark and Barbara walked out on the deck leaving Bill and Carol alone to say their goodnight in the living room.

CHAPTER TEN

THE SKY WAS CLEAR and the stars were shining brightly. There was a full moon coming up behind the house casting long shadows on the beach in front of them. The only sounds were of the waves splashing against the beach and an occasional car going by on the road out front.

Barbara reached up, put her hands on Mark's shoulders and looked into his dark brown eyes. Mark reached out and put his hands on her waist.

"Will you be all right?" Mark asked softly.

"Yes. Do you have to go?"

"No."

"Would you stay a little longer?" Barbara's eyes pleaded with him to stay.

"Sure," he said as he gently pulled her close to him.

Barbara let her hands slide up over his shoulders and around behind his neck as she tipped her head back. He leaned down and pressed his lips against hers and slid his hands around behind her. He held her tightly against his body. He could feel the firmness of her breasts against his chest. She made a soft moaning sound as their lips parted and their kiss deepened in its passion.

"Hey, you guys. I'm going to bed. I have to work in the morning."

Mark and Barbara were startled by Carol's sudden announcement. Carol was standing in the doorway with a big grin on her face.

"You know you could have just gone to bed," Mark remarked.

"Yes. I could have, but it was more fun this way."

"It's okay, mother. I'm a big girl now," Barbara said.

Carol laughed at Barbara's little sarcastic remark, but turned serious rather quickly.

"Mark, are you going to stay overnight?" Carol asked.

Mark had assumed that Bill would be the one to stay with the girls tonight. The seriousness of her tone and the look on her face took him totally off guard.

"I thought Bill would be staying tonight."

"Bill would have stayed if he could, but he has some work to do down at the saltwater treatment plant tonight. Some new kind of test they are working on and he has to do something at midnight to get it started. He will be back tomorrow afternoon. I really would feel better if you could stay," Carol explained.

Mark looked at Barbara to see how she might feel about him staying overnight.

Barbara wanted him to stay, but was afraid to say so. The way she was feeling right now, she didn't want him to ever leave. If it got out that he had stayed overnight it would not look good, nor would it set very well with her supervisor, Lieutenant Halston.

"Barbara, would you like me to stay?" Mark asked softly as he looked into her eyes.

"Yes," she replied softly. "I'm a little afraid to be here alone."

"Okay. I'll stay the night, but I don't think it would be a good idea to let word of this get out."

"Lieutenant Halston can be a bitch. We're not going to say anything to anyone about this, are we, Barbara?" Carol stated firmly.

"No, of course not."

"I'll see you in the morning."

Carol turned and went to her bedroom leaving Barbara and Mark on the deck.

Barbara took Mark's hand and led him into the living room. They sat down on the sofa. Barbara snuggled up against him as he put his arm around her.

She didn't say anything. Her mind was filled with thoughts of this evening with Mark. It seemed to be the simple things that made her the happiest.

"A penny for you thoughts," Mark whispered.

"It would take a lot more than a penny. Would you like something to drink?" she asked in an effort to change the subject.

She was afraid if he pressed her for a response, she might tell him how she felt about him. Her heart said it would be 'okay', but her mind was still telling her to 'slow down, don't tell him, not yet, anyway'.

"Sure. What are you offering?"

Mark understood why she changed the subject, and maybe it was just as well. He had known her for only a short time. It passed through his mind that it might be a mistake to stay overnight. But, on the other hand, he did not like the idea of the girls being here alone.

"I have an idea. Why don't I fix us some munchies? We can sit on the floor in front of the sofa and munch away while we watch a movie on TV," Barbara suggested.

"That sounds good. What's on?"

"I don't know."

Barbara sat up and reached over to the end table. She picked up a TV Guide and handed it to Mark.

"You pick out something and I'll fix the goodies."

Barbara stood up and started toward the kitchen. She stopped suddenly and turned around. Mark looked up at her wondering why she had stopped. She reached out, put her hands on his shoulders, leaned down and kissed him. It was not a very passionate kiss, but rather an 'I love you' kiss, short and sweet.

As she straightened up, she smiled down at him. "Keep that thought."

Turning, she left the room for the kitchen. Mark wondered what she meant by that comment. She was something special, just what he needed in his life.

Mark looked through the TV Guide. There wasn't much to choose from. Most of the movies were old, and he had seen them before. Then he saw an old movie he had always enjoyed, <u>North by Northwest</u> with Cary Grant. He wondered if Barbara would like to see it. He looked at his watch. It would begin in about ten minutes. He got up and went out to the kitchen.

Barbara was putting some cheese and crackers on a plate. She turned and smiled at Mark as he came into the kitchen.

"Did you find something to watch?"

"There isn't much on except old movies."

"I like old movies."

"<u>North by Northwest</u> is on in about ten minutes. Would you like to watch it?"

"Sure. I've seen it before, but I like that movie. Here, you can help me with this," she said as she handed him the plate.

"What would you like to drink?"

"Pepsi would be fine."

"Good, cause that's about all we have unless you want milk or coffee. There might be a beer left."

"Pepsi would be fine."

Mark carried the goodies into the living room with Barbara right behind him with their drinks. They settled on the floor in front of the sofa.

The movie was longer than most movies. By the time it was over, Barbara had fallen asleep with her head in Mark's lap. He didn't want to disturb her and thought about letting her sleep right where she was, but he would not be able to sit that way for very long without becoming very uncomfortable.

Mark had watched her sleep for several minutes before he woke her. It gave him a chance to look at her. Her long shapely legs, the flowing curve of her hips, the smooth lines of her breasts, and the look of her smooth, soft complexion framed by her soft blond hair. She looked so beautiful that he could not keep from touching her. He reached down and gently ran his hand over her soft hair.

Barbara opened her eyes and realized she had missed most of the movie. She didn't move for several minutes. She liked the feel of his hand brushing over her hair.

"I'm sorry. I guess I didn't realize I was so tired."

"It's okay. Maybe, you should go to bed," Mark suggested.

Barbara sat up next to him. She leaned over and kissed him, then stood up.

"I'll get you some sheets and a pillow. You can sleep here on the sofa."

As Barbara left the living room, Mark got up and took the plate and their empty glasses to the kitchen. When he returned to the living room, Barbara was already making up the sofa for him.

After they finished, Mark took her by the hand and walked her back to her bedroom. At the door, he took her in his arms and gave her a long, deep goodnight kiss.

Barbara looked up at him. She had only known him for a short time, yet she wanted him to spend the night with her. She had always thought of herself as the kind of girl who would not sleep with a man until they were married. Yet, here she was ready to ask him to sleep with her.

Mark did not want her to go into the bedroom without him. He wanted her, but quickly came to his senses and, with some effort, decided it was not the time. He needed to give them a chance.

"I'll see you in the morning," Mark whispered.

"Can I come out and tuck you in?"

It was an innocent request, but it made Mark smile. It had been many years since anyone had tucked him in. It seemed strange, but he kind of liked the idea, especially since it would be Barbara who would tuck him in.

"Sure. Just give me a few minutes to get ready for bed."

Barbara reached up and kissed him again.

"I'll get ready for bed, too."

Barbara turned and disappeared behind her bedroom door. Mark stood there for a minute looking at the door. God, she is beautiful, he said to himself. He turned and went to the bathroom. After finishing up in the bathroom, he returned to the living room.

Mark sat down on the sofa and took off his shoes and sox and neatly set them on the floor at the end of the sofa. After taking off his shirt and pants, he crawled under the covers and pulled the sheet up above his waist. Placing his hands behind his head, he relaxed while he waited for Barbara.

BARBARA CLOSED THE bedroom door behind her, leaving Mark standing in the hall. The sound of the latch catching seemed especially loud. It was like the sound of a lock shutting everything out of her life. She was tempted to open the door and ask Mark to come into her bedroom and stay with her.

Barbara backed up against the door and leaned against it as if she were trying to prevent herself from opening it. It was not like her to want a man like this. She wanted him with her, holding her and touching her. Yet, she was afraid he would not want her as much as she wanted him. She had felt the sting of rejection before and did not want to feel it again. She would not give herself to any man without some kind of commitment of love and respect, she told herself firmly. But even her stern resolution was not enough to keep her from wanting Mark.

Barbara moved away from the door and sat down on the edge of the bed. She took off her shoes and sox and dropped them on the floor beside the bed. Normally, she would have taken care of them immediately, but her mind was full of confusion and conflict. Should she do what she wanted to do, or should she do what she had been taught to be right?

Barbara pulled her shirt loose from her slacks, pulled it up over her head and tossed it at a chair. She stood up and took off her slacks, tossing them onto the chair, too.

She went to the closet to select something to wear. The first item she pulled out was a rather sexy powder blue nightgown. Holding it out in front of her, she looked it over. The nightgown was made of a thin, very delicate and sheer material that one could almost see through. The bodice was cut down the front and the back to the waist. The bodice, what there was of it, was fashioned mostly of lace leaving almost nothing to the imagination. It was very alluring. She was sure Mark would like to see her in it, but it would do very little to help her keep things on the cool side, at least for now. Maybe, she would wear it for him when their relationship was more solid and they were deeply committed to each other, she thought as she hung it back in the closet.

The second nightie she picked out was a baby doll nightie in a soft pink. It was not as lacy as the nightgown, nor was the bodice as revealing. However, it was very short and would show off her long shapely legs. She decided it was also a little too sexy for tonight. She was having enough problems controlling her own wants and desires without having to try to control his. She quickly hung the baby doll nightie back in the closet.

She then picked out a pair of white satin pajamas. They were silky and smooth, and far less revealing than the others were. The pajamas had a certain elegance about them. She smiled as she held them up. They were perfect. She knew she looked good in them and liked the way the material felt on her skin. Laying the pajamas on the bed, she took off her bra and panties and tossed them on the chair with the rest of her clothes.

Barbara picked up the pajama bottoms, held them out and stepped into them. The coolness of the satin against her legs felt refreshing like a soft lotion being applied to her skin. It reminded her of Mark at the beach when he rubbed suntan lotion on her legs. The cool soft material caressed her shapely hips and hugged her firm butt as she pulled the pajama bottoms up to her narrow waist.

She picked up the pajama top and put it on. The coolness of the material on her bare back gave her the same sort of sensation as the bottoms had given her on her legs. She slipped her arms into the sleeves. As she pulled the front closed over her firm breasts, the cool material rubbed over her nipples. The sensation caused her to take in a quick breath as it ran through her entire body.

As Barbara buttoned the pajama top, she almost wished she had not said she would tuck him in. She was having a difficult time controlling her emotions. If Mark made any kind of move for her, she knew she would not be able to resist. She wasn't even sure she wanted to resist him. It seemed every move she made, everything she did, brought Mark and her love for him to mind.

She stepped in front of her full-length mirror and looked at her reflection. She saw a woman who was so much in love that it almost frightened her. She shook her head. "Pull yourself together," she told herself. "You don't really know him all that well".

She knew that she had to give herself some time to sort out her feelings about him. Maybe, he has to do the same thing, she thought.

That thought gave her renewed courage. She would listen to what her head told her tonight, not what her heart told her. She took a couple of seconds to remind herself of what she had decided earlier, to give their relationship a chance to grow; and if it was to be, it would be.

She again looked in the mirror, but this time she saw a woman in elegant satin pajamas that showed off her figure, yet, was not too revealing. The top of the pajamas laid soft against her skin showing the smooth lines of her firm breasts, while the bottoms clung to her shapely hips and long legs. She smiled at the reflection of herself. These pajamas may not be as revealing as the nighties, but they were still very sexy. With her resolve to keep things cooled down between them, she was ready to go tuck him in.

BARBARA TURNED AWAY from the mirror, left her bedroom and walked into the living room. The only light on was the table lamp on the end table next to the sofa. Mark was lying on his back with his hands behind his head and his eyes closed. The sheet was pulled up to just above his waist leaving his bare chest exposed. She took a few seconds to look at him. You are one good-looking man, she thought.

She noticed his chest was rising and falling as he breathed slowly. Then it registered in her mind, he was asleep. She smiled as she watched him sleeping. All her worries and fears had been for nothing. Mark had found the perfect solution by simply falling asleep.

Barbara walked over to the sofa. She wanted so much to lean down and kiss him goodnight, but he looked so peaceful. In an effort not to disturb him, she reached over him to shut off the table lamp.

"Aren't you going to tuck me in?" Mark asked in a whisper.

She looked down at him and saw that he was smiling up at her.

"I thought you were asleep. You looked so peaceful that I didn't want to wake you."

"I don't mind."

Mark reached down and patted the sofa next to his hip. Barbara looked where he patted, then back at his face. She had been able to control things up to now. If she sat down beside him, all her resolve might be lost.

"Maybe, we should get some sleep."

Mark patted the sofa again. "Sit with me for awhile."

She could not resist his request and sat down beside him. Reaching out, she put a hand on his chest as if it would help her keep from getting too close to him. His chest felt warm to her touch.

Mark reached out and put a hand on the side of her leg. The satin material felt soft and smooth. With his other hand, he reached up and took her by the shoulder. Gently, but firmly, he drew her down over his chest. She let her hand slide around to his side as she came closer to him.

As their lips met, she let herself down over him. She could feel the warmth of his body through the silky material of her pajamas.

Mark could feel the firmness of her breasts against his chest. As they kissed and he stroked her back through the pajama top, he could feel her melt in his arms. He wanted so much to slide his hands up under her pajama top and touch her soft skin.

Reluctantly, she pulled away and sat up. Barbara could see the love and the passion in his eyes. She was ready to stay right here on the sofa with him, if he would only ask her. Without even thinking about it, she let her hand slide lightly over his chest again. She liked the feel of him.

It took Mark a few seconds to get his desires under control. He wanted her so much, and he was sure she wanted him; but it wasn't right, at least not now. He wanted her; but if he took advantage of her, he might lose her forever.

"I love you," Mark whispered.

The words just seemed to escape from him as he looked into her eyes. It was almost as if his heart had taken over his mind.

She smiled down at him.

"I love you, too," she replied in a soft whisper.

She felt bubbly inside. He had said the words she had needed to hear. He had said them before, but this time was different. This time she was sure he meant it in every sense of the words.

"I think you had better go to your bedroom before I decide to keep you here with me all night."

His remark had invited her to sleep with him, but would that be enough. If he truly loved her, just having her sleep beside him would be enough.

"Do you want me to go?" she asked softly.

She had opened the door. With those few words, she had asked him to let her stay.

"No."

"Can I sleep beside you?"

She was willing to settle for just being beside him for the night. Barbara was sure in her own mind they would simply sleep in each other's arms. She loved him and she knew when the time came for them to make love, it would be beautiful for both of them. She also knew this was not the time.

Barbara turned and lay down on top of the sheet beside him. She laid her head on his shoulder for a pillow and rested her arm across his chest. As she cuddled up against him, he pulled the blanket over her, shut off the light and then wrapped his arms around her.

Mark could feel the warmth of her body through the sheet. Her firm breasts were pressed against his side and her hand was resting on his bare chest. She curled one leg up over his legs. It only took a few minutes for him to tell by her breathing that she was asleep.

Mark thought that this is the way it will be when we are married. That thought surprised him a little. He had not really thought in terms of marriage before. Somehow it sounded pretty good to him. He was not ready to ask her to marry him, but the idea was there. He would have to wait until he was sure this was what they both wanted.

Mark closed his eyes. He was feeling very comfortable with her at his side. What more could a man want were his last thoughts before he drifted off to sleep.

CHAPTER ELEVEN

MARK WOKE WITH THE SUN shining in the front window of the living room. He was not sure if it was the sun filtering in through the drapes that woke him, or the sound of someone moving around in the house. He could hear the sound of water running in one of the several bathrooms of the large old house. He glanced at his watch for the time. It was twenty after six.

Mark heard footsteps coming down the hall toward the living room. He turned his head slightly and watched as Carol came out of the hallway.

Carol glanced into the living room as she passed by. Stopping suddenly, she took a second look and saw that Barbara was sleeping on the sofa with Mark, and that Mark was awake.

"Good morning," she whispered.

Mark simply smiled in reply as Carol turned and went on into the kitchen. Mark did not want to wake Barbara until she was ready to get up.

A slight moan came from Barbara as she began to stir. She was not fully awake, but she knew she was still curled up with Mark. After a couple of minutes of cuddling next to him, she raised her head off his shoulder and looked up at him.

"Good morning," she whispered.

"Good morning sleepy head," Mark replied. "Carol's up. She's in the kitchen."

"Does she know that I slept with you all night?"

"I would think so."

Just then Carol came out of the kitchen.

"Well, you two, did you get any sleep?"

"As a matter of fact, we did," Mark replied.

"I'm off to work. Bill said he would be back about five. He will be able to stay tonight. By the way, Mark, thanks for staying. I slept much better knowing you where here."

For all her kidding around, he knew that both of the girls felt much safer with a man in the house. He felt better knowing that Bill would be here tonight.

"You're very welcome."

Carol smiled, then turned and left for work. Barbara sat up on the edge of the sofa and looked down at Mark. Her satin pajamas were all wrinkled and clung to her body.

"I think we should get up and get dressed," Barbara suggested as she ran her hand across Mark's bare chest.

Mark didn't want her to leave, but it was probably a good idea.

"I should go back to the base and get cleaned up. What would you like to do today?"

"Why don't I fix you some breakfast before you go? When you get back, we can decide what we want to do."

"Okay."

"I'll go get dressed so you can get dressed."

Barbara leaned down and planted a firm, yet loving kiss on Mark's lips. The warmth and the softness of her lips against his, and the brush of her breast across his chest sent a flash of desire through his entire body. Just as quickly as she kissed him, she ended it.

"Think about that while you're getting dressed," she said playfully.

She stood up before he had a chance to respond, and before he could reach out and grab her.

Mark watched her as she walked away from him. He would most likely think about her most of the time, but that kiss would certainly guarantee it.

Mark sat up on the sofa and stretched. He was a little stiff from spending the night without moving. He stood up, slipped into his slacks, then went into the bathroom.

Barbara went into her bedroom and closed the door. She leaned back against the door. That last kiss she had so firmly planted on Mark had not only sent sensations through him, it had aroused desires in her faster than she expected. It took her a minute to catch her breath.

Barbara pushed herself away from the door and took off her pajamas and neatly put them in the hamper. She dressed quickly in the same clothes she had worn the night before. Taking a quick look in the mirror, she thought she looked pretty good for someone who had spent the night on a sofa.

She left her bedroom for the kitchen. As she passed the living room, she looked for Mark, but did not see him. Once in the kitchen, she began to make breakfast for both of them. She had decided on bacon and eggs with toast and orange juice.

Barbara was putting the bacon in the pan when Mark came into the kitchen. He walked up behind her, placed his hands on her hips and looked over her shoulder.

"How do you like your bacon?"

That simple question made Barbara realize she hardly knew the man she loved. She didn't know even the little things, like how he liked his bacon, or his eggs, or much of anything else.

"I'll eat it about anyway except charcoal black."

Mark realized that he did not really know very much about her, either. He decided this breakfast just might be the place for them to get to know each other a little better.

"What can I do to help?"

"You could set the table."

"Okay."

With a lot of help from Barbara, Mark managed to find the glasses, plates and silverware. He poured the juice and made coffee while Barbara made the toast, bacon and eggs. Once all was ready, they sat down at the table to eat.

Mark and Barbara sat quietly while they ate. They both had lots of questions, but were unsure of how to get started.

They were more than half way through their meal before either of them spoke. When they did, they both spoke at the same time.

"I'm sorry. What did you want to say?" Mark was a bit nervous and was more than willing to let her talk first.

"No, you go ahead."

She was as nervous as he was, but she didn't understand why he was nervous. After all, she was the one who was going to ask him about his personal life.

"Please, ladies first."

Barbara smiled at him. Why was it that men always used that as an excuse to get out of leading off a conversation? She was not sure how to get started, but she was sure that he would understand. Nervously she started.

"When I asked you how you liked your bacon, I realized that I don't know what you like and what you don't like. I don't even know the simplest little things about you. What do you like?"

Mark reached across the table, touched her hand and smiled at her. She had been wondering about the same things he had, and it made him love her all the more.

"Well, let's see. I like my bacon just short of crispy, I like my eggs over easy, and I like my toast lightly toasted. I like my woman to be pretty on the inside as well as the outside, just like you. I don't like to be lied to. I like to eat at hot dog stands at amusement parks and I like to eat in fancy restaurants where I have to wear a tie. I like to go canoeing and camping, and I like you, very much."

Barbara was a little embarrassed by his quick response to her question, but his openness reassured her. She felt much more at ease because of his straightforward answer.

Barbara smiled at him and squeezed his hand. She was also amused by the way he rattled it all off. Yet, at the same time, it gave her more insight into the real Mark than she had expected. He liked many of the same things she liked and that made her feel better.

"Now, what about you?"

Barbara hesitated for a second, then quickly decided to give him the same type of response she had gotten.

"Well, ah, I like my bacon crispy, my eggs over hard and my toast a little darker than yours. I like my men to be handsome, but more importantly, I like them to be gentlemen and gentle with me. I like the outdoors, camping and that sort of thing; and I love you."

Mark gave her a broad smile.

"I love you, too. What else would you like to know about me?"

"I would like to know if you are going to let your eggs get cold?"

He looked down at what was left of his eggs, then back at her. He let go of her hand. Maybe, he was pushing her a little too fast, he thought. It might be best if they learned more about each other a little at a time.

They finished their breakfast, then he helped her clear the table and put things away. He wondered if it would be like this if they were married.

"I think I should go shave and clean up. Will you be all right if I leave you alone for a little while?"

"Yes. I'll be fine."

She liked knowing that he worried about her. That thought kind of surprised her, as she had never liked anyone thinking they needed to protect her or take care of her. A boyfriend she had had back in college had been overly protective of her, almost to the point of suffocating her.

It was different with Mark. He showed his concern, but still gave her the space she needed. He always seemed to give her breathing room, taking only as much as she was willing to give, and giving only what she was willing to accept.

Mark took her hand. Together, they walked to the front door. He let go of her hand and wrapped his arms around her. As he pulled her up against him, she slid her hands up over his shoulders and around his neck.

"I'll be back in about an hour and half," he whispered.

"I'll be waiting."

She tipped her head to one side as he leaned down and kissed her. It was a more passionate kiss than the one she had given him earlier. She liked the feel of him pressed against her, savoring the closeness of him.

Reluctantly, he broke off the kiss and looked into her eyes. Mark hesitated for a moment, being unwilling to let her go, but then he released her.

"Wear something comfortable. You will probably want to take a nap before you go to work tonight," Barbara suggested.

Mark smiled, gave her a wink and started out the door. He waved to her as he backed out of the drive.

Barbara waved back at him and waited until his car was out of sight. Someday, he will not have to leave, she thought as she closed the door and locked it.

Barbara went into her bedroom and undressed. She had plenty of time, so she decided to take a nice long shower, maybe even wash her hair.

She went into the bathroom and turned on the shower. As soon as it was warm, she stepped in. The warm water washing over her felt refreshing. It not only refreshed her body, but it seemed to help her put her thoughts in perspective.

Mark was the main line of her thoughts, but as she went over the events of the last couple of days, she realized his concern for her was understandable. He knew people like Thorne and the kind of things they were capable of doing. She had led a fairly protected life, while Mark had been around the world a time or two, literally.

Barbara's thoughts of Thorne and what he had already done made her nervous. Mark's car was gone and there were no other cars around except hers. This was a sure sign to anyone watching the house that she was alone.

The thought that someone like Thorne might be watching the house, along with what he had already done, frightened her. It caused a cold chill to run through her, even in the warmth of the shower.

Barbara quickly got out of the shower, dried off and got dressed. She walked through the house making sure all the windows and doors were closed and locked, even closing the drapes and curtains. It made her feel more secure to be locked in the house.

She returned to her bedroom and sat down in front of her vanity. As she looked into the mirror at her reflection, she shook her head. "You are one big chicken," she said out loud.

But the more she thought about it, the more she realized she was not a chicken, but rather a person who was taking no chances. She was sure Mark would approve of her checking to make sure the place was secure.

Barbara thought of Mark and missed him. She looked at her watch. It would be close to an hour before Mark would be back. There was nothing for her to do, but to wait for him. She was feeling a little tired. A short nap while she waited seemed like the perfect idea. She lay down on her bed and within a couple of minutes, she was curled up with her pillow, sound asleep.

MARK PULLED INTO a parking space behind the men's barracks. His mind was on Barbara and the fact he would be starting to work the graveyard shift tonight. With the two of them working different shifts, it was going to be hard to spend much time with her over the next two weeks.

Mark got out of his car and started toward the barracks. As he walked past James's car, he did not notice that there was someone in it.

"Hi, Mark," a woman's voice called out to him.

Mark stopped, looked toward James's car and saw that it was Pam Williams.

"Hi. Are you waiting for James?" Mark asked as he leaned down on the edge of the door and looked in.

Pam was as sexy as always. She was wearing tight fitting shorts and a halter-top.

"Yes."

Mark noticed that she seemed happier than usual.

"How has everything been going?"

"It's been terrific. James and I have been having a lot of fun. He really is a nice guy. I like him."

"Hey, I told you he was nice once you got to know him."

"I remember. Say, James was saying that Jim Thorne trashed Ensign Miller's room at the beach house. Is that true?"

"Someone trashed her room. We think he had one of his friends do his dirty work for him."

"That sounds like him. Are the police looking for him?"

"They were the last time I talked to them."

"Well, I know where they might find him."

"Where?"

Mark was paying very close attention to her now. This was the first real lead he had to find Thorne.

"Just about every Monday and Wednesday mornings he's down at Muscle Beach showing off for the beach bunnies."

Mark looked at her. He wondered how she would know that about him. She seemed to sense what Mark was thinking.

"I dated him for a very short time. And I mean a very short time. The only person that man will ever love is himself. He's a creep, he's nasty and he's mean.

"He slapped me once, but I was luckier than Miss Miller. It happened on the beach in front of a cop. The cop stepped in and stopped him. I'm sure he would have beat me up real bad, like he did Miss Miller, if the cop hadn't stepped in."

"I'll let the police know where they might find him. And thanks for the information."

"It's my pleasure. I like Ensign Miller. She's real nice. I would also like to see that bum get what he has coming."

Mark nodded in agreement. He didn't know if James knew about Pam having dated Jim Thorne. He thought about asking her, but he saw James coming out of the barracks.

"You trying to steal my girl?" James said with a smile.

"No. I don't think anyone will be stealing her from you."

Pam smiled. She did indeed like James. He was the first guy that she had gone out with who treated her like a lady. Pam knew she had a reputation for being easy, but it was not true. James liked her for herself, and she liked that about him.

"Have they found Thorne yet?" James asked.

"No, not that I know of. But we have a new lead which might help them find him."

Mark did not offer anymore information, besides it was not important now.

"Good. If you need anything, just let me know."

"Thanks, James. Right now I have to get cleaned up."

"You going to see Ensign Sanders?" Pam asked.

Mark looked at Pam, then at James. It was apparently not a secret anymore.

"Yes, I am," Mark said flatly.

"Don't worry, it's not all over the base. Your secret is safe with us. James told me; but I haven't said a word to anyone, and I won't," Pam promised after seeing the look on Mark's face and hearing the tone of his voice.

"I would appreciate it if it didn't get around. There are some who don't take kindly to enlisted personnel dating officers," Mark reminded them.

"I know that, and I know who you mean," Pam said.

"I have to get cleaned up. I'll see you guys later."

Mark turned and walked toward the building. He glanced back toward James's car as he entered the building. James had gotten into the car and was leaning over giving Pam a kiss. It looked to Mark as if things were working out for them.

Mark took his time shaving and cleaning up. He was a little tired and had a lot on his mind. He wondered why life could never be simple.

MARK DROVE BACK to the beach house. When he arrived, he found Laurey and Holland had returned from their trip to the mountains. Barbara had explained what had happened while they were gone and that they were discussing what they could do about it.

Holland was in total agreement with the plan that had been worked out earlier, but Laurey was not so sure. Laurey felt Janice would not press charges.

They had been sitting around discussing the problem when Carol came home from work. She seemed to be in better than usual spirits.

"Guess what? I had a long talk with Janice. She was not going to press charges against Thorne, but she has changed her mind. She will press charges."

"How did you get her to change her mind?" Barbara asked.

"I simply told her that we had seen Thorne with another woman at the amusement park, and how he had hit her for standing too close to him while he tried to play some stupid game. I told her the next time he beats up a women, he just might kill her."

"We know the only people that he beats up on are women. The guy doesn't have the guts to take a swing at a man," Holland stated flatly.

"You know that just may be the answer," Bill said.

No one had noticed that Bill had also followed Carol into the living room. He had arrived at the beach house within a minute of Carol and he had walked in behind her. Carol got up, went to him and put her arms around him.

"Bill, what's on your mind?" Mark asked.

"Well, I was thinking that if we made a show of force, he might just decide it's not in his best interest to bother the girls anymore. Let's face it, he may have muscles as big as a house, but he's still a coward."

"I agree with what you're saying. However, he does have a lot of friends," Holland cautioned.

"Listen to my plan, then decide."

Bill laid out a plan that he was sure would get Thorne out of his and everyone else's life, especially Janice's.

"I personally think we should use Bill's plan as a last resort," Mark said.

"I agree," Laurey replied. "I think we have a chance of getting him out of our lives if Janice will press charges."

"I called Lieutenant Sinclair before I left the base and told him where they might find Thorne. He told me he would check it out, but there was little he could do if Janice would not press charges," Mark explained.

Just then the phone began ringing. Carol was standing next to the phone and picked it up. Everyone was quiet. It was obvious that it was the police calling. After only a short time, Carol hung up the phone.

"It seems the police got a complaint filed by Janice against Thorne. The police have already picked up Thorne and are holding him on charges of assault and attempted murder. Janice went all the way.

"She filed charges of attempted murder because the doctor told her that she could have died among the rocks if Barbara and Mark hadn't found her. He also said Thorne is squealing like a stuck pig. He was threatened with charges of breaking and entering, and the destruction of Janice's room, so he confessed to having someone else do it for him, and named the person who trashed her room."

"That's great. Now all we have to do is let the law take care of him," Holland said.

Everyone was happy with the news. It really looked like Thorne was going to be out of their lives. The charges were very serious and would most likely get him put away for years.

"Excuse me. Excuse me, please. I have something else to tell you," Carol said trying to get everyone's attention.

They all stopped talking and looked over at her. They wondered what could possibly be better news.

"There was one other minor little thing that Detective Sinclair told me about. Janice gave the police Thorne's address. It seems that when they picked up Thorne at his Ocean Beach apartment, they also picked up three of his friends dealing in steroids, which are illegal. So, they also have them for drug dealing, which should put them all away for a very long time."

"I think we should all go out and celebrate," Holland suggested. "How about it, Bill?"

"Damn, I was kind of hoping to get the chance to beat the shit out of him, just so he would know how Janice feels," he said with a disappointed look on his face.

Everyone enjoyed a good laugh over his comment and the way he said it. Mark laughed because Bill's comment had been funny, especially coming from him. Deep down, Mark was relieved it was not going to have to come to a fight. Mark was no coward. He was quite capable of taking care of himself in a fight, but he also knew that a fight rarely settled anything. In fact, it usually escalated the problem.

Mark was not very interested in celebrating. He was tired and just wanted to relax. After all, he was going to have to go to work in a few hours. He took Barbara aside while the others started to make plans for the evening.

"I really don't feel like going out," Mark said softly.

"I don't either. Why don't we just stay here until you have to go to work? I'll fix you something to eat."

"I would like that."

"Say, guys. Mark and I are going to stay here. He has to go to work tonight. I think a little peace and quiet would be nice before he goes to face the rat race at the hospital. I hope you don't mind?"

Everyone seemed to understand and after a discussion on where they would go, they left, leaving Barbara and Mark alone. Barbara took Mark's hand and led him over to the sofa. Mark sat down, but Barbara stood in front of him.

"Why don't you lie down and take a nap. I'm sure you didn't get much sleep last night. I'll get you a pillow," Barbara suggested.

"I think I will," Mark replied.

Barbara went to her room and got a pillow. When she returned, Mark was laying down on the sofa with his eyes closed. He opened his eyes and smiled. He raised his head up and she tucked the pillow under his head. As he settled back down, she leaned down and kissed him.

"I'll wake you when it's time to eat," she said softly.

Mark watched her as she walked toward the kitchen. He closed his eyes and turned his head to cuddle down into the soft pillow. The smell of the pillow was fresh and clean with just a hint of the fragrance of the perfume Barbara wore. The fragrance lingered in his mind as he dozed off.

CHAPTER TWELVE

WORKING NIGHTS in the emergency room had been rather uneventful so far. There had been the usual treatment of some minor injuries and a few drunken sailors. Other than that, it had been very boring.

Mark's time with Barbara had been limited to a few minutes in the morning when she was coming on duty and he was going off, and a couple of hours at her place in the evening before he started work. The short time he was able to spend with her seemed to make the nights drag out.

Their evenings were often quiet evenings together. They would watch a little television, and Barbara would fix dinner for them. It was even hard for them to have any real privacy, especially with Laurey and Carol at home most evenings.

The mornings were different, too. They would see each other at the change of shifts, one of the busiest times on any hospital ward. There was no time to even enjoy a quiet cup of coffee together. There was not a single minute without someone watching them, or at least being in the same room with them.

On the third night, Mark reported for work as usual. Shortly after he arrived, the telephone rang. Mark answered the phone. He listened very carefully to the report he received, making notes. He hung up the phone and went directly to the staff lounge.

"We have incoming injured. There has been an accident on Montgomery Freeway involving a Navy bus, a tanker truck and several cars. We will be getting about six to twelve of the injured here. There may be some burn cases. Let's get a move on!" Mark ordered.

It was Mark's job to make sure the emergency room, staff and all treatment areas were ready at all times for any emergency. Calling up extra corpsmen when needed was part of his job, too. He had just finished making the calls to the barracks for extra corpsman that were on call when he heard the sound of the ambulance sirens. He watched as several corpsmen headed out to the receiving door with gurneys.

"Richard, they are sending most of the serious burn cases here. I want you to set up a triage in the main hallway. Ask the duty nurse to assign a nurse to work with you. We want the most critical cases first."

The duty nurse was Lieutenant Halston. She arrived at the emergency room only seconds before the first ambulance. She looked around as if trying to figure out what she was supposed to do. She acted as if she had never been in the emergency room before.

"Lieutenant Halston, could you help Sherman with the triage in the hallway, please?" Mark suggested.

Lieutenant Halston looked at Mark as if she didn't understand what he was talking about. Without a word, she turned and started toward the door that led into the hallway.

Just as she was about to open the door, the door flew open and two corpsmen came rushing through the door with a patient on a gurney. The victim's clothes were badly burned and his face so covered with soot and blood that it was hard to tell if the patient was still alive.

Lieutenant Halston got only a brief look at the patient, but it was enough. Mark caught a glimpse of her as she ran out the door and quickly turned down the hall to the left. Mark wondered why she had turned left. It was the normal procedure that all the patients are gathered in the hallway to the right, leaving the hallway clear to the operating rooms.

Mark did not have time to worry about what was going on in the hall. A patient had just been transferred to the treatment table and needed his skills, right now.

Mark immediately began cutting away the patient's clothing in order to determine the extent of his injuries. Lt. Commander Wilson made a quick examination of the patient and gave Mark his orders. Mark was joined by another corpsman whose specialty was burn cases.

While Mark cut away the patient's clothing, the other corpsman started an IV of normal saline. Mark discovered that the patient before him was a young boy, not old enough to be a sailor. They washed him in cool sterile water as best they could and looked for open wounds. The boy's most serious burns were to his legs and would require surgery. Since the boy's vital signs were stable, they quickly wrapped the boy's legs in moist surgical wrappings and had him immediately transferred to surgery.

Their second patient was a sailor who had also been burned, but was not as seriously burned as the first one was. He did not require surgery and would be treated, then sent directly to the burn ward where he would be watched and treated.

Other medical teams working in the emergency room had their hands full, too. No one had time to sit around. As each patient was treated and transferred to another department or ward, another one would be wheeled in for emergency treatment.

Just as the third patient was wheeled up to the treatment table in front of Mark, Lieutenant jg, Laurey Michaels came up beside Mark.

"Need a little help, sailor."

"Sure. You can start another IV on that side of him and keep track of his vital signs," Mark said as he started cutting the clothes off the patient.

"What are you doing down here?" Mark asked without even looking up. He had found a blood vessel in the patient's leg bleeding severely, and he was too busy trying to stop the bleeding to look around.

"Lieutenant Halston came up to the maternity ward and told me to come down here and help out. So, here I am. She looked a little pale," Laurey stated as she regulated the flow of the IV.

Mark stopped suddenly and glanced up at her, but quickly returned to his work. So that's where she went in such a hurry, he thought. The woman couldn't handle a real emergency if her life depended on it. Mark smiled to himself and shook his head while still trying to stop the bleeding.

"What's so funny?" Laurey asked, curious about Mark's reaction.

"I'll tell you later. Could you hand me those forceps? I've got a bleeder here. I can't seem to get it stopped. I'm going to have to pinch it off."

Laurey handed Mark the forceps and watched him as he carefully found the bleeder and pinched it off with the forceps. Between taking the patient's vital signs and checking on the IV's, Laurey watched Mark work. She could see why he had such a good reputation as a skillful corpsman. She noticed that he wasted no time, yet he did not rush. He simply did a good job.

"He seems to be stable now. We need to get him prepped for surgery. He will need his leg set and a couple of badly damaged blood vessels repaired."

Laurey called over a couple of corpsmen to help move the patient. They transferred the patient to a gurney and wheeled him out of the room. Mark took off his rubber gloves and began preparing the table for the next patient. Laurey pitched right in and worked right along with the other corpsmen who had been working with Mark.

"Mark, I've got one here that's going to need a delicate touch. Lt. Commander Wilson said for you to get started, and he will be here to help you as soon as he can," Richard said as he helped wheel a patient up to the treatment table.

Mark looked at the young man lying before him. His face was covered with small cuts.

"Fill me in," Mark said as he put on a fresh pair of rubber gloves.

"His face is full of pieces of glass. It seems he went right through the windshield of the bus when the tanker truck hit them. When the tanker blow up, it spread broken glass all over and he got it in the face again. The burns on his face do not seem to be all that severe, but his right arm is badly burned and broken," Richard explained.

"See what you can do for his arm." Mark said.

The corpsman that had been working with Mark had left with the last patient. Mark looked up at Laurey. He was going to need her help.

Mark moved one of the overhead lights down close. He was hoping it would shine on some of the pieces of glass. If it worked, it would make it much easier to find the small pieces of glass and remove them. Mark was glad to see this patient was not awake and did not seem to be having any trouble maintaining good vital signs.

Laurey took a soft surgical sponge and began dabbing away the blood to help Mark find the pieces of glass. She watched as Mark worked very systematically over the patient's face. He first cleared away the larger, easy to find pieces of glass from a small area of the patient's face. As he would remove a piece of glass with a pair of tweezers, Laurey would clean the area of blood so Mark could examine it more closely for any smaller pieces. Once an area was cleared of all the glass, Laurey would place small dressings over the area to prevent further bleeding, though the bleeding on the patient's face was minimal. Mark continued to repeat the process over each area of the patient's face until all the glass that he could find had been removed.

Mark had noticed a small cut in the patient's eyelid and carefully pulled the patient's eyelid up and back. He immediately saw a bright red spot just to one side of the patient's pupil. Getting down as close to the patient's eye as possible, Mark could just barely make out a small thin sliver of glass embedded in the young man's eyeball. He hesitated for just a few seconds, looking up at the patient and then at Laurey.

"His vital signs are stable," Laurey said without being asked.

"I don't know about this," Mark said. He's got a piece of glass in his eyeball."

"You can do it, Mark," Laurey reassured him.

In just this short time of working with him, she had developed a confidence in his ability. His experience of working alone on a destroyer was about to pay off. He had a steady hand and the will to try to help others.

"If I slip, I could cause him permanent damage to the eye."

"If you don't get it out, it will cause permanent damage. You have a steady hand, Mark. You can do it."

Mark let out a long sigh. He knew he had no choice. It had to be done, and done now.

"I need you to hold his head very still. If he wakes up or moves while I'm trying to remove the piece of glass, I could slip," Mark explained.

Mark knew it was going to be very tough, and very touchy. One slip and he could cause the sailor to lose the sight of his eye. That thought haunted Mark as he prepared to remove the glass. He would like to give the job to a doctor, but they had their hands full with other patients.

Laurey leaned down and took hold of the sailor's head. Holding his head tightly in her hands, she nodded to Mark to go ahead and remove the glass.

Mark leaned over the sailor. With very slow and precise movements, he took the small tweezers and carefully gripped the sliver of glass. As he tried to remove it, it slipped out of the tweezers. He took another deep breath, then once again gripped the piece of glass with the tweezers, only the second time he was able to pull the glass from the sailor's eyeball. With the glass removed, the eyeball began to bleed slightly. He took a soft moist surgical sponge and laid it directly over the wound to absorb the blood. It only took a few seconds for the bleeding to stop.

Mark was very much relieved to see the bleeding stop. He was not sure if the sailor would be able to see out of his eye or not, but he had done the best he could. He looked up at Laurey, and she smiled at him. It was clear that they were both relieved it was over.

"How we doing?"

Mark looked up to see Lt. Commander Wilson. The thought of telling Lt. Commander Wilson that it was about time he showed up passed through Mark's mind, but he decided it was probably best not to make any comment at all.

"We're doing fine," Laurey said with a big smile.

She looked over at Mark.

"Good," Doctor Wilson said as he leaned over and examined the sailor's eye.

"You did a good job here. I don't know if he will be able to see out of that eye, only time will tell, but you did a fine job. Let's put a sterile eye dressing on and wrap up both eyes. It will help keep him from trying to look around. We'll give it a couple of days to heal, and then we will see if he will have the use of his eye."

"Yes, sir," Mark replied.

"You did a good job on that arm, too," Doctor Wilson said looking up at Mark.

"I didn't take care of that, Sherman did, sir."

"Well, Sherman, you do good work, too. I'm sure glad I have the two of you on my team. You finish up with this patient and you can take a break. We have seen all the patients. Considering the type of accident these people were involved in, I'm surprised we didn't lose more of them."

"How many didn't make it, sir?" Mark asked.

"We lost one here and three died at the scene of the accident. The reports indicate that there were twenty to twenty-four people involved. We got eight of the worst burn cases and three with other injuries. I have no idea what the other hospitals in the area got for patients."

As soon as the patient was removed from the emergency room, Mark and Sherman began cleaning up their work area. Laurey pitched in to help. When the treatment area was ready for use again, Mark invited Laurey to the staff lounge for a cup of coffee. She gladly accepted the offer.

On their way to the staff lounge, Mark looked over the other treatment areas to make sure that they were ready for the next emergency. He also glanced up at the clock. They had been working for almost four hours.

Once in the lounge, Mark poured two cups of coffee and gave one to Laurey. She took the coffee and sat down on the sofa next to a corpsman.

"I'm glad I don't work here. This place can be a real zoo. I have to admire you guys," Laurey said.

"It isn't always this crazy around here. Sometimes we sit around doing nothing for hours. It's not so much different from any other ward. Sometimes we're very busy, like tonight. Most of the time, it's pretty routine," Mark replied.

"By the way, when I first told you why I was here, you simply smiled and shook your head. What was that all about?"

"Lieutenant Halston sent you here to help. Right?

"Yes, she did."

"She had already been here. She was here when the first accident victim arrived. When she saw him, she disappeared. She left here as if her girdle was on fire," Mark explained.

"You're kidding?" Laurey said in disbelief.

"No, I'm not. It looked to me as if she couldn't get out of here fast enough."

"If that ever gets back to the base commander, she will be out of here in a heartbeat. He would never stand for such conduct from a nurse. Are you going to report her?"

"I don't think I will have to report her. The word will get around fast enough. Almost everyone saw her leave, and you know how hard it is to keep a secret around here."

Laurey simply nodded in agreement as she sipped her coffee. She was wondering what Lieutenant Halston must have been thinking, knowing she had deserted her post and neglected her duty as a nurse. If word of it got around, she would lose what little respect she had from the nurses and doctors, to say nothing of the how the corpsmen would feel about her.

"I better get back to the Maternity Ward. Lieutenant Halston doesn't strike me as the kind of person to enjoy taking care of babies, either."

"Thanks for your help. Anytime you want a job around here, you will certainly be welcome."

"Thanks, Mark, but I think you have a pretty good staff here now," she replied as she stood up and held the coffee cup out to Mark.

Mark stood up and took the cup. He watched her as she walked out of the staff lounge. As she left, Mark glanced at his watch. It was already three o'clock in the morning. His shift was almost half over and it seemed like it had just started. He quickly finished his coffee, then took the cups over to the sink to wash them out.

Mark's thoughts turned to Barbara. He pictured her in his mind's eye all curled up and tucked under her comforter, sound asleep.

THE RINGING OF THE PHONE at the nurse's station suddenly interrupted his thoughts. He stepped out of the lounge and looked toward Richard who was already on the phone. He watched Richard for some clue as to what was coming.

"What's up?" Mark asked.

"We have a marine and a sailor coming in with multiple stab wounds and cuts. It seems they got into a knife fight in a bar. Shore Patrol is bringing them in. It doesn't sound like they are hurt too badly. Shore Patrol just wants us to check them over and patch them up," Richard explained.

"Call Lt. Commander Wilson. He will have to check them over. I might as well get out a couple of suture kits. I'd be willing to bet they are also drunk."

"You'd win that bet," Richard said as he picked up the phone.

Mark went back onto the floor to prepare suture kits at two of the treatment tables. He had just finished setting up when Lt. Commander Wilson arrived.

"Looks like you're ready," Lt. Commander Wilson said as he looked around.

"Yes, Sir," Mark replied. "All we need now are the patients."

Just then they heard noise coming from the hallway. They turned to look as two sailors wearing Shore Patrol patches on their arms pulled a sailor through the door. The sailor's white jumper was all covered with blood and dirt. He had several small cuts on his face and his right arm had a very deep cut on it.

"Where do you want this one?" one of the SP's asked.

"Over here," Mark replied pointing to one of the treatment tables. "Where is the other one?"

"He'll be along in a minute."

"I'll take this one," Richard said.

The SP's took the sailor over to the treatment table. He was instructed to take off his jumper. The sailor did as he was told and then got up onto the treatment table. Lt. Commander Wilson examined him and gave Richard instructions on what to do for him. The sailor was going to require several stitches on his face and a lot of stitches to close the long, deep wound on his arm.

"If you don't mind, I'll stand by this one. I don't think he will give you any trouble, but he is drunk," the SP said.

"Not at all. If he gives me any trouble, I'll simply put him under and he will not be any trouble to anyone," Richard said more in an effort to get cooperation from the sailor than anything else.

The SP simply smiled. "You are going to cooperate with the corpsman, aren't you?" the SP asked to the sailor.

"Yes, sir," the sailor replied with a defeated tone to his voice.

With that response, Richard began preparing the wounds for suturing. Mark helped Richard while he waited for the other patient to show up.

The noise in the hallway sounded like a fight. Mark looked up at Richard. Richard smiled at Mark.

"I think your patient has arrived."

"Yeah, that's what I'm afraid of. I don't think this one is going to be so easy to handle."

Mark turned to see two rather large SP's literally dragging a blood-covered marine into the emergency room. The Marine had a gag over his mouth. The SP's looked over at Mark. Mark simply pointed at the treatment table, stood back and let the SP's set the Marine on the treatment table.

Lt. Commander Wilson had been standing back out of the way. He moved up closer to the Marine to get a better look at him. It was apparent that the Marine had a rather deep diagonal cut across his chest. Although the cut was deep and would require a lot of stitches, it was not deep enough to cause the patient any respiratory problems. The front of the Marine's shirt was cut open and covered with blood.

There was a bruise on his left cheek and a cut over his right eye, which was also going to need stitches. The Marine smelled of alcohol. It was clear to everyone that the Marine was not in any pain. He had had enough booze to take care of that problem.

"We will need to have these cuffs and that gag off," Lt. Commander Wilson instructed the SP.

"Sir, I don't think that's a good idea. He has tried to beat up everyone he has come in contact with tonight. He put a civilian in the hospital with a concussion and caused injuries to several other people at a bar, and that was before these two got to fighting. The reason for the gag is he has bitten one man and has tried to bite several others," the SP explained.

Lt Commander Wilson looked at the SP then at Mark.

"Let's get him secured to the treatment table and run some tests on him. We can stitch him up while we wait for the results."

With the help of the SP's, Mark took the cuffs and gag off the patient, then strapped him to the treatment table. Mark cut the patient's shirt off him. Lt. Commander Wilson drew a blood sample from the patient while Mark cleaned him up.

"Go ahead and suture up the chest wound and the cut over his eye. I will get this blood to the lab. I think we have more then booze involved here," Lt. Commander Wilson said.

Mark began suturing the wounds. Richard finished with his patient and turned him over to the SP's, then turned to help Mark. They were almost finished when Lt. Commander Wilson returned. By this time the patient had passed out and was not giving anyone any trouble at all.

"Well, this guy is not going to the brig, at least not right now. He's on drugs. That's why you had so much trouble handling him. Let's transfer him to the Intensive Care Unit where he can be watched and confined at the same time."

Mark and Richard transferred him to a gurney and secured him to it. Richard called for a corpsman to take him to the Intensive Care Unit with the SP's escorting them, just in case the Marine came around while they were moving him.

With all the excitement they had on the night shift, the night had seemed to go by fast. For Mark, morning and the arrival of his relief, could not come soon enough. He had worked hard, but he still had time to sit and drink a couple of cups of coffee. The emergency room was like that, work hard and fast one minute, then have little or nothing to do the next. Anything can happen in the ER.

He sat at the nurse's station and looked up at the clock. It would not be long now before he could leave and go get some sleep.

CHAPTER THIRTEEN

IT WAS ABOUT 05:30 HOURS when Barbara arrived in the emergency room. It was a little earlier than usual, but she was hoping to have some time for coffee with Mark before he left to get some sleep. She walked into the nurse's station, but Mark was not there. Looking around the treatment area, she did not see him. She wondered where he could be.

Richard had a supply cart and was restocking the medicine cabinets near the treatment tables. He noticed that Barbara was looking around. When she looked his way, he smiled and pointed toward the supply room.

The door to the supply room was open and there was a light on inside. She went directly to the supply room and stood in the door. Mark had his back to her and had not heard her come up behind him. He was busy taking inventory of the supplies and writing a new order to replace the items that had been used.

"Are you about done?" Barbara asked as she stepped into the room.

Mark turned and smiled at her.

"Just about," he replied as he looked at his watch. "What are you doing here this early?"

"I thought if I got here a little early, we might have a cup of coffee together."

"That sounds good, but I would rather have a good morning kiss."

Mark stepped past her and shut the door. As he turned, she stepped in front of him. Setting the clipboard down on one of the shelves, he reached out, put his hands on her waist and drew her toward him.

She reached up and put her hands on his shoulders. Barbara liked the way he looked at her. Better yet, she liked the way he held her. She always felt warm and loved in his arms.

"Don't you think this might be a little risky with Lieutenant Halston stalking around?" she asked looking into his eyes. She knew full well how much trouble the lieutenant could cause them if she caught them together.

"I wouldn't worry about her," Mark said softly.

"Where is Lieutenant Halston? Wasn't she on duty here last night?"

"We don't know where she is, nor do we care. We haven't seen her since she ran out on us last night. When we needed her help, she ran off to the maternity ward and sent Laurey down to help."

Barbara looked into Mark's eyes. She found it difficult to believe that a nurse would run off.

"I'll explain what happened later. Right now, I would like a good morning kiss."

Mark pulled her tightly against him. She wrapped her arms around his neck and pressed her body tightly against his. She tipped her head to one side and closed her eyes as their lips met. It was a warm gentle kiss that sent a warm rush through her.

"You sure smell good," he whispered as he smiled at her.

"Thank you," she replied. "I think we better get back to work, don't you?"

"Yes. I better help Richard."

Just as he took his hands off Barbara, there was a light knock at the door. "Lieutenant Halston is on her way," the voice from the other side said.

Mark opened the door and looked out. He did not see anyone except Richard.

"Thanks," Mark said as he held the door for Barbara.

"Why don't you go sit in the staff lounge? I'll join you as soon as I can."

Barbara nodded and quickly went into the staff lounge as Mark returned to the nurse's station. He was checking to make sure that the ward was ready to be turned over to the next shift when Lieutenant Halston came in.

Lieutenant Halston looked at Mark and then at Richard. It was apparent that neither of them was going to speak to her unless she spoke first. There was no doubt in her mind that they felt she had deserted her post.

"Is the ward ready for the change of shifts?" Lieutenant Halston asked in a rather demanding voice.

"Yes," Richard replied.

The tone of his voice was less than pleasant. In fact, it had a note of dislike for her to it. It also showed a lack of respect, as he did not respond with the usual "Yes, Ma'am".

It was apparent to Lieutenant Halston that Richard had responded this way intentionally and meant it to show a lack of respect for her.

Mark also noticed the tone in Richard's voice. Mark could see the anger growing in the lieutenant's eyes. He did not want to see his friend get into trouble, even though he felt the same way about her. He had to do something to prevent this from going any farther.

"Richard, we didn't get the staff lounge cleaned up. I want you to do it, now," Mark ordered.

Mark felt very uncomfortable giving an order to Richard. He had never had to use an order to get Richard to do anything. Being the senior corpsman on duty, it was Mark's responsibility to make sure everything was in order at all times. Richard did not like the way Mark had made it an order and he hesitated.

"Now," Mark insisted.

Richard looked at Mark, then at Lieutenant Halston. He realized Mark was not just pulling rank on him, but trying to keep him out of trouble. Richard turned without saying a word and went directly to the staff lounge.

"It's good to see you have some control over your subordinates," Lieutenant Halston said with a tone of arrogance.

"Richard may be my subordinate, but he is also my friend and one of the best corpsmen on this base. He will do anything for anyone he respects," Mark added sharply.

"Just what do you mean by that, mister?"

Mark quickly cooled his temper. It would do him no good to get into a shouting match with Lieutenant Halston. That type of situation would only cause him problems.

As Barbara stepped out of the staff lounge onto the ward, she could not hear, but she could see that Lieutenant Halston and Mark were in a very heated discussion. She hesitated for a second, but she felt she should go to Mark's rescue before he ended up in front of the base commander and lost his stripes for insubordination.

As she approached the nurse's station, she could see it was Lieutenant Halston who was all heated up. Mark seemed to be keeping his cool. She decided it would be best if she did not interfere, but simply listened.

"You are the one who neglected your duties, Ma'am, not me," Mark said flatly.

"Who do you think you are? You are nothing but a peon. Who do you think will believe you when you run and tell?"

Lieutenant Halston's voice was getting louder. There was both the fear someone might believe him and anger that he had the nerve to throw this up at her.

"I'm not going to tell anyone about this," Mark said quietly and calmly.

"I don't believe you. If you don't tell, do you think it will give you something you can hold over me?"

Barbara stepped back behind a door, out of sight. She could just visualize the lieutenant getting Mark shipped out to sea. She also knew there was nothing she could do to help him.

"Lieutenant Halston, I don't have to tell anyone about what happened here. It will be all over the base by noon. Not only will this base know, but so will the other bases in the area."

Mark was doing very well at keeping control of his temper. After all, he had more to lose by yelling back at her. She was going to do whatever she wanted, and there was little he could do about it.

Just then, Lt. Commander Wilson came into the emergency room. Barbara saw he was about to speak to her, so she put a finger over her lips in hopes the doctor would not speak out loud. He noticed Barbara's strange action and walked up to her.

"What's going on?" he asked rather quietly.

"I think you should hear what is going on in the nurse's station before you go in there," Barbara suggested.

"I don't approve of listening in on other people's conversations, Ensign Sanders," his tone of voice showing his disapproval.

"I don't either, but I think you should make an exception this time."

Lt. Commander Wilson was curious about what Ensign Sanders' thought was so important for him to hear. He didn't like to listen in, but if Ensign Sanders thought it was important, he would listen, just this once.

"Don't you dare threaten me. I'll have your stripes, and you will be out to sea before you know what the hell happened," Lieutenant Halston yelled at Mark.

Lt. Commander Wilson looked at Barbara. He couldn't believe what he was hearing. Lieutenant Halston was threatening Mark. He knew Mark to be an excellent corpsman and a good enlisted man. What could he have done that would cause such a rage from Lieutenant Halston?

"I did not threaten you. All I said was that when word that you deserted your post and neglected your duties gets around, you will be the one who will have the explaining to do," Mark said quietly."

"Yes, and you are the one who is going to tell everyone I ran off and sent someone else down here to work."

Lt. Commander Wilson could feel the anger in her voice. He also heard her admit that she had left the ward when she was needed. He felt it was time to put a stop to what was going on, but he had to be sure he understood what he had heard.

"No. I won't have to tell anyone, lieutenant. You deserted your post in front of at least three corpsmen from this base, at least two from the ambulance team from 32nd Street Naval Station and two from the ambulance team from North Island Naval Air Station."

Mark was not gloating or holding this over her head, he was simply making a statement of fact. He was not going to show her any respect, nor was he going to try to force any of his so-called 'subordinates' to show her any respect.

Lt. Commander Wilson decided he had heard enough. It was clear to him what had happened and who was threatening who. He stepped out from behind the door and entered the nurse's station.

Lieutenant Halston saw him just as she was about to say something more to Mark. The surprised look on her face made it clear that she knew that she had been overheard by someone in authority. Someone who could cause her to lose her bars, maybe even her commission.

"Lt. Commander Wilson!" Lieutenant Halston said with surprise.

"Mark, I want a full report of what happened here last night," Lt. Commander Wilson ordered.

"I can give you a report," Lieutenant Halston said holding her head up high.

"Lieutenant Halston, you have exactly five minutes to get off this ward. You will report to my office at 0800 and you will wait there until I get there. Do you understand?"

"I - - I."

She didn't know just what to say. She had done one of the worst things a nurse could do, and now there was no way to explain her way out of the mess she had put herself in.

"Do you understand?" Lt. Commander Wilson repeated, demanding an answer.

"Yes, sir," she replied quietly.

She looked over at Mark. If looks could kill, that would have been the one that would have done Mark in. She turned sharply and left the nurse's station in a walk that was just short of a run.

"I want a report on my desk before you leave, a full report of all that happened last night with regard to Lieutenant Halston leaving her post. Is that clear?"

"Yes, sir," Mark replied.

Lt. Commander Wilson turned to leave. Just as he stepped out of the nurse's station, he turned back and looked at Mark.

"I wouldn't worry too much about this. She is in no position to do anything, except try to get herself out of trouble."

Mark watched as Lt. Commander Wilson left the nurse's station and Barbara entered. Mark looked at her. She seemed worried.

"Don't worry. Lieutenant Halston is all through here."

Mark made an effort to relieve Barbara's worries, but he was not sure his problems with the lieutenant were over. As long as she was around, he could not be sure of anything.

"I hope you are right. I would hate to see you shipped out to sea."

Barbara had not had much experience in the Navy, but she had heard about enlisted personnel having run-ins with officers. She had heard they suddenly were transferred to distant duty stations or to ships that were almost always out at sea.

"I have to get a report written for Lt. Commander Wilson. It looks like you are in charge now. It's all yours. Besides, it looks like your first customer of the day has just arrived," Mark said looking over her shoulder.

Barbara turned around and saw a young woman with a small child wrapped in a baby blanket come into the receiving room. The woman looked very worried. Barbara turned back toward Mark.

"Please see me before you leave." she asked.

"Sure. I'll write my report in the staff lounge. If you get a minute, stop in."

While Mark gathered up paper and pen to write his report, Barbara went to help the woman with the child. It wasn't long before Richard's and Mark's replacements had arrived.

Richard had seen Mark going into the staff lounge instead of going to the mess hall for breakfast, something they did every morning. He went into the lounge to see what was keeping Mark.

"What's up? Are you coming to breakfast?"

"I can't. I have to write a report about what happened last night for Lt. Commander Wilson."

"So that's what all the noise was about."

"Yeah."

"Well, I guess I'm off to breakfast. I'll see you later. I'm glad I'm not in your shoes."

Mark simply nodded his head. He wished he were not in his shoes either. Writing the report was not what he wanted to do, but he had no choice. He didn't like Lieutenant Halston, but he could not let it show in his report. He knew the type of person Lieutenant Halston was, and he knew that she would challenge everything he put in his report.

Just as Mark was finishing, Barbara came into the staff lounge. She did not want to disturb him, but she was concerned about him.

"How are you doing?"

"I think I have it done. How are things going out there?"

"It's pretty quiet right now. It will get busy about eight when the clinics open."

"I guess I had better get this report up to Lt. Commander Wilson's office."

Mark didn't seem to be in any hurry to go. Yet, he knew he would have to cover his actions since Lieutenant Halston had made it clear she was going to take her troubles out on him.

"Are you worried about what might happen as a result of your report?"

Barbara was hoping Mark would share his feelings with her.

"No. Well, maybe a little. I don't think she can hurt me much, but she could get me transferred if she really tries hard enough. A month ago, or even a week ago, I wouldn't have cared, but things are different now."

Barbara understood what he was trying to tell her. A couple of weeks ago, it wouldn't have bothered her very much if Mark was transferred, or if she was transferred, but now it would. Just the thought of Mark being transferred sent a cold chill down her spin. She could hardly keep the tears from forming in her eyes.

"I've got to go. I've got to get this to Lt. Commander Wilson's office."

Mark stood up and started to walk past her, but stopped. He reached out and touched her cheek with his hand.

"Can I come over tonight?"

"Yes." She hesitated for a second then added, "Why don't you go to the house and sleep? I'm sure it will be quieter there. No one will be home."

Barbara looked at him. She wanted so much for him to be there when she got home, but she was afraid to tell him. She wanted to be there when he woke up, just in case he needed someone who would listen to him.

"What about Laurey. Won't she be there? She worked last night, too."

"No. She is going over to Holland's. He worked last night, too. You would have the whole house all to yourself. Carol is going over to Bill's after work so she won't be home, either.

"You can sleep in my bed, if you want. My room is quiet. If you shut the drapes, it's fairly dark."

Mark looked into her eyes. It would be quieter, that's for sure, he thought as he tried to justify accepting her offer. It also would be nice to have her wake him.

"I'll think about it while I deliver this report. I need to get something to eat first," he said smiling at her.

"You can pick up my key on your way out."

She smiled at him. He never said that he would, but she felt he would come back and pick up her house key.

"I'll see you in a little while, okay?"

"Okay."

She decided to leave it at that and not say anything more. If he picked up her key she would be very happy. If he didn't, she would most likely be disappointed. Either way, she would not love him any less.

Mark was not thinking about the report when he entered Lt. Commander Wilson's office, he was thinking about Barbara's offer for him to sleep in her bed. He could remember the fresh smell of her when he kissed her in the staff lounge, and the fresh smell of her pillow that he had used the other evening. Remembering things like that made it hard for him to turn down her offer.

LT. COMMANDER WILSON was not in his office. He was not sure what he should do with the report. He didn't want to leave it where someone might find it. Just as he was about to leave, Lt. Commander Wilson came in.

"You have your report ready for me?"

"Yes, sir."

"Good. Let me look at it."

Lt. Commander Wilson reached out his hand and Mark handed the report over to him. He motioned for Mark to sit down and immediately began reading it. Mark waited in silence, noticing every reaction the doctor had as he read it.

"Well Mark, this seems to be very complete. You've even listed your witnesses. Very good. I guess you are a little nervous about this."

"Yes, sir."

Mark thought the doctor's comment was an understatement. He would have preferred that the report be burned.

"I don't intend to use your report unless Miss, ah, Lieutenant Halston gives me any trouble."

"I don't understand, sir." Mark wondered why he had been required to write the report if Lt. Commander Wilson was not going to use it.

"Lieutenant Halston had requested a transfer to the Hospital Corps School at Great Lakes in Illinois. I'm going to try to get her that transfer. She does know her stuff, but she is not cut out to work in the emergency room. I'm sure that is not what you wanted, but at least her talents will be used and no one will have to worry about her deserting her post when she is really needed. What do you think?" Lt. Commander Wilson asked.

Mark thought about it for a minute. It would be a shame to lose her teaching skills. Transferring her seemed to make sense. It would get her out of his life and out of the hospital setting. At the same time, it would get her what she wanted most. It seemed like a good solution.

"It sounds all right to me, I guess."

"Good. You go ahead and get some sleep. By the way, things are working out very well with Ensign Sanders. She has been doing an excellent job. I'm glad you talked me into keeping her."

Mark did not reply. Instead, he simply nodded in agreement. He stood up and left the Lt. Commander's office without further comment.

MARK WENT TO THE MESS HALL to get something to eat. As he ate, he thought about Barbara and her offer to let him sleep at her place. There was no reason for him to stay on base. Yet, he still had his reservations. If word got out he was sleeping at her place, it could make things difficult for her. On the other hand, she seemed to really want him there when she got home. He made up his mind that he would take her up on her offer, but then what was the big deal? He knew deep down inside he was going to from the very beginning.

After he finished eating, he returned to the emergency room. Barbara was busy with a patient. He was about to change his mind and go to the barracks to get some sleep when she looked up and saw him watching her.

She smiled at him and excused herself, leaving the patient in the care of a corpsman. She motioned for him to meet her in the staff lounge. Mark followed her into the lounge and shut the door.

"I decided to take you up on your offer."

"I'm glad," she said with a smile.

She went over to her locker and got her purse. She dug out her house key and handed it to him.

"There are extra towels in the bathroom cabinet if you would like to take a shower. What time would you like me to wake you?"

"When you get home would be fine."

"Sleep well," she said smiling at him.

"I will."

Mark reached out and put his hand on her cheek. He leaned forward and kissed her lightly.

"I better get back to work. I'll see you later."

Mark nodded and followed her out of the staff lounge. He watched her for a second as she returned to her patient, then left the emergency room for the barracks to get his shaving kit and a change of clothes.

It was almost nine when he arrived at the house. He went directly to her bedroom and took off his clothes. After a shower, he slipped on a pair of briefs and crawled into her bed.

The sheets felt cool against his skin and the fresh smell of her sheets and pillow filled his senses. The large bed was firm, yet very comfortable. His last thoughts were of Barbara before he fell into a deep restful sleep.

CHAPTER FOURTEEN

BARBARA ENTERED THE HOUSE as quietly as possible. She did not want to wake Mark if he was still sleeping. He had had a tough night and he needed his rest.

Barbara went directly to the kitchen to check out the refrigerator to see what was on hand for dinner. There were two nice sized steaks and all the fixings for a fresh tossed salad. It would make a good dinner for the two of them. This would be the only night this week when the others would not be home. They could make it an evening for just the two of them, at least until he had to leave for work.

Mark had told her to wake him when she got home, so she went to her bedroom. Slowly and quietly, she opened the door. The sun shining against the closed window curtains dimly lighted the room. She smiled as she looked in on him lying there, sound asleep. The satin sheet was pulled up to his waist. His strong shoulders, broad chest and flat stomach were that of a man who took very good care of himself.

"I love you." she whispered.

He looked so comfortable she decided not to disturb him, not yet anyway. She would take a quick shower and change clothes before waking him.

Barbara tiptoed past him and went into the bathroom. She took one last look at him before she closed the bathroom door. After taking off her clothes, she turned on the shower. As soon as the water was warm, she stepped into the shower and let the water run over the smooth lines of her body. It felt soothing, like soft hands lightly caressing her body.

Barbara thought about Mark sleeping in her bed. She was sure he loved her as much as she loved him. He was gentle, sensitive and considerate. Yet, he was strong. He could be forceful if he needed to be or wanted to be.

She had heard about his reputation with some of the nurses. Much of it was not true. Sure, he had dated several nurses, but that was all there was to it. She certainly couldn't hold that against him. After all, she had had several boyfriends in her past and the past should be left where it belonged, in the past.

Barbara was sure that she was not just a nurse that he was dating. Yet, a little twinge of doubt stuck in her mind like an annoying little sliver in your finger. Not very painful, but a constant reminder that it was there. She understood the reality that they had not known each other very long, but time was not a factor in how she felt about him.

She took a mental trip back to when they first met. She was sure she loved him from the first time she saw him in the emergency room.

Barbara turned off the water and stepped out of the shower. As she stood in front of the mirror and dried off, she looked at her reflection. What she saw was a mature woman with a beautiful figure, smooth skin and a pleasant personality. She also saw a woman who was unsure of herself and unsure of what she really wanted. A woman with a lot of confusion going on within her, and a lot of doubts inside her head.

She had loved like this before, only to get rejected. It was a deep wound that would not easily heal if it was opened again. The question that came to her mind now is is Mark going to reopen the old wound or will he heal it forever? It was a question she knew only time could answer.

She finished drying herself off and slipped into her terry cloth beach robe that had been hanging on the bathroom door. After she tied the robe closed, she opened the door and went into the bedroom.

Mark still appeared to be sleeping. She needed to get into her closet to get a change of clothes. As she opened the closet door, it squeaked.

"Hi," Mark said as he watched her close the closet door.

Mark liked the way she looked fresh from the shower. The robe she was wearing was rather short and showed off her long shapely legs. Mark watched her as she turned and smiled at him.

"Good afternoon, sleepy head. I didn't mean to disturb you. You were sleeping so peacefully I thought I would let you sleep a little while longer."

"Come over here," Mark said softly as he patted the bed next to him.

She looked at the bed and moved toward him. She sat down on the edge of the bed and placed her hand on his chest. His skin was warm and smooth. She rubbed her hand lightly over his chest.

Mark laid his arm across her lap and rested his hand on the side of her leg. Her skin felt warm and soft from her shower. He reached up and placed his other hand on her shoulder and gently pulled her down over him.

As their lips met, she wrapped her arms around his neck. He could feel the firmness of her breasts through the robe as she lay across his chest. He slowly let his hand slide up the outside of her leg and up over her hip. He slid his hand around behind her and over the smooth curve of her shapely butt.

The depth of their passion increased with each passing moment. She moaned softly as he ran his hand gently over her skin. She liked having him touch her and caress her that way. All her doubts vanished from her mind.

With their lips still in a passionate kiss, she raised herself and stretched out along side him. As she rolled up against him, he moved his hands to her hips and gently lifted her up on top of him. She could feel the hardness of his body and the passion he was feeling for her.

He slid both his hands under her robe and gently touched her. With the full length of her body lying over him, he could sense her desire for him, and she was showing her love for him in return with their passionate kisses. He wanted her more than anything.

Wrapping his arms tightly around her, he carefully rolled over on his side, rolling her onto her side with him.

Barbara curled her shapely leg over his legs as she looked into his eyes. This was the man she loved. Nothing else mattered. She would give herself to him and trust that he loved her as much as she loved him.

He put a hand on her cheek and gently touched her as he kissed her lightly. She moved her hand from behind his neck on down his side to his hip.

Gently, as if not to frighten her, Mark slid his hand down off her shoulder, pushing her robe down her arm and exposing one of her firm breasts. He laid his hand over her breast and gently let the palm of his hand slide over her nipple.

Her eyes showed the passion she was feeling. She took her hand off his hip and reached between them. After untying the belt of her robe, she tipped her shoulder back so he could push the robe off her.

Mark pushed her robe down her arm and back behind her. He gently and lightly ran his hand down her body from her firm breast, down over her narrow waist, over the smooth curve of her hip and down her hip onto her long shapely leg.

She reached over and put her hand on his waist. As he slid his hand up her leg to her hip and on up to the small of her back, she looped her fingers into the waistband of his shorts and pushed them down off his hips. She bent down and lightly kissed his chest as she pushed his shorts and the sheet off his legs.

She stretched out, pressing her body against him once again. Mark encircled her in his arms and rolled her back up on top of him. She put one arm around behind his neck, and put her other arm down at her side so that Mark could push her robe off her arm. With her robe loose in his hand, he reached out and dropped it on the floor next to the bed.

With her completely naked and stretched out over him, he ran his hands up and down her body as they exchanged passionate kisses. She moaned softly as he caressed the warm contours of her body.

They kissed each other; their lips touching, parting; their tongues touching, tasting. Her breasts were pressed firmly against his chest and her flat stomach pressed firmly against his hard body. Their passion and desire for each other were building with each second.

She rose up a little and looked down into his eyes. Softly and quietly, almost pleading, she whispered, "Love me."

He slid his hands up her firm, smooth body, across the small of her back and up onto her shoulder blades. Holding her tightly, he rolled her over on her back. They wrapped themselves in each other and in their love for each other; and they made love.

MARK LAY ON HIS BACK with Barbara's head on his chest and shoulder. She had one leg bent up over his legs, and her breasts pressed against his side. Her arm lay across his chest with her fingers making slow tiny circles on his skin.

Barbara was warm and comfortable. She could hear his heartbeat and feel the rhythmic rising and falling of his chest with each breath he took. She had never felt so loved, so wanted, as she did right then. He had been gentle with her. Their lovemaking had been everything she was sure it would be. She wanted this time to last forever.

Mark was feeling warm and comfortable, too. He wanted to savor this moment. He stared at the ceiling while he gently rubbed her back. It was an unconscious thing he was doing, but her skin felt soft and smooth.

Creeping slowly out of the back of Mark's mind came his doubts and fears. They came to haunt him and make him question their relationship. She was a nurse with a college education, while he had only a high school education and the medical training he had received in the Navy. She had a future when she got out of the Navy. What did he have?

If he made the Navy a career, he could only offer her long lonely weeks or months at a time while he was out at sea. If he didn't make a career of the Navy, what then? What did he have to offer her? What would he do? This was all he knew. He could go back to school, but then she would have to support him while he was in school.

"Are you getting hungry?" Barbara asked in a whisper.

"What?" he responded suddenly?

Her question had surprised him and interrupted his thoughts. She did not want to spoil the moment, but he had to go to work. She was sure he would be hungry.

"Are you okay?" she asked worried about him.

"I'm sorry, honey. I was thinking about something. What did you ask?"

"I asked if you were hungry?"

"Yes, a little, I guess."

Barbara was curious to know what was on his mind. Yet, she was afraid to ask for fear it would be something that she would rather not hear. She laid her head back down on his chest. Putting her head in the sand like an ostrich was not the way to build a loving and happy relationship, so she decided to ask.

"What were you thinking about?"

Mark hesitated for a minute. He was not sure just how to tell her what was on his mind. He decided the only way was to just come out with it and hope she would understand.

"I was thinking about us. You and me."

"What about us?" she asked reluctantly, almost wishing that she had not asked.

"I was thinking about how little I have to offer you."

Barbara didn't look up at him, she didn't even raise her head off his chest. She could see it coming. He was trying to dump her as easily as he could, she thought as tears began to fill her eyes.

"I don't have very much to offer you," he said, then paused as he tried to pick his words carefully.

Here is where it all ends, she thought. It hurt her to think he would do this to her, that he would use her, then dump her. She wanted to tell him that his love was enough, that they could work things out, but she couldn't say it.

"We can make it together," he said thoughtfully. "It will take a bit of planning and a little adjusting, but I think we can do it."

Although it was what he had been thinking, he had not stated it very well. However, it was what he wanted. It was what he felt deep inside. No matter what his fears, he loved her.

Barbara did not move for several seconds. Had she really heard what she thought she heard? Her mind had a hard time believing it. She raised her head off his chest and looked at him. She had been so sure he was going to dump her that she never expected this. He wanted her, and not just for tonight, but forever.

Mark noticed the light from the window reflecting on the tears in her eyes. He didn't know what to think, or what to say. Maybe, it was too soon. Maybe, she felt he was pushing her too fast.

"Did I say something wrong?"

The worry and concern he felt showed in the tone of his voice.

"No. Oh, no. You said everything just right," she cried softly

She pulled herself up over his chest and rolled over on top of him again. She wrapped her arms around his neck and planted a hard kiss on his lips that she was sure he would feel all the way to his toes.

He wrapped his arms around her and held her tightly against him. The full length of her warm soft body pressed against him. A sexy, naked body full of love just for him.

Barbara rose up and looked down into his eyes. She could hardly speak as she saw the love he felt for her in his dark brown eyes. She could also feel the love he had for her in his touch as he gently ran his hands up and down the full length her back.

"There is something I have to ask you," Barbara whispered.

She looked down at him, hoping to find the answer to her question without asking. She hesitated, still not sure she was understanding just what he had tried to tell her.

"What is it?" he asked smiling up at her while he continued to let his hands lightly glide over the smooth skin of her back.

"Did you just suggest that we get married?" she asked shyly, a little afraid that she was reading more into what he had said than was really there.

"Yes, I am suggesting that very thing, but you know something?"

"What?" she asked, a little relieved that she had understood him.

"I think it is a crock that men are the ones who have to do the asking. Why can't women do the asking once in awhile?" Mark asked teasing her.

Barbara looked at him. It seemed so perfectly logical to her. She saw no reason why a woman couldn't ask a man to marry. She started to smile at him and in a soft loving whisper spoke.

"Will you marry me, Mark?"

"Yes," he replied simply and quietly. "I would love to marry you, Miss Sanders."

Mark slid his hands up to her shoulders and to the back of her neck. He gently guided her head down to him until their lips met. Their lips held in a long, soft and loving kiss.

It was a kiss that was not driven by passion or lust, but rather by their deep love for each other.

It was getting late and the sun was beginning to set. She once again rose up and looked down at his face. She didn't want to let go of him, but she would have to if he was going to get something to eat and still get to work on time. Reluctantly, she rolled off him, swung her legs over the side of the bed as she sat up.

"It's getting late. Let me use the bathroom first. You can get cleaned up for work while I fix something to eat," she said as she looked at him over her shoulder.

"Okay," he agreed reaching out to touch her back.

He watched her as she bent over and picked up her beach robe. Even in the dim light of the bedroom, he could admire her figure.

She stood up and put the robe on as she went into the bathroom. While she was in the bathroom, Mark lay there looking up at the ceiling. He no longer had thoughts about what he could possibly offer her. She wanted to marry him and that was enough for now. They could work things out.

Barbara returned still wearing the beach robe.

"It's all yours. I'll go get our dinner started. Steak and salad okay?"

"That would be great."

He watched her as she walked out of the bedroom. Mark sat up and swung his legs over the side of the bed. He sat there for a minute in the dark to think before he went into the bathroom.

After shaving and showering, he got dressed. He would have to make a quick stop at the barracks for a uniform, but otherwise he was ready for work.

Barbara was cutting up some cheese to add to the salad when Mark entered the kitchen. She looked over at him as he stood in the doorway looking at her.

"What are you looking at?"

"I am looking at the sexiest woman in the world. And do you know what's so amazing about that?"

"No, what?" she said with a grin.

"She has agreed to marry me."

Barbara smiled as Mark walked up to her. She put the cheese and the knife down on the counter, then threw her arms around his neck.

He wrapped her in his arms and held her tightly as he leaned down and kissed her. Their kiss was a kiss of love and desire. The kind of a kiss that makes the heart race and takes the breath away. When they broke off the kiss, Barbara looked up at him and smiled.

"If we don't quit this, you will end up going to work hungry. It can be a long night if you don't eat."

"Then let's get it on the table. The sooner we eat, the sooner we can get back to necking," Mark said teasing her.

"You are crazy."

"Yes, crazy about you. Now, what can I do to help?" he asked taking a little more serious tone.

"Would you like to cook the steaks?" she replied as she took her arms from around his neck, and he let go of her.

"Sure, how do you like yours?" he asked as he let go of her.

"Medium rare, just like you."

Mark took the plate of steaks out to the grill on the deck. As he waited for the gas grill to get hot, he watched Barbara set the table for two. She was beautiful, but that was not what was on his mind right now. He knew it was going to get difficult for both of them when some of the old hard-liners found out that an officer was going to marry an enlisted man. It would be especially difficult for Barbara since she was the officer. It didn't seem to be as much of a problem when the officer was a man.

Mark put the steaks on the grill. It did not take long before they were ready to eat. Mark put the steaks on the plate and returned to the kitchen.

"The steaks are ready," he said as he put a steak on each of their plates.

Barbara sat down next to him. She took a little salad and passed the bowl to him. After their plates were full, they started to eat. Barbara looked over at Mark. He seemed to be preoccupied, rather distant, she thought. This evening should be a happy evening for both of them. She was wondering if he was possibly having second thoughts.

"What are you thinking about?" she asked.

Her tone was that of a woman who was very worried about something. She wanted this time to be special.

"I was just thinking that things could get a little hard for you if the wrong people found out about us before we have our plans made. Maybe, we should keep this quiet until all our plans are completed. What do you think?"

Barbara wanted to tell the whole world, but she knew it might not be a good idea to say too much, at least not yet.

"You're probably right."

Mark could see that she was a little disappointed. He was sure that she wanted to tell someone, her best friend at least.

"I think we can tell Bill and Carol, and of course Laurey and Holland," Mark said in an effort to cheer her up.

"I don't think we should say anything to Janice," Barbara said. "She has a hard time keeping her mouth shut sometimes. We should call my parents. I would like to introduce you to them, at least on the phone."

She wondered if that was going to be hard for Mark. She was not sure how he would accept the idea.

"I think that's a good idea. We can call your folks on Sunday afternoon. After we talk to your folks, we can call mine in the early evening," Mark said with a grin.

They did not say much until dinner was over. Mark helped her clear the table and put things away.

"Mark, do you have time for a cup of coffee?" she asked.

Her tone was that of a woman who had something important to say to him, something that she needed to talk about with him.

"Sure. Why don't we sit out on the deck? I'll get the coffee."

Barbara went out on the deck, sat down and waited for Mark. He stepped out onto the deck with a cup of coffee in each hand.

"What's on your mind?" Mark asked as he handed her one of the cups, then sat down beside her.

"Well, I was just wondering. Do you like children?" she asked nervously.

"Sure. I like children."

"I'm glad," she said with a sigh of relief and a smile.

Mark reached over and touched her cheek. She leaned toward him and he met her. Their lips met in a tender, loving kiss. She looked into his eyes as their kiss ended.

"I have an idea. Bill and Holland will be here with the girls Saturday night. I don't have to work Saturday night, so why don't we tell them then, that is if you can keep it a secret that long," Mark suggested with a hint of teasing.

"You!" she replied as she hit him playfully on the shoulder. "What makes you think that I can't keep it a secret?"

"You know, the usual reason, you're a woman," Mark joked.

"Mark! You are asking for it. Men are worse gossips than women."

Mark laughed. Barbara knew he was kidding. She glanced at his watch as he sipped his coffee. She noticed it was time for him to leave.

"I think you better get to work," she suggested reluctantly.

Mark looked at his watch. He still had to change into his uniform and it was getting late. He set his cup down on the table, stood up and reached out to Barbara. They walked to the front door together. Mark turned to face her and put his arms around her waist and she slipped her arms around his neck.

"Be sure to lock up. I'll see you in the morning."

"I will, and you will," she replied with a grin.

Mark leaned down and kissed her. He left her standing in the door watching him walk out to his car. She waved to him as he backed into the street and started off to work.

As soon as he was out of sight, she went back in the house, locking the door behind her. She went out onto the deck, retrieved the cups and locked the patio door.

After putting the cups in the sink, she went into her bedroom and got ready for bed. She took off her robe and crawled into bed. She chose not to wear any kind of nightie tonight. She didn't always wear one anyway, but tonight she wanted the feel of the satin sheets against her skin. It wasn't long until she was sound asleep with thoughts of Mark to keep her warm.

MARK ARRIVED AT THE barracks just in time to change and get to roll call. He walked with Richard to the emergency room, but he was not as talkative as usual. He was content to listen to Richard, and think about the evening he had spent with Barbara.

"Is there something wrong?" Richard asked.

"No, not a thing," Mark replied with a smile.

Mark said nothing more about it, although he was dying to tell his friend about asking Miss Sanders to marry him. As they walked, Richard filled Mark in on his day. A good part of it had been spent at the beach with his girlfriend from La Jolla.

CHAPTER FIFTEEN

MARK AND BARBARA had very little time alone together for the rest of the week. Laurey and Carol were home in the evenings, and sometimes Bill or Holland would come over, too. Mark and Barbara would often go for walks along the beach just to have time to themselves. Occasionally, they would sit out on the deck and watch the sunset.

It was difficult for Barbara not to tell her very best friend Carol, that Mark and she were planning to marry. She was sure Carol had figured out something was going on, but doubted she had figured out just what it was. Carol had commented on how much happier Barbara seemed to be lately.

Thursday evening, Mark and Barbara were sitting on the sofa with Bill and Carol sitting across from them. It was Mark's last night on the graveyard shift and they were planning a party for Saturday evening.

"I talked to Laurey, and she said Holland would be happy to chip in on whatever we decide to do," Carol said.

"I thought if the guys brought the steaks, then the three of us girls could make potato salad, maybe some baked beans and a relish dish," Barbara suggested.

"Sounds good to me. What do you think, Mark?" Bill asked.

"I think that would work. What about something to drink?"

"We could get some beer and pop," Carol suggested.

"Okay, I think that will just about do it. I'll pick up the steaks. Mark, why don't you pick up a case of beer and some pop? We can settle up with Holland later," Bill suggested.

"Sounds good. What do you girls think?" Mark replied.

"Sounds good to me, too." Barbara agreed.

"Me, too." Carol replied.

"Ah, just out of curiosity, would anybody mind telling me what this party is all about?" Bill asked.

Mark looked at Barbara, then turned and looked at Bill.

"Bill, do we have to have a reason for a beach party?"

"Well, no. I guess not."

Barbara smiled at Mark. It was the perfect answer. At least it seemed to satisfy Bill. When Mark and Barbara announced their engagement Saturday night, everyone would know the reason for the party.

Mark stood up and put his hand out to Barbara. She looked up at him, smiled and took his hand as she stood up.

"We're going for a walk, we'll see you later," Mark said.

Mark and Barbara went out on the deck, down the stairs and onto the beach. He slipped his arm around behind her, tucked her up against his side and began walking slowly along the beach.

"I got a call this morning from Lieutenant Halston just before I left work."

"What does she want?"

Barbara could just see it now. Lieutenant Halston was going to have Mark transferred to a ship and he would be gone for months at a time. Barbara just knew that Lieutenant Halston was going to get even for the report Mark was forced to file against her.

"She wants to meet with me tomorrow afternoon, right after lunch. She said she wanted to talk about the future. I think she meant my future."

"Oh, no. I was afraid she would try something like this," Barbara said with a tone of disappointment in her voice.

Mark stopped and stepped in front of her. He took her in his arms and looked into her eyes.

"Everything will be okay," he tried to reassure her.

Mark wished he believed that as much as he wanted Barbara to believe it. He was sure Lieutenant Halston was going to make things as hard as she could for them.

Barbara laid her head on his shoulder. She could not keep the tears from rolling down her cheek. They were just getting to know each other, and this woman was going to do everything she could to keep them apart. It wasn't fair.

Mark knew she was crying and he could not blame her. He did not want to be separated from her, either. All he could do was to try to calm her. As he held her, his mind was trying to work out a possible solution. Since Lieutenant Halston had not made any move to get him transferred, it was hard to decide what to do next.

"I have an idea," Mark said suddenly.

Barbara raised her head off his chest and looked up at him. He took his finger and gently brushed the tears away from her cheek.

"I'm going to talk to Lt. Commander Wilson. I'll tell him about the meeting Lieutenant Halston wants with me and see if he will come along. She wouldn't dare try anything if he is there as a witness."

"Do you think he will go with you?"

"I don't know, but I can always ask. The worst thing that can happen is he will say no."

The tone in Mark's voice gave her a small ray of hope. She needed that right now.

Mark turned and walked with her a little further down the beach. They didn't say very much. Each was lost in their own thoughts.

Barbara was worried about the outcome of the meeting. She knew the type of person Lieutenant Halston was. The lieutenant would use her authority to get what she wanted, or to get even with someone she didn't happen to like. She was also the type of person who did not take the blame for her own actions. It was always someone else's fault, never her own. Barbara knew that Lieutenant Halston was not dumb.

She knew the system and how to make it work for her, and that scared Barbara.

Mark was also thinking about Lieutenant Halston. He knew she would try to use her position as an officer, but he had been around for a while and knew how the military worked, too. If he played his cards right, he could get Lieutenant Halston to hang herself.

When they arrived at the rocks at the end of the beach, Barbara turned in front of Mark. She put her hands on his shoulders and looked into his eyes. He reached out and put his hands on her waist.

"Hold me," she whispered softly.

Her eyes were pleading for him to make her feel safe and secure. Mark slid his arms around her as he pulled her close. She let her arms slide around his neck as she pressed her body against his. As she laid her head on his shoulder, she hung onto him tightly. She needed the secure feeling she always had when he held her.

Mark could understand her need to be held. He often felt the same way. He needed her to hold him just as much as she needed it.

Barbara raised her head off his shoulder and looked up at him. She tipped her head back as he leaned down and kissed her. It was a long passionate kiss.

As they broke off the kiss, Mark reached up and took her hand from around his neck, turned and started back down the beach toward the house. After they had gone a short distance, he stopped and they sat down on the sand together.

The bright orange sun was just starting to sink into the ocean. She leaned against him as he wrapped his arm over her shoulder, tucking her under his arm and holding her close to his side. They sat in silence on the warm sand and listened to the surf wash up on the beach. They also watched the sea gulls that fluttered in the air along the shore, and the sun as it slowly sank into the ocean.

There was little to say. It was a time they could be close to each other and shut out the rest of the world. There was no need to even share their thoughts, for they were wrapped in their love for each other.

When the sun had finally set and all that was left was the faint orange glow in the western sky, Mark looked over at Barbara. The gentle breeze stirred her hair ever so slightly. He reached up from her shoulder and touched her soft hair. When he did, she turned, looked at him and smiled.

"I love you," she whispered softly.

"I love you, too," he replied.

Mark leaned over toward her and she leaned toward him. Their lips met in a soft, loving kiss. She shivered slightly. Mark pulled back and looked at her.

"Are you chilly?"

"A little."

"Let's go back to the house."

She nodded her approval of the idea. Mark stood up, took her hands in his and pulled her up onto her feet. Once again, he slipped his arm around behind her as they slowly walked back toward the house. They were in no hurry to have this time together end. As long as his arm was around her, she did not feel the cool breeze.

It was getting close to the time when Mark would have to leave for work. They decided not to go inside, but to walk around to the front of the house instead. When they got around to the front, Mark leaned back against his car. Barbara stood in front of him with her hands on his shoulders while he rested his hands on her hips.

"What time do you think you will be coming out tomorrow?"

"I really don't know for sure. I'm going to try to get a couple of hours of sleep in the morning before I have the meeting with Lieutenant Halston. I also have something I have to do tomorrow. I don't know how long it will take," he said with a bit of a devilish grin.

"Could you possibly make it for dinner?"

"Sure. How would you like to have a late dinner, say about seven o'clock? We could go to the Italian Village for a spaghetti dinner."

"I'd like that."

She leaned against him, sliding her arms around his neck. He slid his arms around her to the small of her back.

"You spoil me, do you know that?"

"I try," he replied with a grin.

"You better get going if you're going to make it to work on time."

She was reluctant to let go of him, and she didn't want him to let go of her. He leaned down and planted a passionate kiss firmly on her soft lips. She moaned softly as he squeezed her tightly against his body. As he kissed her, he let his hands slide down from the small of her back onto her firm shapely butt.

Barbara pulled back slightly and looked into his eyes. Her eyes sparkled as she smiled at him. She took her arms from around his neck and reached around behind her back and took hold of his hands. She gently, but firmly removed his hands from her butt.

"You'll have to save that kind of touching for some other time. We don't have time to start that now."

Barbara liked it when he touched her, she liked it very much. She would have preferred to let him continue to touch her, but she knew she might have trouble controlling her own emotions.

"I will, will I?" he said as he folded her arms up behind her back and pulled her tightly against him.

Her breasts pressed hard against his chest as he kissed her. She returned his kiss with as much passion and desire as he had put into it. Mark let go of her arms, and she quickly throw her arms around his neck. The passion of their kiss was so intense they had to stop to take a breath.

Barbara laid her head on his shoulder. The more she was with him, the more she wanted to be with him. She held onto him as he rubbed her shoulders and neck.

"I better go," he said reluctantly.

She lifted her head from his chest and looked up at him. He leaned down and kissed her lightly. She smiled up at him as she straightened up. Reluctantly, they let go of each other. She walked with him around to the driver's side of the car and stood there while he got in.

"I'll see you about six-thirty," he said as he looked up at her.

She leaned down and gave him a kiss. He started the engine of the little car. Stepping back, Barbara stood in the driveway and watched Mark as he backed out into the street. She waved to him as he drove off down the street and disappeared from view.

It was still fairly early, but Barbara wanted to be alone. She went into her bedroom, closed the door, and lay down on top of the covers. Her mind was in a state of confusion. She was worried about what would happen tomorrow when Mark met with Lieutenant Halston. Would Lt. Commander Wilson attend the meeting with Mark? Are they going to have to learn to live without each other for months at a time? It was the last question she asked herself that disturbed her most.

Suddenly her mind began to put things in a more positive perspective. If Lieutenant Halston got her way and had Mark shipped out, they would make the best of it. She loved Mark and she was sure they could stand the long months of separation. She would write to him every day. Others had managed, although it was often very difficult. They would make the most of the time they had together. She knew Lieutenant Halston could not beat them. Their love for each other would grow in spite of her.

With that very positive thought and the resolve to make things work out, she felt a sense of relief. She closed her eyes and pictured Mark in her mind. It didn't take long and she had fallen into a deep and pleasant sleep.

MARK ARRIVED AT THE barracks in plenty of time to shave and change into his uniform. When he arrived, he found James setting on the edge of his bed just staring at the floor.

"You okay?" Mark asked.

"Yeah. I was just thinking," James replied, then hesitated.

"You want to talk, or would you prefer I leave you alone?"

"I guess I would like to talk."

"Okay. I have to shave, so come along."

James followed Mark to the washroom. He just stood there leaning against the doorjamb as Mark began to shave.

"I thought you wanted to talk."

"I do. It's about Pam."

"What about her? Say, why aren't you two out on the town?"

"She has to work tonight."

He paused to think a little.

"I need a little advice."

"Okay."

"Pam is a very nice girl. She certainly has one fantastic figure. She is a lot of fun to be with and she seems to like me. We have a good time together and we can talk pretty freely with each other."

Mark didn't say anything. He simply listened to James as he rambled on and on about all the things he had in common with Pam. When Mark finished shaving, James followed him back to the room.

"I really think she likes me a lot. I don't know for sure if she loves me, at least not yet, but I'm pretty sure she will as we get to know each other better," James was saying.

Mark had put on a clean uniform and was ready to go for roll call. He didn't have a great deal of time left. James was normally the quiet type. He had never heard James talk so much about anything.

"James," Mark interrupted, "is there a point to all this? Maybe there is something you want to ask me, or are you just telling me all this so you can hear yourself think out loud?"

"Mark, I think I love her," he blurted out.

He looked at Mark as if he had just discovered it at the very time he said it.

"Great. How does she feel about you?" Mark asked as he smiled at James.

"Well, I guess she loves me. She said she did when she gave me a big kiss at her front door a little while ago."

"Great. Sounds to me like everything is working out just fine."

"It is, isn't it?" James replied somewhat surprised to discover things were turning out just the way he wanted.

Mark just shook his head in disbelief. How could a guy as smart as James get his head all messed up over some woman, Mark thought. Mark knew James was not the only one. He could probably put himself in the same category.

Mark left the room for muster before reporting to the emergency room. This time Mark was much more talkative. He told Richard about James, and they both had a good laugh. Mark thought the thing that made it so funny was both of them had been in James' shoes before.

They arrived at the emergency room right on time. The place was very quiet. Mark and Richard relieved the staff and took over in the emergency room.

"Let's hope it's a quiet night tonight," Richard said.

Mark agreed, but did not respond to Richard's comment. He began checking over the emergency room to make sure all was in order, while Richard went into the staff lounge and made a fresh pot of coffee.

"Mark, who is our staff nurse tonight?" Richard asked as he returned to the nurse's station.

"I'm not sure. I think it will be Lieutenant Halston. She's been on all week."

"Not if what I heard is true."

"What did you hear?"

"I heard the base commander got a call from a doctor friend of his about Lieutenant Halston. It seems the doctor is at the North Island Naval Air Station Dispensary. Apparently, the ambulance team from North Island told the doctor about Lieutenant Halston running from the emergency room when she was needed. The doctor reported what his ambulance driver told him to our base commander," Richard explained.

"Needless to say, our base commander hit the roof and called her in on the carpet. I understand she was relieved of all nursing duties until he can decide what to do with her. She has been transferred to personnel until he decides just what action he is going to take."

When Mark heard where she had been re-assigned, his heart almost stopped. The last place he wanted her to be was in personnel. From there she could make transfers with little or no questions asked.

This also caused another problem for Mark. He did not know if all this occurred before or after she had called him to meet with her. If it occurred before, then what did she want to talk to him about? Transferring him? Maybe. If it occurred after, did she still feel the need to talk to him?

It was too late to do anything about it now. He would have to wait until morning. Mark thought about calling Barbara, but thought better of it. If she was already asleep, there was no sense waking her when there would be nothing she could do but worry. He might as well let her get her sleep. If she was awake, there was no sense having her worry all night and not get any sleep at all.

Mark was deep in his thoughts when Laurey Michaels walked into the nurse's station. Mark looked up when he heard her enter.

"What are you doing here?" Mark asked.

"Lieutenant Halston was pulled off nights, and they told me that I was to be the Night Supervisor tonight. It sure looks quiet here," she said as she looked out over the treatment area.

"So far. Would you like a cup of coffee?" Mark asked.

"No, thanks. I thought I would stop here first, then make rounds of the wards I have to supervise. I'll stop back later for some coffee. Call me if anything happens?"

"We sure will," Mark replied.

Laurey turned and walked out of the emergency room. She had offered no new information. Mark wondered if Laurey really knew why Lieutenant Halston was not on duty tonight.

Mark settled back in the chair at the desk. It looked like it might be a slow night. He almost wished it were busy so he didn't have so much time to think about what might, or might not happen with Lieutenant Halston, and the problems she might or might not cause.

CHAPTER SIXTEEN

MARK WAS SITTING at the desk in the nurse's station with his head in his hands. It was hard for him to keep from falling asleep. It seemed as if the clock on the wall had come to a complete stop. It was two-thirty in the morning and nothing had happened. Suddenly, the phone rang, startling Mark. He reached over and picked up the receiver.

"Emergency, Walker speaking."

"We had a city ambulance just clear the main gate with lights flashing. No idea what's going on," the voice at the other end said.

"Thanks," Mark replied and hung up. He stepped out of the nurse's station.

"We have an incoming ambulance. No other information."

While Mark notified Laurey, Richard and another corpsman grabbed a gurney and headed for the receiving entrance. He looked up just as the gurney was wheeled into the treatment area. The patient had an IV in one arm, an oxygen mask over her face and blood soaked dressings on her wrists. In the few seconds it took to get the gurney from the door to a place alongside a treatment table, Mark surmised that the patient had tried to commit suicide by cutting her wrists.

Mark helped move the patient from the gurney to the treatment table, then quickly removed the dressing on the patient's wrist nearest him. He noticed her wrist had been slashed pretty deep, but she had apparently failed to cut the maim artery. Glancing up at the patient's face as he turned to get a suture kit, he stopped suddenly.

"My God!"

"What's the matter?" Lt. Commander Wilson said as he came up behind Mark.

Mark turned and looked at Lt. Commander Wilson.

"It's Lieutenant Halston. She's cut her wrists."

Lt. Commander Wilson looked at Mark in disbelief, then moved past Mark to look at Lieutenant Halston. He looked up at Richard who had just finished taking her vital signs.

"Pulse is slow and weak, blood pressure 70 over 30 and falling," Richard reported.

"Start another IV, get some blood started. Mark take care of that wrist, get the bleeding stopped," Lt. Commander Wilson ordered as he started to remove the dressing from her other wrist.

Richard was sitting on a stool near the head of the treatment table keeping track of her vital signs. He had to adjust the oxygen mask and as he did he detected the strong odor of alcohol.

"Sir, from the smell of her breath, I think she has been drinking rather heavily."

Lt. Commander Wilson looked around for someone who was not busy. He saw Laurey Michaels just as she came into the emergency room.

"Miss Michaels, get help and pump Halston's stomach."

Laurey saw another corpsman standing by. She motioned for him to come with her. She quickly moved around to the head of the table and set up a stomach pump. She pushed a stomach tube down Lieutenant Halston's throat and started pumping.

There were six members of the emergency room staff working to save Lieutenant Halston's life. With Halston's wrists repaired and the bleeding stopped, IV's running in both arms, oxygen running and the stomach pump having emptied her stomach of both liquor and pills, Lieutenant Halston's vital signs slowly, very slowly, began to stabilize.

Lt. Commander Wilson just stood there for a long time just watching her. He had done all he and the rest of the staff could do. It was just a matter of time to see if she would have any permanent damage.

"Listen, all of you. I want everything that happened here kept quiet, at least for now. We will keep her here until morning. I do not want her left alone for even one second," Lt. Commander Wilson ordered.

Mark looked at Lieutenant Halston, then at Lt. Commander Wilson. He felt a bit guilty about what she had done to herself. Mark felt that if he had not written that report on her, she might not have tried to kill herself.

"Mark, I would like to see you in the staff lounge."

"Yes, sir."

Laurey and Richard took charge of the treatment room. They wheeled the treatment table over into a corner and pulled the curtain around it. Laurey stayed with Lieutenant Halston.

"Close the door, Mark," Lt. Commander Wilson instructed after entering the staff lounge.

"It is my guess you're feeling a little responsible for Lieutenant Halston being in here tonight. Am I correct?"

"Yes, sir. If I hadn't written that report on her, she might very well not be here."

"You shouldn't feel guilty about it. I never showed her your report. I had a talk with her about her conduct in the emergency room. I told her if she put in for a transfer to the Hospital Corps School at Great Lakes to teach, and if she didn't cause you or anyone else any trouble, I would approve her transfer and say nothing to anyone about her conduct."

"What Richard told me about the doctor from North Island was true then."

"I don't know what you were told, but probably. Yes. You had nothing to do with it. By the way, she knew the base commander found out from the North Island doctor. I don't think she was blaming you."

Mark felt somewhat relieved that she had no animosity toward him. He could understand how she could try to take her own life. Lieutenant Halston had always set the strictest standards for everyone, including herself. Yet, on one night, she discovered she could not live up to those standards.

"Do you think she will be all right?" Mark asked.

"I think so. It will take a while, but with some help she should do just fine."

"I suppose her Navy career is over?"

"I would think so," Lt. Commander Wilson agreed.

"I hope she can get a job as a teacher in some nursing school somewhere. She has a lot to share with others."

"I hope so, too. You can be sure I will do all I can to help her."

"Thanks, doc."

Mark had never addressed Lt. Commander Wilson like that before. He did not do it out of a lack of respect, but rather out of gratitude for the doctor's concern for Lieutenant Halston.

Mark turned and left the staff lounge. Everyone seemed to be watching to see if he had gotten into some kind of trouble. He noticed the emergency room was not busy and his friend Richard was waiting for him at the nurse's station.

"You okay?" Richard asked.

"I'm fine. I'd like you to take over the ward. Miss Michaels has rounds to make, I'm sure. I'll stay with Lieutenant Halston."

"Sure."

Mark walked over to the corner, pushed back the curtain and stepped behind it. Laurey looked up at him. She had just finished taking Halston's vital signs.

"She seems to be stable. She has not given any sign of coming around yet," Laurey reported.

She sensed Mark was very concerned about Lieutenant Halston.

"Are you all right?"

"Yes, I'm fine. I'll take over here for a while. You must have rounds to make."

"Yes, I do. You will call me if anything changes?"

"Yes."

Laurey smiled at Mark, then stepped out from behind the curtain. Mark looked down at Lieutenant Halston. She seemed so weak, which was not the way he had always seen her. This whole experience most have been terribly hard on her.

Mark took her vital signs. They seemed to be stable when compared to the other recorded vital signs. He recorded the vital signs, then sat down on a stool beside the treatment table. For some reason, he felt he should be there when she came around.

Time passed very slowly. It had been a slow night for everyone. Mark continued to take her vital signs every fifteen minutes throughout the rest of night. Others brought him coffee from time to time, but he stayed with her.

Mark could not understand why he felt he should be at her side. He really didn't like her very much and didn't think much of her as an officer. Maybe that was the reason he felt the need to be at her side, to give her a small measure of support, something she would certainly need.

Mark was sitting on the stool looking down at the floor when he noticed a pair of white nurse's shoes in front of him. He looked up to see Barbara looking down at him.

"Hi. How is she doing?" Barbara asked softly.

Her concern for Mark, as well as Lieutenant Halston, was apparent in the tone of her voice and the look on her face.

"Hi. She's stable. That's about all I can say. She has been stable for the past three hours or so."

"You look tired, why don't you go get some sleep. Lt. Commander Wilson filled me in on what happened and the rest of the night crew has already gone," she said as she reached out and touched his cheek.

Mark reached up and put his hand over hers. He was tired and he needed some rest.

"I guess you're right. There is nothing more I can do here."

Mark stood up and took hold of her hands. It felt good to have her support and understanding.

"You get some sleep. I'll see you this evening," she said as she smiled up at him.

Mark nodded in agreement. He leaned down a little and gave her a light kiss. If he had been anywhere else he would have taken her in his arms and held onto her.

Barbara watched him as he pushed the curtain aside and walked away. He left the emergency room and went straight to the barracks. He set his alarm for noon, striped down to his underwear and dropped into bed. It was only a matter of seconds before he was sound asleep.

MARK WOKE UP TO the irritating sound of his alarm. He reached up above his head and shut it off. He lay there for a couple of minutes just looking up at the ceiling. His first thoughts were of Barbara. Being Friday, he didn't think she would be very busy. Friday was often slow during the day, but the night shift could get busy.

He also thought about Lieutenant Halston. He wondered how she was doing as he glanced at his watch. By now she would be on a ward.

Mark got up, took a quick shower and got dressed in civilian clothes. He decided not to eat at the mess hall, but rather pick up something to eat while he was out. He drove out to a nice shopping area in La Jolla. After parking his car, he started looking for a place to get something to eat. He found a little sandwich shop. It was just what he was looking for, so he went in and sat down near a window.

He had just finished ordering when he heard a knock on the window. Looking out, he saw Laurey and Holland smiling back at him. He motioned for them to come inside and join him.

"Hi. What are you doing here?" Laurey asked as she approached the table with Holland right behind her.

"I came over here to do some shopping," Mark replied as he held out his hand in a gesture for them to sit down.

Holland held a chair for Laurey. She sat down, and then Holland sat down beside her.

"Holland and I have been doing some shopping, too."

Laurey held out her hand. There on her finger was a diamond ring. Mark reached out and took her hand as he examined the ring.

"Congratulations. When is the big day?"

Laurey looked at Holland, then back at Mark.

"We are planning a fall wedding, most likely in October."

"I'm happy for both of you. I hope you will invite me."

"Sure thing," Holland replied. "You are the first one to know she has her ring."

"I feel honored," he said just as his lunch arrived. "Would you like something?"

"No. No, thank you. We have already eaten, but you go right ahead, please," Laurey said.

"Say, when are you and Barbara going to get your act together?" Holland asked.

Mark had just taken a bite of his sandwich. He stopped in the middle of chewing and looked at Holland. That question had not been expected.

"Holland!" Laurey exclaimed looking at him. "Give them a chance to get to know each other. Besides, maybe that is none of our business."

Mark swallowed and looked over at Laurey.

"You know, I might just ask her one of these days, but I don't know. We will have to see how things go. Laurey is right, we haven't known each other very long. This is not something to rush into," Mark said casually as if he hadn't even given the idea of marriage a thought before that very minute.

"You stick to your guns. Don't let anyone push you into marriage. When it is right for the two of you, you will know it."

Laurey gave out her advice as if she were a mother talking to her son. Mark could hardly keep from laughing. He took another bite of his sandwich so he wouldn't have to say anything.

"Laurey, we have to get going. I hope you don't mind, but we have some things to do before I have to report to the base," Holland said.

"No, I don't mind. Are you going to be able to make the party Saturday night?"

"We sure are. Keep this under your hat, but we plan to announce our engagement at the party," Laurey said with a broad smile.

"Just how do you expect to keep it a secret until Saturday if you're wearing an engagement ring now?" Mark asked.

"We just picked up the ring. I'm not going to wear it for good until tomorrow night. I couldn't resist wearing it for a little while."

"We have to go," Holland said as he stood up. "We'll see you tomorrow night."

"Okay," Mark replied.

Mark watched them as they left the restaurant. He thought that tomorrow evening was going to be a big surprise to Laurey and Holland.

After Mark finished his lunch and paid the cashier, he left and went directly to a jewelry store. He spent the next hour or so looking at rings. He had a good idea of the type of ring Barbara would like, but was not absolutely sure. After the jeweler explained that if she was not happy with the setting or it didn't fit just right, he could bring it back and exchange it. He picked out one he was reasonably sure she would like. He just hoped it was the right size.

He paid for the ring and returned to his car. By the time he got back to the base, it was a little after three o'clock. After checking at the Information Desk, he found out Lieutenant Halston had been admitted to a private room in the psychiatric ward. He went directly to the ward.

After talking briefly with the nurse on duty, she agreed to let him see Lieutenant Halston. The duty corpsman led Mark to Lieutenant Halston's room. Mark was let in after the corpsman checked to see if she was awake. When Mark entered her room, she slowly turned her head to the side to see who had come in.

"Hi, Lieutenant Halston. How are you feeling?" Mark spoke very quietly.

He was a little nervous and not sure just what he should say.

"They tell me you're the reason I'm alive."

Her speech was slow and there was no emotion in her voice. Even her statement gave him no indication of any meaning other than that of a simple, flat out statement.

"I was there," Mark replied.

"Why didn't you just let me die?"

Again, there was no emotion in her question.

Mark knew Lieutenant Halston to be a person who understood things in a logical and orderly manner, so he decided to answer her in a way she might understand, even now when she was under fairly heavy medication.

"One, it was my job. It is not my job to let people who come into the emergency room die without doing all I can to prevent it.

"Two, you were not able to tell me what you wanted. I had to assume that you really didn't want to die, that you have things to live for.

"Three, you are much too valuable a person, and a nurse, to let you just throw your life away over such a stupid mistake. Not everyone is cut out to work in the emergency room. Some nurses are good in the emergency room, some are not. Some nurses are good teachers, some are not. You happen to be a very good teacher, and I was not about to let you throw that skill away just because you were feeling sorry for yourself."

Mark stopped suddenly. He hoped he had not said too much. It was not his intention to upset her. He watched her for some reaction. He could tell she was thinking over what he had said.

"Do you really think I would make a good teacher?" she finally asked.

Her voice seemed to show just a hint of emotion, something she had been lacking up to now. She seemed to understand what he had said.

"Yes, I do. Lt. Commander Wilson thinks so, too. He said as soon as you are feeling better, he will help you find a teaching job. Your knowledge of nursing and your skill as a teacher shouldn't be wasted. You could do more to help people through teaching others, than any one single person could do through direct contact with patience."

Mark could see that what he was saying was slowly getting through to her. He hoped what he had to say would give her some hope for a future.

"Do you think Lt. Commander Wilson will really help me?"

"Yes. He is a man of his word. Right now, all you have to do is get better. I have to go, but if there is anything you need, just let me know."

Lieutenant Halston did not say any more. Mark could tell she was turning over in her mind all he had told her. It was a slow process for her right now, but once she had it all sorted out, she would most likely feel better about herself.

Mark was let out of her room. He glanced back at her as the corpsman closed the door and locked it. Lieutenant Halston was still deep in thought, although he was not sure just how much of what he told her she would be able to remember five minutes from now. Somehow, he was sure things would work out for her.

Mark returned to the barracks and got dressed for his dinner date with Barbara. He was feeling a little tired, but he was looking forward to seeing her.

He arrived at the house a few minutes after six. Parking his car behind Barbara's, he checked his pocket to make sure the engagement ring was still there. He noticed that Bill's car was in the driveway. He got out of his car and walked up to the door. Just as he was about to reach out and take hold of the knocker, the door opened.

"Hi. Come on in. We are just leaving," Carol said.

"Have a good time. We'll see you tomorrow night," Bill said as he gently pushed Carol out the door.

"Mark's here," Carol called back over her shoulder.

Mark smiled at them as he shut the door. Mark turned around to see Barbara standing across the room smiling at him. She was wearing her beach robe.

"Hi. You're a little early," she said.

"Would you like me to leave and come back later?"

"No, silly."

She walked up to him and put her hands on his shoulders. He slipped his hands around her waist.

"I missed you, today," Mark said as he looked into her eyes.

"I missed you, too. Did you get everything done you had planned for today?"

"Yes."

"Did you get any sleep?"

Barbara was very concerned about him. She could see in his eyes that he looked very tired. If he got any sleep at all, she was sure it was not enough.

"I got a couple of hours."

"Would you rather stay here tonight?"

Barbara was almost hoping he would say "yes". Everyone else was out for the evening and they had the house to themselves. They had not had a chance to be alone for most of the week.

"Let's go out and get something to eat, then we can come back here. Maybe, we could watch a movie or something," he suggested.

"Okay. I'll get dressed."

She tipped her head back as he leaned down and kissed her lightly on the lips. It was a warm, tender kiss.

Mark let her go so she could get dressed for dinner. He watched her as she walked toward the living room.

"You are beautiful," he said softly.

Barbara looked back over her shoulder and smiled at him. She gave her hips a wiggle and blew him a kiss, then disappeared around the corner into the hall.

Mark walked into the living room. A knickknack shelf caught his attention. He walked over to it and looked at the hand blown glass figurines. There were about twenty-six of them and right in the middle was the glass angel he had purchased for her. It seemed to have a special place all its own.

"Do you like where I put the angel?" she said as she walked up behind him.

"Yes," he said as he turned and looked at her. "You look beautiful."

She did look beautiful in her light blue summer dress. It was an elegant dress that showed off her figure very well. The bodice was fitted and had thin shoulder straps and narrow waist. The skirt was full and flowing.

"Thank you," she said with a smile. "Are you ready to go?"

They locked up the house and drove to the Italian Village for dinner. They were shown to a table in a corner where they sat down. Mark ordered dinner for the two of them. After they had eaten, Mark leaned across the table and took Barbara's hands in his. He looked into her eyes.

"Barbara, I love you very much and I want to marry you."

He had said he loved her before, but this time he looked so serious about it. She was caught a little off guard by the seriousness of his statement.

Mark reached into his pocket and pulled out the small box that contained the engagement ring. He opened the box and held it out to her.

Barbara looked from the ring to Mark and back to the ring. She knew they were planning to announce their engagement tomorrow night, but they had not even discussed a ring.

Mark watched her as she looked at the ring. She did not reach out to take it, she just looked at it.

"You don't like it?" he asked.

"No, I like it very much," she said as she looked up and saw the hurt look in his eyes. "I just wasn't expecting it."

Mark gave a sigh of relief.

"If you would prefer some other style or shape, we can take it back and get one you would like better," he said as he took the ring out of the box.

Mark put the box on the table, took her hand and slipped the ring on her finger. He was a little relieved that it fit her finger perfectly. She looked at the ring as tears started to fill her eyes, then looked up at Mark.

"I like it. I don't want to exchange it for any other," she said as she smiled at him. "I love you and, yes, I will marry you."

Mark picked up his napkin, reached across the table and dabbed the tears from her cheeks. She held his hand tightly as if letting go would end this happy moment.

After several minutes had passed, Mark suggested they go back to the house and she agreed. He left a tip on the table after paying the check. They walked arm in arm out to his car. All the way back to the house there was little said.

Barbara had a difficult time letting go of Mark's hand so he could shift gears. She also kept looking at the ring on her hand as if she did not believe it was truly there.

After arriving at the house, Barbara went to the kitchen to get them some coffee. When she returned Mark had fallen asleep on the sofa. She set the coffee down on the end table, then sat down on the sofa next to him. She reached over and gently pulled him over toward her. He woke up.

"I'm sorry," he said.

"It's okay. It's been a long hard week for you," she said with a smile.

"Maybe, I should just go back to the barracks. I don't want to be too tired for the party tomorrow."

Mark stood up and helped Barbara to her feet. They walked to the front door. Mark turned and wrapped his arms around her while she wrapped her arms around his neck. He pulled her up tightly against him as he kissed her.

Barbara moaned softly as their kiss became more passionate. She felt warm, secure and loved in his arms. She did not want to let him go. She wanted him to stay the night with her. But she also knew they would not have the house to themselves all night tonight.

Mark wanted to stay, too. The full length of her body was pressed against his. He let his hands slide down past the small of her back, pulling her tightly against him. He pulled back slightly and looked into her eyes.

"I love you," he said in an almost breathless whisper.

"I love you, too," she replied.

Mark kissed her again, only it was a much lighter kiss. He took his arms from around her and took her hand. She opened the door for him.

"Be careful, you're very tired. Would you like me to take you back to the base?" she asked as he leaned down and gave her another light kiss.

"No. I'll be careful."

"Okay."

"I'll see you tomorrow. I'll call you around noon."

Mark kissed her again, then turned and walked to his car. He saw her standing in the doorway as he backed out into the street. He waved to her as he drove away.

CHAPTER SEVENTEEN

BARBARA WENT INTO THE house after Mark's car disappeared around the corner. For some reason the house seemed very empty. She went directly to her room, turned on the bedside lamp and sat down on the edge of her bed. Leaning backwards, she let herself fall back on the bed. She raised her hand up in front of her. Holding her own hand, she looked lovingly at the ring Mark had placed on her finger only a short time ago.

Barbara smiled as she thought how Mark had really surprised her with the ring. She hadn't thought much about a ring, other than that Mark would get her one someday. A ring was not that important to her. She did not need a sign on her hand to tell everyone that she had someone who loved her.

It was still early, but she was feeling tired. Tomorrow was the big day when they would tell their closest friends they were engaged. She sat up on the edge of the bed, bent over and slipped off her shoes. Standing up, she put them neatly on the floor inside her closet. Reaching behind her back, she unhooked the back of her dress and pulled the zipper down past her waist. Slipping the thin shoulder straps down her arms, she allowed the dress to fall away from her breasts and down to her waist. Hooking her fingers into the waistband of the dress, she pushed it down over her hips, letting it fall to the floor. She stepped out of the dress, picked it up and placed it neatly over the chair.

Barbara went into the bathroom and prepared herself for bed. When she was finished, she returned to the bedroom. She took off her bra and panties and placed them on the chair along with the dress. She pulled the covers back on her bed and crawled into it. Reaching over to the nightstand, she turned off the bedside lamp. As she lay down, she pulled the satin cover up over her body.

The cool satin sheets felt good on her bare skin. She closed her eyes and her thoughts turned to thoughts of Mark and herself. It seemed a little strange, but she could not think of herself without Mark, or Mark without her. Her skin tingled slightly as she remembered Mark's hands sliding lightly over her skin, especially the way he ran his hands down her back.

Barbara began to feel a little lonely. Remembering their evening of making love made her wish he was here with her now. She remembered how smooth his skin was, how passionate his kisses were, how firm his body felt under her and how gentle he had been with her. These thoughts made tears come to her eyes. Not tears of sorrow, but tears of love for him.

Barbara had always been a shy person, but with him, in the privacy of her room, she felt no embarrassment in being completely naked with him. She had always felt that making love should be something done only after marriage, but with him, it seemed so natural, so right. There was no feeling of guilt about having made love to him without a marriage license, even though it had not been the way she had been brought up.

She curled up with her pillow, tucking it up against her. It was not long before she was sound asleep, off in a dream world all her own.

MARK TURNED IN THROUGH the main gate of Balboa Naval Hospital and took the most direct route to the men's barracks. He parked his car behind the building where he sat for a minute thinking about the evening's events. He had made a commitment to Barbara and gave her a ring to show her that he meant it. His whole life was going to be changed. He was no longer going to be able to do just what he wanted without having to think about someone else. He could no longer be selfish and not share himself with at least one other person.

But on the other hand, he loved Barbara and he wanted to share himself and his dreams with her. He wanted her to be a part of his life, a very big part of it. There was going to be some adjustments for both of them. He knew his life was going to be even better because he had someone to share it with.

Mark needed some time to think, to really organize his thoughts. He got out of his car and snapped the tonneau cover over the seats. Mark decided he would walk over to one of the enclosed garden patios near the administration building, maybe to the one with the Roman style courtyard with its small pool and fountain.

He knew that they would have a lot of things to work out. He had originally planned to make the Navy a career, but now he would have to discuss it with Barbara. Maybe, a career change would be the best thing, then again, maybe it would not. They would have to work these things out together.

Mark was tired, very tired, but his mind was so filled with thoughts and ideas, he knew he would have difficulty getting to sleep. He walked around the Roman style courtyard and then headed back toward the barracks.

The only lights that were on at the barracks were the lights that were left on all night. He glanced at his watch and wondered if James would be in yet. Being as quiet as possible, Mark slipped his key into the lock. He opened the door and entered the room. James had left the desk lamp on again, and was not in the room.

Mark gathered up his toothbrush and toothpaste, and went down the hall to the washroom. After brushing his teeth, he returned to his room. He stripped out of his clothes, down to his shorts, and lay down on his bed. Putting his hands behind his head, he laid there looking up at the ceiling.

His mind was filled with thoughts of Barbara when he dozed off.

JAMES RETURNED TO THE base rather late. He dropped Pam off at the women's barracks. After several long goodnight kisses, he went directly to the men's barracks to see if Mark was in.

When he arrived at the barracks, he parked his car. He was sure Mark would be in because Mark's car was in the parking lot. Being as quiet as possible, he slipped his key into the lock and opened the door, then entered the room.

James found Mark sound asleep. He didn't want to wake him, but he had to deliver an important message to him. He walked over next to Mark's bed, then reached down and touched Mark on the shoulder.

"Mark," he said as he gently shook Mark's shoulder.

"James, is that you?" Mark asked through a slight fog of sleep.

"Yeah. Sorry, I didn't want to wake you, but I have to," James said apologetically.

"That's all right. What's up?"

"I have a message for you from the guard on duty at the front gate."

James hesitated just slightly. He wanted to be sure Mark was awake.

"What's the message?"

"He said they want you over at the Master-at-Arms office as soon as possible. They said it didn't matter what time you got in, they wanted to see you."

"You know what it's about?"

"No. They didn't tell me anything. I got a brief look at the list of people they were calling up and from the list something big has happened, or is about to happen."

"What list?"

"A list the guard had in his shack."

"Are you on the list?" Mark asked.

"No. From what the guard said and from what little I saw of the list, it looks like they are putting together several medical teams. A good many of the people on the list have experience with burn cases, like you."

Mark looked at him wondering what might be going on. Why would they need personnel that have experience with burn cases, Mark wondered.

"I guess I better get over there and see what this is all about."

"I'm coming with you."

"Okay."

Mark swung his feet out of bed and onto the floor. He looked over at the clock before standing up. It was late.

"I have a quick call to make while you get dressed," James said.

Mark went to his locker as James picked up the phone. He could hear James talking to Pam. James hung up the phone just as Mark finished dressing. They walked out of the barracks together.

"Pam says no one will let them know what is going on, but the corpswaves have all been placed on alert. She thinks that all the corpsmen have been placed on alert, too."

"She works on the same ward Janice Miller is on, doesn't she?" Mark asked.

"Yes."

"Do you know how Janice is doing?"

"She told me earlier Janice was doing much better. They are going to let her start getting around in a wheelchair, possibly tomorrow. She seems to be making pretty good progress."

They turned a corner and entered the administration building. The duty officer was standing at the counter looking over some papers when they arrived.

"Sir, I'm Second Class Hospital Corpsman Mark Walker. I understand you wanted to see me?"

"Yes, Walker. We are putting several medical teams together. You are to report to the supply building next to the helicopter platform at 0600 hours tomorrow. Your breakfast will be served there during a briefing. You are to be in dungarees and ready to go. All the gear you will need will be waiting for you when you get where you are going," the duty officer explained.

"Just where are we going, sir?" Mark asked.

"You, along with the rest of the medical teams are to be flown out to a carrier to assist their medical staff. That is all I can tell you. You'll find out what you need to know at the briefing in the morning. I suggest you get as much sleep as you can. You're dismissed, Walker."

With that, the duty officer turned around and walked away.

Mark turned and looked at James. He knew it had to be something really big. Large carriers are like small cities, they have a complete hospital on board. Though the hospital or sick bays on carriers are fairly small, they are well supplied and well equipped for almost any kind of an emergency. There must have been some kind of an explosion or big accident to require a ship the size of an aircraft carrier to request medical help be flown out to them.

Mark and James walked back to the barracks. Neither of them said a word. Each was deep in his own thoughts. All sorts of thoughts passed through their minds. Maybe, there was a collision at sea between the carrier and some other ship. Maybe, there was a fire on board the carrier from an explosion or from an aircraft that crash landed.

The one thing they both understood from their years in the military was no matter how many possible reasons they could come up with, they would not know what happened until the briefing in the morning. There was nothing they could do tonight except to get as much sleep as possible.

"I better get a shower and some rest," Mark said as they entered their room.

"Yeah. That's a good idea. You may not get much rest tomorrow, and you will probably not get a shower, either."

"Tomorrow!" Mark said out loud.

He suddenly remembered he had other plans for tomorrow.

"What did you say?" James asked.

"Yeah. I said 'tomorrow'. I had plans for tomorrow."

"Well, I think your plans have been changed for you."

"No kidding."

Mark said nothing more. He undressed and wrapped a towel around his waist and left the room for the showers. He hung his towel on a hook just outside the showers, then stepped into the showers and turned on the water. As soon as the water was warm, he stepped under the shower and let the warm water splash over his head and face.

Mark thought of Barbara. He wondered how she would feel if he didn't show up tomorrow. The idea of calling her crossed his mind, but it was very late and she could be in bed. He could not see waking her and letting her worry all night when there was a possibility by morning the medical teams might not be needed.

Mark quickly dismissed that thought. The Navy did not call up medical teams on the possibility they would be needed. The only reason they were waiting until morning was because of the dangers involved in getting medical teams to where they were needed in the dark.

Maybe, he would get the opportunity to call Barbara in the morning once he found out what was going on. There was no sense ruining her rest when there was nothing either of them could do about it. She would certainly understand, after all she was in the Navy, too. They would just have to delay the announcement of their engagement by a day or two.

Mark took the soap and lathered up. After rinsing off, he dried himself. He then wrapped a towel around his waist and went back to his room. Entering the room, he saw that

James was asleep. He set his alarm clock for 0515 hours. It would give him plenty of time to get dressed and get down to the supply building for the briefing.

Mark climbed into bed and lay on his back with his hands behind his head. His mind shifted between thoughts of Barbara and thoughts of the call-up. With so many things on his mind, Mark had to force himself to close his eyes and force himself to seek the sleep he needed. His last thoughts before he finally got to sleep were of Barbara.

CHAPTER EIGHTEEN

MARK'S ALARM WENT OFF right at 0515 hours. Reaching over his head, he quickly shut it off and sat up in bed. He looked over to see if James was awake. James had apparently slept through the alarm. Mark quickly got ready and left the barracks for the short walk to the supply building.

The morning air was cool, but not cold. The ice plants along the street were wet with morning dew. Mark looked up at the sky. It looked as if it would be a beautiful day, with blue skies and lots of sunshine. The sun was beginning to show its light in the east and the morning star was giving out its last few flickers before it would disappear from the sky.

Mark arrived at the supply building at about 0550 hours. There were several cooks and cook's helpers setting up to serve a buffet style breakfast. Mark was about to ask if he could help when the door opened behind him. He turned to see three officers come into the building. Mark knew only one of the officers, Lt. Commander Wilson. The highest-ranking officer among them was a Rear Admiral, a line officer. The other officer Mark did not know was also a line officer. He seemed to be just following the Rear Admiral around. Mark wondered what was going on. It was unusual to have line officers at a medical briefing.

Lt. Commander Wilson saw Mark and excused himself from the presence of the line officers.

"Hi, Mark. I'm glad they found you. I was afraid you would be gone for the weekend."

"I got the message late last night. Say, what's going on, Sir?"

"I don't really know. No one has said much, but I think we will be finding out very soon. Rear Admiral Hamilton from Westpack will be giving the briefing. He has all the details and so far he has been very closed mouthed. I was told to meet them and bring them here to give a briefing."

Mark made no more inquiries into what was going on. Mark and Lt. Commander Wilson just stood there and watched as the rest of the personnel on the list reported as ordered.

Lt. Commander Wilson was about to say something to Mark when Chief Petty Officer Johnson began his announcement.

"I want all of you to get something to eat and find a place to sit down as soon as possible. Rear Admiral Hamilton will begin the briefing while we eat."

There were four doctors and twenty hospital corpsmen including Lt. Commander Wilson and Mark. They all formed a line and passed in front of the serving trays. As soon as they had their serving trays filled, they sat down and began to eat. Once everyone had settled in, Rear Admiral Hamilton stood up in front of the men.

"Gentlemen, I want you to eat up. This may be the last regular meal you get for a couple of days," Rear Admiral Hamilton began.

Mark was sitting next to Lt. Commander Wilson. They turned and looked at each other. It was clear to both of them that whatever was going on, it was not a drill to see how ready they were. This was the real thing.

"I know you are all wondering what this is all about. What I am about to tell you is not to go beyond this room.

"At about 2200 hours, yesterday, there was a large explosion on board the aircraft carrier Ranger. The damage was originally limited to the engine room. The explosion put the ship dead in the water.

"While the damage control parties were working on putting out the fires resulting from that explosion and attempting to get the Ranger back in operation, another explosion occurred either on or below the hangar deck, just aft of the superstructure. The second explosion ignited fuel storage areas and has set several aircraft on fire. It has also set the flight deck on fire and made it unsafe to land or takeoff. This has limited our ability to get on and off the ship quickly. It has also caused several other smaller explosions on board the ship.

"I'll let Lieutenant Beckman fill you on the current situation. Lieutenant."

Rear Admiral Hamilton moved aside and Lieutenant Beckman stood up.

"Right now, the Ranger is still sitting dead in the water. The ship is listing several degrees to port. Communication with the Ranger has been severely interrupted and information is limited. Based on the information we do have, the ship is apparently in a very critical condition.

"We do not know very much about the status of the personnel on board the Ranger, but what we do know is this. There are several hundred sailors aboard the Ranger who have been severely burned and an untold number with other injuries. We have no accurate information on the number of deaths. However, it could easily run into the hundreds.

"Up until now, we have been unable to get the dead or injured off the ship because of the thick smoke that lies over the ship and because of the fires that continue to burn on several decks, including the flight deck.

"Our reports of the situation coming in at this time have improved now that we have other ships nearby. Currently, the destroyer Hickox is standing by off the port side, and the submarine Skipjack is off the starboard side of the Ranger. We have several other ships headed to the area at full speed.

"To put it simply, the reason for this briefing is medical aid is needed aboard the Ranger very badly. The sub and the destroyer do not have much of a medical staff to help deal with this situation. Apparently, from what we can find out, nearly half of the medical staff on board the Ranger were injured during the second explosion and resulting fires. That has not been confirmed yet, but we feel this is no time to doubt the worst. As best we can determine, the second explosion did a great deal of damage to the sick bay.

"We must consider the worst, plan for the worst, and go from there. It is our plan to fly you people out to the Ranger and get you aboard as quickly as possible."

"Excuse me, Sir, but just how do you plan to get us aboard if the ship is on fire and we can't land on the flight deck?" Lt. Commander Wilson asked.

"That is a very good question, doctor. We plan to fly you out there in helicopters. Our last report indicates we should be able to put a helicopter down on the flight deck near the bow. The water is calm and there has been very little wind out there until just recently. This has kept the smoke hanging over the Ranger making it difficult for the ships standing by to see what the extent of damage to the flight deck really is. However, a little bit of a breeze has come up off the starboard side of the Ranger. We plan to use that breeze to clear the smoke away from the bow.

"As I said, the destroyer Hickox is standing by. We plan to use the destroyer to tow the bow of the Ranger into the breeze so the forward part of the fight deck will be cleared of smoke, kind of like a tugboat would pull a ship. We understand the forward part of the flight deck has not been damaged," Lieutenant Beckman explained.

"Gentlemen, I wish you God's speed. The men of the Ranger are waiting for your help. Let's not make them wait any longer," Rear Admiral Hamilton said as he stood up and put an immediate end to the briefing.

"There are two helicopters on the pad, the Chief explained. "We will be split up into four teams, two teams to each helicopter. Each team will be led by one of the four doctors assigned to this operation. I will call off the names of each team member. Teams A and B will go in the first helicopter, teams C and D in the second helicopter. Your gear is already in the helicopters, so let's go."

The Chief started calling off names. Mark was in B team along with Lt. Commander Wilson. As soon as his name was called off and he had dropped off his food tray, he began running toward the first helicopter, followed by the rest of the team.

As soon as the two teams were all on board, the helicopter lifted off the ground. As it rose straight above the helicopter platform, it slowly turned its nose toward the open sea. The nose of the helicopter tipped down and it began to pick up speed rapidly as it continued to climb well above the surrounding buildings. As the helicopter moved away from the Hospital, Lt. Commander Wilson turned to Mark.

"I want you as the team leader for team B," Lt. Commander Wilson said.

"Yes, sir," Mark replied.

"We are to establish a clearing place for the wounded on the hangar deck, if possible. Based on what little information we have, it will most likely be near one of the forward aircraft elevators. We will have to find a way to get the injured out and up on the flight deck, or out onto ships standing by,"

Mark acknowledged Lt. Commander Wilson's statements with a nod. Mark knew very little about aircraft carriers. Most of his time at sea had been spent on destroyers. He settled back in the seat and mentally reviewed what little he knew about the interior. If there was no danger of fire and the smoke was not too thick, the area near the forward aircraft elevators could prove to be a good location to establish a clearing area for the injured.

He sat next to a small window. Mark turned toward the window and looked out. He could see north up along the coast for several miles as the helicopter headed out to sea. The sky was clear and the sun cast long shadows out onto the beach. He caught a glimpse of the house where Barbara lived. He glanced down at his watch, it was only 0655 hours.

Mark tipped his head back against the back of the seat as the coastline disappeared from his sight. He was tired and could use some rest. It would take at least a couple of hours before they would reach the aircraft carrier Ranger.

His thoughts turned to the two airmen he had helped treat just a short time ago in the emergency room. There was no doubt that what Mark would see today was going to be worse than anything he had seen before. He closed his eyes in an effort to shut out those thoughts, at least for now.

With his eyes closed, he thought of Barbara. He wondered if she was getting up yet. She was most likely still sound asleep. He certainly couldn't blame her for sleeping in. He was tired enough that if he had not been called up for this rescue mission, he would still be sleeping. He took a deep breath and let his body relax. It did not take long before he was asleep.

"MARK, TAKE A LOOK out there." The voice was that of his friend, Richard Sherman.

Mark opened his eyes, looked at Richard, then turned and looked out the window. The sight toward the horizon was like nothing he had ever seen before. It caused him to sit up and look more carefully at the scene ahead and a little below them.

Off in the distance, maybe six or seven miles away, he could see a thick black cloud of smoke. All around, the sky was a perfect blue, except for the large column of black, ugly smoke which rose from the sea and slowly faded away into the deep blue of the sky. At this distance it was impossible to see what was burning.

As they got closer, Mark could make out a large aircraft carrier under all the smoke. Mark knew from the color of the smoke that it was jet fuel and diesel fuel burning.

It was several minutes before Mark realized there were two other ships down there. They were much smaller than the aircraft carrier. The smoke from the carrier had grabbed his attention and held it so completely that he hadn't noticed the smaller ships at first.

All of the vessels lay still in the water. From this distance, they all looked like model boats.

The aircraft carrier Ranger had everything from the bridge aft covered with the thick heavy black and dark gray smoke. There were no flames visible at this distance. Most of the smoke seemed to be coming from the flight deck and the hangar deck below and aft of the bridge.

The destroyer Hickox had its stern toward the bow of the carrier Ranger. It seemed almost impossible that such a small ship would be able to move the large aircraft carrier. The destroyer was certainly no tugboat, but it had done its job well.

It had managed to pull the bow of the carrier Ranger into the breeze. The breeze had cleared the smoke away from the bow of the carrier, leaving the forward portion of the flight deck clear of smoke and visible to the helicopter pilots.

The USS Skipjack, a nuclear submarine, was quietly setting off the port side of the carrier. It lay about three hundred yards away from the carrier. The submarine just lay there, waiting. It reminded Mark of a big, black cigar floating in the water.

As the helicopters approached the carrier, it became possible to see a number of sailors on the flight deck manning the fire hoses. It was apparent the flight deck was indeed on fire. Thick black smoke billowed out of the two rear starboard aircraft elevator ports much like smoke from factory smokestacks. The starboard aircraft elevator, forward of the bridge, had some smoke coming from it, but it was much less than that from the rear elevators. This was a good indication that the fires below the flight deck were confined to the stern of the ship.

The helicopter moved around to get into position to land on the bow of the carrier. Mark noticed for the first time the carrier's slight list to port. It was enough of a list that Mark was sure there had to be damage to the ship below the water line. To Mark, this meant there would be injuries to sailors deep in the lower levels of the ship.

The helicopter touched down hard on the flight deck. It jarred the corpsmen, causing one to fall down as he was getting the equipment ready to unload from the helicopter. The doors flew open and the medical teams jumped out onto the deck. Supplies were quickly unloaded and moved away from the helicopter.

Mark turned just in time to see the forward port side aircraft elevator come up even with the flight deck. On the elevator were about a dozen stretchers with an injured sailor on each one. Standing on the elevator among the stretchers were about a half a dozen sailors. The face of each sailor told the story of pain and death they had witnessed. Their faces were covered with streaks of sweat and soot from the smoke and dirt. Several even had minor burns that had not been taken care of yet. There was no time for the minor burns with so many seriously burned sailors.

Both the A team and the B team ran over to help get the stretchers off the elevator and load them onto the helicopters. In the rush to clear the elevator, no one really noticed a lone officer in a dirty, soot covered uniform bending over a stretcher. Mark did not notice him until he started to go get the stretcher.

As Mark approached him, he realized the man was a priest. Although his uniform was so covered with soot and sweat, and was even burned away in a few places, it was clear who the man was and what he was doing. He was giving a severely burned sailor his last rights.

Mark walked up to the stretcher and stopped. The priest slowly turned and looked up at Mark. Mark knew from the look in the priest's eyes that the sailor was dead.

As Mark bent down to pick up one end of the stretcher, the priest took hold of the other end. Mark noticed blood on the priest's right sleeve. Yet, together, they carried the dead sailor to the helicopter for his last trip home. After placing the stretcher on the helicopter, Mark motioned for the priest to get in, but he simply shook his head and started to walk back toward the aircraft elevator.

"Son, I'm needed here," the priest stated flatly as he walked past Mark.

Mark looked at the open wound on the priest's right arm. It did not look to be all that serious, but it did need some attention as blood was trickling down his arm.

Mark looked over at the aircraft elevator and saw all their supplies had been placed on the elevator. He walked up beside the priest and took hold of his arm. Together, they stepped onto the aircraft elevator. As the elevator descended to the hangar deck, Mark picked up a first aid kit.

Once the elevator got to the hangar deck, the men began removing the supplies, setting up a treatment area and a clearing station among the aircraft. Mark took the priest aside and immediately began to treat the priest's wound. He washed the wound out with normal saline, applied an antiseptic, and bandaged the wound with a pressure dressing.

"That should hold you for awhile. What the hell happened here?" Mark asked as he looked around.

"I think 'hell' is the appropriate word. We really don't know what went wrong," the priest explained. "By the way, I'm Owen, Father Owen."

"Mark."

"Well, Mark, what do we do now?"

Mark looked around. The fires seemed to be pretty well contained toward the rear area of the hangar deck. There appeared to be a couple of aircraft at the rear of the hangar deck that were still burning.

In the forward part of the hangar deck, the air was filled with a thin gray smoke and there was the heavy smell of burned fuel. There was a great deal of confusion everywhere he looked. Some of the medical teams were already working on the injured near the port side aircraft elevator where the breeze was keeping the air clear. The rest of the medical teams were just about finished setting up the area and making it ready for more of the injured.

"It looks like I have plenty to do right here," Mark replied as he looked over rows of injured sailors that had been grouped together around the aircraft, waiting to be treated.

"Me, too."

Father Owen let out a deep sigh. He was almost overcome with a deep feeling of being overwhelmed by the death and destruction that had taken place here. Father Owen could not and would not let down those who depended on him.

Mark nodded that he understood what was going on in Father Owen's mind. He turned around, bent down beside the first patient he came to and began tending to his immediate needs. Mark cut the sailor's clothes away from his neck and shoulder while Richard started an IV to help replace the vital body fluids the sailor had already lost. The sailor was burned so badly the skin around the open wounds was charred black. The sailor was in a great deal of pain.

While Richard was giving the sailor a shot of morphine for pain, Mark cleaned the wound as best he could, under the circumstances. Mark placed thin pieces of sterile Vaseline gauze directly over the burned area to slow the loss of vital body fluids and to keep the area moist. After covering the entire wound, he wrapped the sailor's neck and shoulder with a bulky sterile dressing. He then covered the dressing with elastic bandages.

Once he had done all he could for the sailor, he was ready to move him out of the way. With Richard's help, they moved the sailor over next to several others. By placing the sailors who had been treated close to each other, it made it easier for one corpsman to look after several of the injured at one time while they waited for the helicopters to come back and airlift them to a hospital.

Mark and Richard worked as a team throughout the day, caring for one burned or injured sailor after another. It seemed as if there was a never ending stream of burned and injured sailors being brought to the clearing area. They did not have time to see what was happening around them. All they knew was, if the other medical teams were as busy as they were, there were hundreds of burned and injured sailors aboard this ship.

Mark had no idea what time it was. He did not have time to concern himself with unimportant things. He had no idea how long they had been working or how long it had been since they had eaten, but he did know he was starting to feel tiredness creep into his bones.

As Mark and Richard knelt down beside the stretcher of their next patient, they realized the young sailor was already dead. Mark let out a deep sigh, as much from the frustration of not being able to do anything for the sailor as from the tiredness he was feeling. Mark looked up at Richard. He could see Richard was tired, too. Just then Mark felt a hand on his shoulder. He turned and looked up to see who was behind him.

"You and Richard take a break. Go over there and get something to eat." Lt. Commander Wilson said.

Mark looked over in the direction the Lt. Commander had pointed. He saw a large coffee urn set up along with several trays of sandwiches.

For the first time since he started treating the injured, Mark took time to look around. Over by the aircraft elevator, sailors who had been treated were being loaded on the elevator and taken topside to be flown to hospitals or transferred to other ships. All around him were other members of A team and B team, huddled over the injured and doing their best to save them.

"Mark, everyone else has had a break. Go get something to eat and take about twenty minutes to relax. It looks like it will be a long night. They are still bringing injured sailors up from some of the lower decks," Lt. Commander Wilson explained.

Mark nodded his head. He understood it was going to be only a break. Their job here was far from over.

Mark stood up. He had not realized how stiff he had become kneeling over so many injured sailors. He stretched his aching muscles in an effort to take some of the soreness out of them. Richard was right behind him.

They got some coffee and a couple of sandwiches, then they found a place against the bulkhead to sit down. Mark was almost too tired to eat, but he knew he had to eat something if he was going to keep going at this pace.

Mark could see a long ways down the hangar deck. The deck, bulkheads, and overheads where charred black and covered with black soot. He could also make out the twisted remains of what, only hours ago, were some of the finest fighter aircraft in the world. Now they were twisted, half-melted piles of junk littering the hangar deck.

He could also see a few pockets of smoke coming from some hot spots. As he sipped his coffee and took small bites of his sandwich, he watched some sailors continue to pour water and fire retardant foam on the hot spots. He watched the water flow across the deck from the starboard side to the port side and on out over the side of the ship. He had been so busy taking care of the injured that he had forgotten the ship was listing slightly to port.

Mark looked over at Richard. He had leaned back against the big steel support beam and had fallen asleep. Mark decided that Richard had a good idea and leaned back to rest his eyes. Maybe, he could catch a little catnap, too.

CHAPTER NINETEEN

SUDDENLY, WITHOUT ANY WARNING, a deep rumble came from way down deep inside the big ship. It caused the ship to shake and shiver, much like a building during an earthquake. Everyone seemed to freeze right where they were. They waited and held their breath, not sure what was happening. They had no idea what they were waiting for, but whatever it was they were all sure it meant more injured, and more dead.

The rumble and shaking of the big ship woke Mark. He sat up quickly and listened as he looked around for some sign of what was to come. All of his senses were alert to even the slightest change.

Mark's mind told him there was nothing to be afraid of, but he could not help thinking of the dead and injured he had already seen. There was an uneasy feeling that seemed to penetrate his whole body. He knew deep in his being that there were going to be more burned bodies and more sailors that would die this day.

"Richard, there's been another explosion."

"Yeah. It sounded like it came from down deep, like maybe in the engine room," Richard replied.

It was suddenly quiet again, almost too quiet. It was as if all life had ceased to exist. The silence was broken by the sound of an approaching helicopter getting ready to set down on the flight deck above them. The helicopter setting down seemed to bring everything back into perspective, back to reality. And things started to move again.

Those who could walk, walked to the aircraft elevator; those who could, helped those who needed help; while still others carried those who could not get there any other way. There was no pushing or shoving. There was no panic.

Mark knew the helicopters had been taking the injured off the ship as fast as the medical teams could get them ready to be transported. Up until now, all the victims had been brought to the medical teams from the lower levels. Mark had seen several corpsmen that were injured. He assumed what he had heard at the briefing was true, that the sickbay had been damaged or completely destroyed.

Mark and Richard returned to work. The first patient they encountered after their short rest was an officer. The right side of his face and his side down to his waist was covered with second and third degree burns. As Mark began cutting away the officer's uniform, he noticed the officer's collar pins.

"This guy's a doctor."

It felt strange to Mark to have this man laying there. They should be working with him, not bent over him trying to save his life. It should not have made any difference who the man was, yet it did. They had seen death all around them today. Yet seeing him brought death even closer. It brought the realization that it did not matter who you were or where you were from, everyone was vulnerable.

Mark quickly washed away the dirt and soot, and cut away the charred skin around the edge of the deepest areas of burned skin. The officer's arm was covered with second-degree burns and his face had some first and second degree burns around his nose and mouth. The right front part of his shoulder and his chest where covered with second and third degree burns. From the looks of his injuries, he had been in an explosion of some kind, most likely a fuel explosion.

Mark rinsed the opened burned areas, cleaning them as best he could, then he began covering them with sterile Vaseline gauze. The officer's burns were then wrapped in thick gauze and bandages.

After all the dressings had been completed, Mark did a final check of the doctor's vital signs before they were ready to move him. Mark and Richard had done all they could do for him. His condition was fairly stable and it was time to transfer him to a hospital where his treatment would continue.

Up to now the doctor had been unconscious. Richard had just finished adjusting the drip on the IV and had moved to the foot of the stretcher when the doctor opened his eyes. Mark was ready to stand up when he noticed the doctor had regained consciousness.

"Hang in there, Doc. We'll take care of you," Mark said.

Mark could see the pain in the doctor's face.

"Please, - - - - help - - them," the doctor pleaded.

His voice was so weak Mark could hardly hear what he had said. Mark leaned down closer.

"Help who?"

"The - - others."

His pain showed on his face as he tried to speak.

Mark looked around the area and saw all the corpsmen busy working on the injured. What he was saying did not seem to make sense.

"We're helping the others."

"No," the doctor said as he grabbed Mark's arm. "Help - the - others, - - - please."

"Richard, give him a shot for pain."

As Richard prepared a shot of morphine to give to the doctor, Mark was trying to understand what the doctor was telling them. Several questions came to Mark's mind. Was he talking about these patients or was he talking about some others, somewhere else on the ship? Mark looked at Richard, then down at the doctor.

"What others, doctor?" Mark asked.

"In - - - sick - - bay," he replied.

The pain of his burns was reflected in his voice. Richard gave him the injection in a hope of relieving some of his pain.

"Are there still others in sickbay?" Mark asked.

"Yes, - - there - are - - - others - - trapped - - down, - down - - - there."

The doctor slowly closed his eyes as he once again passed out.

Mark looked up at Richard. He took the doctor's hand and checked his pulse. Mark let out a sigh of relief.

"He's passed out. Let's get him out of here."

Mark and Richard picked up the stretcher and carried it over to the aircraft elevator. They passed it off to two sailors who were ferrying patients to the flight deck. They watched for a second as the doctor was carried aboard the elevator.

"We have to get down to sickbay," Mark said.

Richard did not need any further conversation. He knew that without some help, some more sailors were going to die. They could not just let it happen. They had to do something and do it, now.

Mark started running down the middle of the hangar deck toward the center of the ship. Richard was right on his heels.

Mark stopped as he saw someone come out of a passageway carrying an injured sailor over his shoulder. The man's head was tipped down, but Mark was sure he knew the man. Mark and Richard ran over to help Father Owen with his burden. Soon others came over to offer aid.

"Take this man over there," Mark instructed the sailors as he pointed to the area where others were being treated.

"Father Owen, we need your help. Have you been down on some of the lower decks?"

"I've been down as far as the third deck. Why?"

"There are several corpsmen trapped in sickbay. If I remember right, the main sickbay on this ship is on the third deck just above and forward of the boiler and machinery spaces."

"That's right, but when the boiler exploded it did a great deal of damage in that area. As far as I know, no one has been able to get into that area," Father Owen explained.

"Someone has gotten out of there. Richard and I just treated a doctor who came from sickbay. He told us that there are others still trapped down there. We have to get down there to help them."

"You know, we might be able to get to them if we go down below them on the first platform level and come back up the ladder behind the sickbay. Follow me."

Father Owen wasted no time as he started off toward a ladder that would take them down into the ship. Mark and Richard followed right behind.

THE MORNING SUN BROKE through the lacy white curtains of Barbara's bedroom window like it did on most other sunny mornings. Shadows moved back and forth across the floor and the foot of her bed as the white curtains moved with the gentle breeze blowing in the window.

Barbara began to stir, reluctant to open her eyes. She could see no reason to get up this early. There were some things she had to do in order to get ready for the party in the evening, but she had most of the day to do them.

Carol had already started the baked beans before she left for work. Laurey was going to fix the relish tray at Holland's apartment and bring it with them to the party. All Barbara had to do was make some potato salad and get a few things organized around the house.

She rolled from her side onto her back. Reluctantly, she opened her eyes and looked up at the ceiling. She raised her hands above her head and stretched. The sheet clung to her as every muscle stretched. It felt good to lie on the smooth cool satin sheets for awhile before getting up.

Barbara laid for several minutes just staring at the ceiling. Her thoughts soon turned to Mark and what had happened last evening. Lifting her hand up, she looked at the ring she was wearing and smiled. She took a quick look at the clock. It would be at least three hours, maybe four, before Mark would call.

Barbara rolled over and sat up on the edge of the bed. The sheet slid down off the smooth lines of her body as she once again stretched. She was feeling very much alive this morning and could not think of a more beautiful day than today. She picked up her robe from the chair, slipped into it as she stood up and went into the bathroom.

Barbara came out of the bathroom with a towel wrapped around her head. She had washed her hair, and was ready to fix it. As she sat down in front of the mirror, she took the towel from her head and began to comb her hair.

A pang of loneliness for Mark passed through her, causing her to shiver. It caused her to wonder where he might be. Was he still in bed or had he already gotten up? Had he eaten breakfast or was he just relaxing in his room?

Her thoughts of him brought a deep feeling of loneliness that seemed to wash over her. She had wondered if the feeling she was experiencing might be the way some of the wives of sailors felt when their men left for long tours of duty at sea. It could hardly be the case for her because Mark was not at sea, she told herself.

After she finished combing her hair, she went to her closet and looked over her choices of things to wear. She picked out a colorful pullover knit shirt that would be comfortable for the work she had to do in the kitchen. She also picked out a pair of plain gray, well-tailored slacks that would go very well with the pullover shirt.

After laying out her clothes on the bed, she took off her robe. She hung the robe on the back of the door and got dressed. As soon as she was ready, she looked in the mirror. She liked the way the pullover shirt accented her firm breasts, and the way the tailored slacks showed off the smooth curves of her hips. She smiled at her reflection as she thought of how much Mark would like her in the outfit. Looking nice for Mark made her feel special.

Barbara went out into the kitchen, put a bunch of potatoes in a pot and began cooking them to make her potato salad. While she waited for the potatoes to cook, she made some coffee and sat down at the table with the local newspaper. By the time the potatoes were cooked, she was finished with the parts of the paper she wanted to read.

After putting the potatoes in the refrigerator to cool, she went to her room. She spent the next couple of hours doing some housework. She changed the bedding, cleaned her bathroom, and picked up her bedroom.

By lunchtime, she had her part of the house cleaned up. She returned to the kitchen where she peeled and cut up the potatoes. As soon as she was finished making the potato salad, she placed it in the refrigerator. She poured herself a glass of milk and made herself a sandwich for lunch. While she ate, she watched the clock and waited for Mark to call.

It was almost one o'clock and still no call from Mark. She was worried that something might have happened and he could not call her. Her imagination could come up with all kinds of reasons for him not calling her, like an auto accident on his way out to see her or maybe he had an accident on the base and broken something like an arm or leg.

As the time passed, her worries turned from worries about him to worries about them. Maybe, he was having second thoughts about marrying her. Maybe, he didn't want to spend the rest of his life with her after all. It seemed all her doubts and insecurities were creeping back into her mind. She had loved him and cared deeply for him. She had given herself to him and now he was dumping her.

Tears began to come to her eyes. Was he really dumping her, she asked herself? She could not believe they could have something so special and he would simply throw it away. There had to be a reason for him not calling. It had to be a logical reason, but what? She knew he loved her. After all, he had given her a very expensive ring. He would not dump her like that if there was any way he could prevent it.

She wiped the tears from her eyes and went into the bathroom. After washing her face, she went out on the deck. She picked up a magazine, sat down and began to thumb through it.

Barbara was about halfway through the magazine when she stopped and looked out toward the ocean. Barbara realized she had not been fair to Mark. She had once again judged him before she had all the facts.

She quickly resolved that whenever something did not go right between them, she was no longer going to jump to any conclusions. She would wait until she knew all the facts. She had jumped to conclusions before, and it almost ruined any chance for them to build a loving relationship. She would not let that happen again.

She smiled to herself at the decision she had made and the conviction with which she made it. Mark would be proud of her, she thought.

Barbara looked again at the magazine and began reading an article. The article she happened to start reading was on the subject of building trust between you and your man. She smiled at the relevance of the article. After becoming engrossed in the article, time passed without her noticing.

Barbara heard the front door open and close. It didn't seem late enough for Carol to be getting home. She put down her magazine and glanced down at her watch, it was two fifteen.

"Barbara," Carol called out as she came in the door.

"I'm out here."

"Have you seen the news?" Carol asked as she rushed out onto the deck, obviously excited.

"No. Why?"

It seemed strange that Carol was concerned about the news. Carol usually showed very little interest in local or world news.

"Come on."

Carol grabbed Barbara by the arm and almost dragged her into the living room. Barbara wondered what could be so important that it would get Carol so excited.

"Take a look at this," Carol said as she turned on the television.

Barbara watched as the picture came on the screen. The newsman's voice was describing the scene.

"Last night, at about ten p.m., an explosion took place on the aircraft carrier USS Ranger. The carrier was returning from routine maneuvers off the coast when the explosion occurred. The Navy has not released any figures on the number of injuries or deaths at this time. However, it is estimated that the number of deaths and injuries could easily run into the hundreds.

"There has been no official word yet, but it is assumed the injuries are very heavy as Balboa Naval Hospital has air lifted several medical teams to the disabled carrier.

"As you can see from the film, a large column of smoke is rising from the carrier's flight deck and from the deck below, called the hangar deck. The carrier is listing several degrees to port, to the left side. Numerous helicopters have been shuttling injured sailors from the ship to military hospitals throughout the area."

Barbara sat there watching the film and listening to the newsman. It took a minute for her to realize just what was going on. If helicopters were carrying injured to shore hospitals, she was sure the emergency rooms would be flooded.

"Has there been a call up at the hospital, yet?" Barbara asked.

"When I left they were getting ready to start calling all off duty personnel to report to the Master-at-Arms office for assignment," Carol replied.

"Why did they let you go?"

"They hadn't started the call up before I left. Besides there is something I think you should know before we go back to the base."

Carol had a worried look on her face that Barbara had come to know. She always looked like that when she had bad news. Carol did not know just how Barbara would take what she had to tell her, but it was best done here where Barbara could express her feelings without strangers around.

"Well, what is it?" Barbara asked impatiently.

"Just before I left the base, I found out that Mark is on one of the medical teams that were airlifted to the burning ship early this morning."

Carol waited for the news to sink in. Barbara just sat there and looked at Carol. She could not believe what Carol had told her. Barbara's head slowly tipped downward until she was looking at the floor just in front of her feet. She sat there for several minutes, just staring at the floor.

All her worries about Mark being in danger were well founded. This time she had something to worry about. For several seconds, all she could think about was the danger Mark was in. He could get hurt out there, even killed. She suddenly looked up again.

"We better get over to the hospital. They will be needing us soon," Barbara said as she stood up.

Carol watched Barbara as she hurried to her bedroom. It was difficult to believe Barbara was taking the news so calmly.

Once Barbara was in her bedroom, she went straight to her closet and got out a fresh uniform. Laying the uniform down on the bed, she pulled her shirt up and over her head. She no more than got her shirt off when her eyes began to fill with tears.

Barbara understood Mark was in a great deal of danger, and her mind filled with all the things that could go wrong. He could get trapped below deck while he was trying to help someone, he could get seriously burned himself, or maybe die out there.

She stood next to her bed with her hands over her mouth and tears running down her face. Barbara was frightened for him.

Barbara suddenly realized that this was not what Mark would want her to be doing. It was not what she knew she should be doing, either. She straightened up and wiped the tears from her face with her hands, and quickly put on her nurse's uniform. Barbara was now ready to do what she had to do. But before she left her bedroom, she took a moment to say a little prayer.

"Please watch over him, God, please," she pleaded softly.

Barbara came out of her bedroom to find Carol waiting in the kitchen. Barbara forced a smile to reassure her friend she was ready.

"You mind if I ride to the hospital with you?" Barbara asked.

"No, not at all."

Carol was trying to understand what Barbara must be going through. How could she possibly understand what was going on in Barbara's mind? She had to admire Barbara's courage, under the circumstances.

Together they went out and got into Carol's car. Carol backed out of the driveway and headed for Balboa Naval Hospital.

CHAPTER TWENTY

MARK AND RICHARD followed Father Owen as they worked their way down to the first platform level, the first level below the third deck. The smell of burning fuel was heavy in the air making it difficult to breathe. The closer they got to the boiler room the thicker the smoke seemed to become. They could hear a racket coming from down the passageway.

They rounded a corner and stepped through a watertight door into a machine room. The noise in the room was almost unbearable. There must have been a dozen sailors in the large room. Some were manning fire hoses while others seemed to be trying to cut through the steel bulkhead. Off to one side stood a Chief Petty Officer directing the work.

"What's going on here?" Mark yelled above the noise.

"We're trying to cut through this bulkhead to get into the boiler room. We have at least four men trapped in there," the chief said as he turned to see who was asking.

"What the hell are you doing down here?" the chief asked as he looked Mark over and saw he was a hospital corpsman.

"We're trying to get to the sickbay. There are corpsmen trapped in there," Mark explained.

"Well you're not going to get up there through here," the chief yelled.

"Yeah, I can see that. Is there any other way we might be able to get to them?"

"You might try the ladder on the other side of the storage room. I doubt you will be able to get into sickbay though. It's had some pretty severe damage. No telling what it's like up there."

The chief coughed. Between the smoke, the flumes and trying to make himself heard above all the noise, the chief's throat was getting raw.

"You need one of us to help you here when you get through the bulkhead?"

"To be honest with you, I don't think we are going to find anyone alive in there, but we have to make sure."

It was as if the chief was preparing himself for the worst. Yet, it was easy to tell from the way he was directing his men that he was hoping for the best.

"I understand. We are pretty sure there are a couple of sailors alive in the sickbay."

"You'd be better off trying to get to them than wasting your efforts here. Good luck to you. If you need some help, let me know. I'll send somebody up there once I get this place checked out."

"I hope we won't need your help, but thanks for the offer."

"Don't thank me. You will have all you can handle just getting there, and then you have to get in. I can't spare anyone right now, but we'll come up and help as soon as we can," the chief said.

"Thanks," Mark said with a nod of understanding.

The three of them turned and left the machine room with Father Owen leading the way to the ladder.

"Mark, there is no telling what we might run into up there," Father Owen said.

"Yeah, I know. We still have to find out if any of them are alive."

Mark reached out and put his hands on the railing of the ladder. He tipped his head back and looked up through the hatch above him, but he was unable to see anything except a small part of the bulkhead on the next level. He had no idea what to expect once he got up there. All he knew was that he could feel his heart beating inside his chest and the sweat running down his face and neck.

Slowly, Mark climbed the ladder, poked his head through the hatch and looked around. Down the passageway toward the sickbay, he could make out the faint glow of the red emergency light through the smoke. It was eerie to see the red glow in an otherwise dark, smoky passageway. It sent a chill through Mark's whole body.

"How's it look?" Richard asked.

Mark wanted to tell him it was scary as hell, but decided it probably would not be what Richard really wanted to hear.

"Can you see anything?" Father Owen asked.

"Not very much. It's pretty smoky up here. The red emergency light near the sickbay is working."

"Can you get down there?" Father Owen asked.

"I don't know yet. I'm going to try."

"You be careful," Father Owen warned.

Mark pulled himself up through the hatch and rolled onto the deck. Father Owen's last comment ran through Mark's mind. "I don't think you have to worry about that, I plan to be damn careful," Mark whispered to himself.

Mark sat down on the deck and leaned against the bulkhead. He took a few minutes to let his eyes adjust to the darkness. The passageway was like a long dark tunnel filled with fog, except the bluish gray fog burned his eyes and made his throat raw. In one direction was the glow of the red emergency light. In the other direction, the passageway went from a dingy gray to totally black. It seemed strange to Mark that the direction that led toward the bow of the ship and safety was pitch black and looked fearsome. Yet, in the direction that led to danger, there was a red light to guide him. He knew what he had to do.

"What's happening?" Richard asked.

Mark was startled by Richard's question.

"I'm just getting my bearings."

Mark rolled over onto his hands and knees. Slowly, he worked his way toward the glow of the light. At first he was not sure, but it seemed the closer he got to the sickbay, the warmer the decking under his hands became. If that was true, then it meant the fires were not out on the decks below.

"How you doing down there."

Mark turned and looked back toward the hatch. In the darkness he could just barely make out someone's head sticking up through the hatch. The sound of the voice told him it was Richard.

"I'm all right. I can see the red light now. I can't be more than about fifteen or twenty feet from the sickbay door."

"Can you see anything else?"

"No, not yet, but the deck seems to get warmer the closer I get to the sickbay."

Mark turned back and continued crawling toward the sickbay. In a matter of minutes he was at the sealed, watertight door to the sickbay. He wondered if it had been closed before or after the explosion.

Testing to see if the steel bulkhead was hot, he quickly touched the bulkhead near the door. It was not hot. He tested the watertight door in the same way. It was not hot either. If they had been hot, than the chances of any survivors would have been almost none.

Mark took hold of the hand wheel in the center of the door. His first attempt to turn the wheel was unsuccessful. He tried a second time, putting all he could into turning the hand wheel. Slowly, the wheel began to turn. He could tell the "dogs", which held the door closed and helped make it watertight, were opening. Once the "dogs" had let loose of the doorframe, the door should have opened easily, but it didn't. Mark pushed on the door as hard as he could, but it would not budge.

"Richard, I need some help. I got the door loose, but it won't open. I think the doorframe is twisted. There's a fire ax on the bulkhead near the ladder. We'll need it to pry the door open," Mark explained.

"I'll get it." Richard answered.

Mark sat down and leaned up against the bulkhead while he waited for Richard. He began to think about the situation. If anyone was still alive in the sickbay, they would need a way to get the injured out. It would be difficult to help an injured person through the small hatch. It was obvious that the only way out would be to go down past the hatch and through the dark, smoky passageway until they found a way to the upper decks.

Mark heard the sound of steel hitting against steel. He could hear Richard crawling along the deck with the fire ax. Suddenly, Richard appeared through the smoke.

"This watertight door seems to be twisted or jammed. If we can get the fire ax in next to the seal, we might be able to force it open," Mark explained as he stood up.

"Okay. Are you sure the door is twisted? Maybe there's something inside keeping it closed?"

"I'm not really sure, but I don't see that we have any choice but to force it."

"Well, let's do it then."

Richard moved over in front of the door. He worked the pick end of the fire ax in between the door and the doorframe. As soon as he had good contact, he looked over at Mark indicating he was ready. Mark took hold of the ax handle with Richard.

"Let's do it," Mark said.

Richard nodded. Together they applied pressure to the ax handle. The door creaked and gave way under the pressure. However, it moved only a few of inches. The seal was now broken and a light from inside the sickbay shone through the crack.

"Wait," Mark said. "I heard something move inside. I think there's something up against the door."

Richard removed the fire ax and looked through the crack. The air inside the sickbay showed no sign of smoke.

"It looks clear inside. I can't see much though."

"What's keeping the door from opening?"

"I can't tell. What little I can see looks like a bulldozer went through there. There might be a cabinet up against the door. Hey! There's someone in there and he's alive. I just saw a foot move," Richard exclaimed.

"We have to get in there. Father Owen, we are going to need your help," Mark called out.

"I'm coming."

Breathing was hard with the smoke-filled passageway. When Father Owen joined them, they gave him a minute to catch his breath while they explained what they were going to try to do.

As soon as Father Owen was ready, the three of them put their shoulders against the watertight door. On the count of three, they all pushed against the door. They could hear the sound of metal scraping against the deck as the door slowly opened.

Mark was the first one through the door. Stainless steel medical cabinets had been thrown around as if they were matchboxes. There was glass from the cabinet doors all over the room. Vials of medicine and medical supplies were scattered around, many of them damaged and unusable.

Mark immediately saw a hospital corpsman trapped under one of the stainless steel cabinets. He rushed to see if he could help him while Richard went to the aid of the hospital corpsman lying behind the treatment table.

Mark bent down beside the corpsman. He put his fingers on the neck of the corpsman to see if he was still alive. There was a pulse, a strong pulse. Mark was sure the cabinet had simply knocked him out. It may have also broken some of the corpsman's bones, but he couldn't be sure until the cabinet was set up.

"Father Owen help me get this cabinet off him." Mark said.

Mark and Father Owen took hold of the cabinet and set it upright. As Mark knelt back down beside the corpsman,

Father Owen went to the aid of another injured sailor who was lying up against the wall in the corner.

Mark rolled the corpsman over on his back. The corpsman was in a semi-conscious state and let out a groan as he was rolled over. Except for a few minor cuts, the corpsmen appeared to have no other injuries. Mark started to check him for broken bones when he came around.

"What the hell happened?" he asked as he looked up at Mark. "Who are you?"

"I'm Mark Walker. We don't know what happened. All we know is the ship has had several explosions on it. How do you feel?"

"I'm okay, I think," he said as he sat up and reached back to feel the size of the bump on his head.

"Mark, I think you better look at this fellow," Father Owen said.

"Richard, how are you doing?" Mark asked.

"I could use a little help," Richard replied.

"Do you think you could help him?" Mark asked the corpsman.

"Sure. By the way I'm Bill Barns."

Mark simply nodded, then moved across the room to help Father Owen. As he knelt down beside the injured sailor, the first thing Mark noticed was the bright red color of blood on the sailor's left leg. He immediately tore away the pant leg from the wound. It was clear that the sailor had a compound fracture of the femur. There was almost nothing that could be done for him here, except to try to stop the bleeding and immobilize the leg to prevent any further damage until they could get him to a hospital. It was going to take surgery to repair his leg. It was just as well that the sailor was not conscious.

Mark did what he could in an effort to see if any major blood vessels were damaged. With no major blood vessels apparently damaged, he applied a dressing to the wound to reduce the loss of blood and to keep the wound as clean as possible.

"That's about all I can do for him here," Mark said as he looked up at Father Owen.

"I'll stay with him. You see if anyone else needs help," Father Owen suggested.

"Keep him quiet if he comes around, and keep checking his pulse. Let me know if it gets weaker or irregular."

"I will," Father Owen replied.

Mark looked over at Richard and Bill. They were both leaning over the injured sailor on the floor.

"Need some help?" Mark asked.

"No. We have things under control here. This guy has some broken ribs, probably, and his arm is broken," Richard reported.

"Is there anyone else down here?" Mark asked of Bill.

"No. We were treating the guy in the corner for a sprained ankle when the first explosion occurred. Our doctor stepped out the door to see what was happening when a second explosion happened. I don't know what happened after that. I don't even know where our doctor is," Bill explained.

"We know where he is. The last time we saw him, he was being airlifted to a hospital.

"Where is the rest of the medical staff?" Richard asked.

"I don't know. I would guess most of them are around doing what they can to help."

"We'll need a couple of stretchers," Mark said.

"There are two stretchers in the wall cabinet over there," Bill said as he pointed to a cabinet in the bulkhead.

One of the large medical cabinets had fallen across in front of it. Mark and Bill got up and moved the medical cabinet out of the way. Mark opened the cabinet and found a cloth litter and a Stoke's stretcher.

"We can use the Stoke's stretcher for the guy with the broken leg. It will help keep his leg from moving around. We can use the litter for the other guy," Mark suggested.

Mark pulled the Stoke's stretcher out of the cabinet and placed it next to the sailor with the broken leg. As carefully as possible, Father Owen, Bill and Mark lifted the sailor up and put him into the basket-like stretcher. Mark tied him into it to prevent as much movement as possible.

As soon as Mark had his patient secure in the Stoke's stretcher, he checked on how Richard was doing with his patient. Richard and Bill had their patient on the litter and were ready to move.

"You ready?" Mark asked.

"Yeah," Richard replied.

"Are you okay, do you think you can help carry a stretcher?" Mark asked Bill.

"I can help," Bill replied.

"Father Owen, you ready?" Mark asked.

"Ready," he replied.

"Let's get out of here," Mark said.

Mark and Father Owen bent down to pick up the Stoke's stretcher and start for the door. Richard and Bill were right behind them with the litter.

Once out in the passageway, they started moving toward the bow of the ship. The passageway was dark, so they moved slowly in order to keep from running into something. They didn't dare fall or drop either one of the stretchers. If they did, they could cause more injuries to their patients. If that happened, they would not be able to see well enough in the darkness to help them.

"I can make out a light up ahead," Mark told the others.

"That should be the ladder to the mess hall. We should be able to get out that way," Bill said.

It was slow going from one level to another. After climbing several ladders, they finally reached the hangar deck. The hangar deck was well lit with lights all over the place. The smoke had pretty well cleared, although the smell of burned jet fuel still hung in the air. As they passed by the opening of one of the aircraft elevators, Mark noticed it was dark outside. He realized they had been below deck for much longer than he had thought. It was good to be up on the hangar deck where he could breathe air that was a little fresher.

As they approached the treatment area, several men came running over. They stepped in and took the stretchers. Mark saw Lt. Commander Wilson approaching.

"We were worried about you two. Where have you been?"

"We were down in sickbay. These guys are from there. I talked to a chief down in the machine shop. He said there were four men trapped in the boiler room. We should get some help down there."

"They're already out. They came up just ahead of you. They were asking if you had gotten back. They were getting ready to go back after you."

"How are things going?" Richard asked.

"All the fires are either out or under control. The ship is stable. They have called for an ocean tug to pull the ship into port tomorrow.

"It doesn't look like it will be long before we can be flown back to the hospital. They will be sending out replacements for us. Some of the guys have already started to get things packed up," Lt. Commander Wilson explained.

"That sounds good," Mark replied with a sigh of relief.

"Things have slowed down a lot here. Why don't you and Richard get a cup of coffee and relax a bit. There might be some sandwiches left, if you're hungry."

"Thanks, Doc."

Mark and Richard walked over to the coffee urn. Mark poured two cups of coffee while Richard picked up a couple of sandwiches. They sat down next to one of the airplanes and began to eat.

As Mark bit into his sandwich, he looked over at the activity near the aircraft elevator. Father Owen was kneeling down and talking to one of the injured sailors. He watched as the priest comforted the sailor. It was hard not to admire the man for his dedication to his calling.

Father Owen stood up as the sailor was lifted up and taken out onto the aircraft elevator. He turned and looked around as if trying to see if anyone else needed his help. He saw Mark watching him. A broad smile came over his face. He started walking toward Mark.

Mark returned the smile and held up his cup of coffee.

"I hope you will excuse me for saying so, but you look like hell," Mark said with a big grin.

"Well, you don't look so good either, but then considering everything, maybe we don't look so bad," Father Owen said as he sat down beside Mark.

"How's your arm?"

"It's funny, but it didn't really hurt that much until now."

"I think you better get it looked at before long."

"I will."

Just then Lt. Commander Wilson walked up to them.

"Okay guys, it's our turn to fly back to the hospital. By the way, Father Keller, your commanding officer said you are to fly back with us and get your arm looked after."

"Well, I guess we better get moving before they decide to leave without us," Mark said as he stood up and pitched his coffee cup into the trash can.

Father Owen and Richard looked at each other and smiled. Without any further delay, they stood up and followed Mark to the aircraft elevator for the ride to the flight deck and then the helicopter ride to Balboa Naval Hospital in San Diego.

CHAPTER TWENTY-ONE

THE ACTIVITIES IN THE emergency room of Balboa Naval Hospital could only be described as confusing and chaotic to the untrained eye. People seemed to be running everywhere, but seemed to be getting nowhere. Orders were being called out, but no one seemed to hear them. Gurneys were being wheeled around as if no one knew where they were going. But with closer observation, it was easy to see these people did know what they were doing, and they were doing it very well.

Gurneys and stretchers lined the hallways. Several doctors and nurses where quickly going from one patient to the next, evaluating each patient's condition and determining in what order each patients would be treated.

Inside the emergency room, every treatment table had a patient on it. The more seriously injured or burned patients were being stabilized and then sent to the operating rooms for surgery. Those who could be taken care of in the emergency room, were treated than transferred to wards where their treatment could be continued.

Carol and Barbara came into the emergency room and went directly to the locker room. They did not talk as they changed into surgical greens.

Carol was worried about Barbara. She was convinced Barbara would be distracted by the thought that the next injured sailor who was brought into the emergency room might be Mark. She was not sure Barbara could stand that kind of pressure.

Barbara had looked at the injured sailors as she passed them on her way to the locker room. With each dirty face and each burned sailor she saw, she thanked God it was not

Mark. She had never experienced such a rush of burned and injured patients before. Today was truly going to be a test of her endurance and her ability to cope.

She thought of Mark and of what he would want her to do. He always seemed so unshakable in an emergency, and he would want her to be the same way. If Mark were injured or even dead, he would not want her to stop and worry about him until everything had been done for the living. As she closed her locker, she said another little pray.

"Keep him safe for me and help me to help those I can," she said silently.

"You ready?" Carol asked.

"Yes, I'm ready."

Barbara was indeed ready. She had set her mind to be ready to face whatever it was she had to do.

Carol followed Barbara out onto the emergency room floor. Barbara looked around and saw all the treatment tables had at least four people working on each patient. She did not wait for someone to assign her a place to work or to assign her duties. She stepped right in and began to help the others at the very first table she came to.

The nurse was working on the sailor's neck, cleaning the wound and preparing it for a dressing. Barbara took a quick look at the sailor from head to toe. Noticing the sailor's pant leg was burned and soaked with blood, she immediately began cutting away the sailor's pants. As she pulled the pant leg way from his leg, she saw a rather long cut on the sailor's leg with a piece of steel embedded in it.

"I'm going to need a surgical kit here," she ordered.

One of the corpsman grabbed a surgical kit and began setting it up on a small table near Barbara. She began giving the corpsman instruction to clean the area and drape it so she could remove the piece of steel and suture the wound.

"Doctor, I have a patient with a piece of steel in his leg. Would you take a look at this, please?"

Barbara was used to getting doctor's orders before doing anything other than minor or emergency treatment. It was standard procedure to have wounds that required suturing to be seen by a doctor first.

"I don't have time to look at it now. Just pull the steel out and suture up the wound. Be careful. If he starts bleeding profusely, pinch off the bleeder and get him to surgery. That piece of steel may have cut an artery. Do what you have to do and get on with it," the doctor told her.

Barbara realized the doctor was not being rude, but was himself busy with a patient. She looked at the wound, then at the corpsman standing by to assist her. The corpsman just stood there looking at her, waiting for her to do something.

She bent down over the leg of the sailor and with a pair of forceps took hold of the piece of steel. Taking a deep breath, she pulled the piece of steel from the sailor's leg. Blood filled the space left by the removal of the steel, but did not seem to be profuse. She quickly, but carefully cleaned and sutured the wound.

After she finished suturing the wound, she checked with the others who had also been working on the sailor. The sailor had some severe burns to his face that would require surgery, possibly some skin grafts. All had been done for him that could be done here. It was time to transfer this sailor to surgery.

As soon as the sailor had been taken away, the team began preparing for another patient. Barbara pitched right in with the others. Within a few minutes there was another sailor on the table.

The afternoon continued like this, finish with one sailor and another one was ready to take his place. There seemed to be no end to the number of injured.

As evening began to approach, each corpsman and nurse was given a short break. When it was Barbara's turn, she was reluctant to leave, but she knew she would not be able to keep going if she didn't get something to eat. She went directly to the mess hall.

She poured herself a cup of strong black coffee and picked up a tray that had already been prepared with a complete meal. Barbara sat down at a table in the corner by herself. Before she started to eat, she closed her eyes and took a deep breath to help her relax and slow down.

As she began to eat, she thought of Mark. She wondered what he was doing, whether or not he was able to get a hot meal, or any kind of meal for that matter. She wondered where he was at this moment, and if he was safe.

When she finished her meal, she leaned back to relax for a couple of minutes before returning to the emergency room. She happened to glance at her hand. For just an instant, she thought she had lost her engagement ring, but gave a sigh of relief when she remembered she had taken it off and left it in her locker before reporting to work.

Barbara glanced at her watch. It was already early evening and she wondered if today could be an omen. She really didn't believe in such things, but today would have been the day they announced their engagement. In fact, they probably would have already announced it, if they could have had the party.

The sudden crash of a pan hitting the floor in the kitchen brought Barbara back to the reality of the moment. It was time for her to return to the emergency room. There was still much to be done there.

Barbara left her tray at the exit on her way out of the mess hall. There was no spring in her step tonight. It had been a long hard day and looked like it was not going to get any better, at least not for some time.

Barbara quickly relieved another nurse as soon as she arrived in the emergency room. She joined two hospital corpsmen at a treatment table where a new patient was just being transferred to the treatment table. One of the corpsmen began checking the sailor's vital signs.

Barbara began carefully removing the burn dressing that had been put on the sailor while he was still aboard the USS Ranger. The dressing had been put on with care, obviously in an effort to make sure the sailor arrived at the hospital in as good a condition as possible, and that often meant simply alive.

As she cut away the dressing, Barbara wondered if this might have been some of Mark's work. Right now, she had to think about the sailor lying in front of her. There was nothing she could do to find out if Mark was safe. The sailor needed her help, and he needed it now.

The sailor had a very severe chest wound along with second and third degree burns of his chest and neck. The sailor's breathing was labored and shallow. His pulse was slow and weak.

Barbara prepared the wound for stitches while the corpsman prepared the suture kit. The team at the table worked like a well rehearsed play, each one doing their part in their effort to save a life.

During the whole procedure, the sailor's vital signs remained fairly stable. Barbara brought the sailor's treatment chart up to date while the corpsmen moved the sailor from the treatment table back onto a gurney.

"He's ready to transfer to the burn ward," Barbara said as she slid the sailor's chart under his pillow.

She watched as the corpsmen rolled the gurney out of the treatment area and out into the hall. Barbara turned around and pulled the soiled rubber gloves from her hands and dropped them into a stainless steel bucket next to a medicine cabinet.

Taking only time for a deep breath, she began preparing the treatment area for the next patient. The two corpsmen who had been assisting her returned quickly. It did not take them long before they were ready for the next patient.

One of the corpsmen signaled to a corpsman standing next to the door that they were ready for another patient. He quickly turned and in a matter of seconds a gurney with another patient was wheeled through the door.

Barbara watched as the corpsmen transferred the patient from the gurney to the treatment table. She quickly read the tag pinned to the dressing on the sailor's right arm.

"Am I going to lose my arm?" the young sailor asked.

His face showed he was scared. Barbara looked at the sailor than back at the tag.

"I don't know. We will do all we can. Are you in pain?"

"No, not really. I'm more worried than in pain," he admitted.

"You just relax and let me take a look at this," Barbara said as she began carefully removing the dressing from his arm.

From the sailor's elbow, all the way to his wrist, there was almost no skin left. The wound had been cleaned very well and packed in sterile Vaseline gauze. The tissue had remained moist and there seemed to be almost no bleeding. There was apparently no damage to the underlying blood vessels. She checked his fingers and there seemed to be good circulation to his hand.

"How does it look? The corpsman on the ship said I had a good chance of keeping my arm," the sailor said.

Barbara wanted to ask the sailor to describe the corpsman to her in the hope she would learn Mark was all right, but quickly decided it would have to wait. Instead, she called the doctor to look at the wound.

The doctor turned around and looked down at the sailor. He quickly examined the sailor's arm. Looking up at the sailor, he said, "Son, I'm sending you to surgery. They will need to do a skin graft on your arm and some other tissue repairs."

"Am I going to lose it?" the young sailor asked fearful that once they got him to surgery they would cut off his arm.

"No. You're not going to lose your arm, although it will be a long time before you will get full use of it," the doctor explained.

"Moist wrap on the arm, doctor?" Barbara asked.

"Yes. Also start a new IV and get him down to surgery as soon as possible."

"Yes, sir."

The minutes stretched into hours. Just about everyone had lost track of time. It was somewhere around ten or ten-thirty that a young sailor was wheeled in and transferred to the treatment table where Barbara was working. The young sailor did not appear to be burned nearly as badly as some of the others they had treated.

One of the corpsman immediately took the patient's vital signs. Even Barbara could see he was having difficulty breathing. She put an oxygen mask over his face and turned it on high.

"His pulse is weak and irregular, BP is 60 over 30 and falling rapidly. We're losing him," the corpsman reported.

"Doctor, we're losing this one," Barbara called out.

"His heart stopped. I've got nothing," the corpsman said.

The tone of his voice showed the urgency of the moment. Barbara immediately began external cardiac massage while one of the corpsman quickly put a tube down the patient's throat and began "bagging" him. The corpsman that had been keeping a watch on the patient's vital signs continued to check and recheck the patient for some signs of life.

Barbara put all the strength and determination she could muster into saving the young sailor, but it was no use. There was nothing anyone could do, and they tried everything possible to save him. Barbara was reluctant to stop trying.

Finally, the doctor reached out and touched Barbara on the arm. She looked over at the doctor.

"It's over," he said quietly.

Barbara turned and looked down at the young sailor, then back at the doctor. She straightened up, looked back at the young sailor, then slowly pulled the surgical cover up over the sailor's face. As she did, tears came to her eyes. It was not easy for her to accept the death of such a young man.

"Are you all right?" the Doctor asked.

He asked her because he was really concerned for her. Everyone knew how difficult it was to lose a patient. Everyone was very tired, which tends to make emotions run even higher.

To Barbara, he seemed worried that she might not be able to continue, that she might not be able to do her job. But in point of fact, he did not want to lose such a good, dedicated nurse. He needed her skills.

"I'm all right," she answered as she pulled her shoulders back and stood tall. She was afraid he might dismiss her from the emergency room like Lt. Commander Wilson had wanted to do. She could not let that happen, she would not let it happen.

"Take a short break and get a cup of coffee," the doctor said.

"I'm all right, sir," she said strongly in an effort to show him that she could continue.

"Ensign, take a break and get a cup of coffee. It just might be a long night. That, Ensign, is an order."

"Yes, sir," she replied weakly.

At first she felt he was dismissing her. It took her a minute to realize that he was not dismissing her from the emergency room, but simply giving her a break, something she really needed.

"By the way, take your team with you," the doctor said with a smile. "They deserve a break, too. We'll take care of him."

"Yes, sir."

She looked back at the young sailor, then looked over at the two corpsmen who had been working with her. It was clear they needed a break as much as anyone.

"Take ten, and thanks."

The three of them went to the staff lounge. They all got a cup of coffee and sat down to relax. Barbara wondered if the doctor was right, was it really going to be a long night? Everything pointed to it.

She leaned back in the chair, tipped her head back and closed her eyes. It would not have been hard for her to go to sleep, but she did not have time to sleep, not now. She thought of Mark and wished he were here to work with her. She missed him and wondered if he was getting a break now and then, too.

It was strange, but Barbara suddenly realized she did not seem to be worried about Mark's safety any more. Somehow, she knew in her heart he was safe and that he was not taking stupid chances, but was working hard to keep a bunch of sailors alive. He was doing the same thing she was, he was just doing it in another place. Maybe, it was the dressings she was seeing on the wounded that reassured her that he was all right. Maybe it was simply the fact that the wounded were still coming in from the ship. She wasn't sure what it was, but she somehow knew he was okay.

Barbara took another sip of her coffee and looked across the room at the two corpsmen. They were sitting quietly on the sofa, sipping at their coffee. She glanced at her watch. It was getting pretty late. She was about to get up and tell the others it was time to return to work when the door opened. It was one of the staff doctors.

"Ensign Sanders, I would like you and your team to come out and help clean up the treatment areas and re-stock the treatment cabinets. It seems the last of the wounded are already here, and we are about finished taking care of them. I'm told some of the medical teams are on their way back."

"That is good news, sir," she replied. "We will be right out."

With their spirits lifted by the news, the three of them went back out to the emergency room treatment areas. Barbara began by taking inventory of the supplies and making a list of what was needed. The corpsmen began the job of cleaning the entire area as the last patient was wheeled out on a gurney to another ward. It took the three of them at least an hour to finish. As soon as they were done, Barbara dismissed the corpsmen to return to the barracks where they would remain "on call", just in case.

Barbara checked in with the oncoming duty nurse and the night staff of the emergency room and turned the duties over to them. She went to the locker room where she changed back into her uniform and carefully placed her engagement ring back on her hand.

Barbara was not sure if Mark would come to the emergency room or go directly to the barracks when he got back. She decided she would go sit in the staff lounge for a little while before going home.

She went into the staff lounge and poured herself another cup of coffee. She took a sip and then sat down in an overstuffed chair that looked very comfortable. She was feeling very satisfied with how she had handled things today and thought how proud Mark would be of her.

Barbara realized that the doctor had not said when they expected the flights to arrive that would be bringing in the medical teams. It could be a long wait. It could be an even longer wait if Mark went directly to the barracks. She reassured herself that to wait for awhile would do no harm. She wasn't in anyone's way, and she needed a few minutes to relax.

She took another sip of her coffee, set the cup down on the end table and leaned back in the chair. Barbara was glad she did not have to work tomorrow and that Mark was off, too. Maybe, they could spend the day just relaxing. Maybe even take a nap together, she thought with a little smile.

The pleasant thoughts of spending the day with Mark seemed to help relieve some of the tension and her tired muscles relaxed. It wasn't long before she had fallen asleep in the large overstuffed chair.

CHAPTER TWENTY-TWO

MARK SETTLED BACK into the seat as the helicopter lifted off the deck of the carrier. Tipping his head back and closing his eyes, he wondered what Barbara was doing at this very minute. He had not heard anything. With the large number of injured they were sending to shore based hospitals, he was sure she had been called up to help.

"Mark, I'm sorry to disturb you, but I think I have a problem."

Mark opened his eyes and looked at Father Owen. He could see that he was in pain.

"What's the problem, Father? Is it your arm?"

"Yes. My fingers tingle, like they are going to sleep."

Mark moved over next to Father Owen. He had Father Owen move his fingers as he checked his circulation. Father Owen's arm appeared to have swollen which caused the dressing to become so tight that it was cutting off some of the circulation. Mark started removing the dressing. As he removed the dressing, he noticed that it was almost completely saturated with blood.

"It looks like you have re-opened the wound and have some swelling. It will require some sutures to close it up. I'll put a new dressing on it for now, but when we get to the hospital I'll have it looked at and suture it closed."

"I would appreciate that."

Mark opened a medical kit and found a clean dressing. He redressed the wound and wrapped it with an elastic bandage to help keep the bleeding to a minimum, and to allow for the swelling.

"Thank you. That feels much better," Father Owen said wiggling his fingers.

"You're welcome."

Mark put away the rest of the medical kit and sat back in his seat. He once again closed his eyes, but it was hard for him not to open them every once in a while to check on Father Owen. Father Owen had also leaned back in his seat and had closed his eyes.

Time seemed to pass rather slowly. The noise of the helicopter did not make it any easier to rest. It seemed to take longer to get back to the base than it had to get out to the carrier.

As the helicopter approached the coast, Mark could see the lights up and down the coast for miles. It was almost like a line of lights had been set out to mark the boundaries between the ocean and the land. As the lights grew brighter, he was able to make out a few of the landmarks.

The pilot set the helicopter down with great care, as if he was carrying a load of eggs. Everyone got off the helicopter and began unloading the supplies. Father Owen reached for a box of medical supplies.

"Hold it right there, Father. You are not going to carry anything more. You have already done enough damage to your arm. You are going right to the emergency room and have your arm looked after," Mark insisted.

"Mark, you go ahead and take him. We'll get the rest of the stuff," Richard suggested.

"Thanks, Richard. Come with me, sir," Mark said as he pointed the way toward the emergency room.

Mark led Father Owen directly to the emergency room and a treatment table. One of the corpsman on duty came over to the treatment table to see who these two men were.

"Oh, hi, Mark. I didn't recognize you. You look like hell. Are you all right?"

Mark kind of smiled. With all the soot, dirt and sweat on him, not to mention the blood, he doubted his own mother would know him.

"Yeah, I'm fine. Nothing a shower, a change of clothes, and some rest won't take care of. This is Father Owen Keller from the USS Ranger. I would like a doctor to take a look at his arm. I think it will need some stitches."

"Hi. Sorry about the comment, Father," the corpsman said.

"No problem. I guess we do look like we spent a little time in hell," Father Owen replied with a grin.

Mark filled the corpsman in on the injury Father Owen had to his arm. He also briefed him on the treatment that had been done and what probable treatment would be needed.

"I'll get a doctor right away."

Mark watched as the corpsman went to the nurse's station and paged the duty doctor. Mark sat down on a stool next to the treatment table. He leaned over and put his head in his hands.

"You look tired, and I might add, a little worried. Is there a problem with my arm you're not telling me about?" Father Owen asked.

"No. I think a few stitches, a clean dressing and a lot of rest, and you'll be fine. I was just thinking about someone."

"Your wife, or girl friend, maybe?"

"My girl friend, I guess."

"What do you mean, 'you guess'? Don't you know?"

"We were supposed to have had a party at her house tonight to announce our engagement. As you well know, I didn't keep my date."

Father Owen noticed a nurse coming out of a room off to the right of the nurse's station. She was stopped by a corpsman that pointed in his direction. The nurse saw Father Owen looking at her. As she approached from behind Mark, she put her finger over her lips to signal Father Owen not to say anything.

"Would this girlfriend of yours happen to be a nurse?" Father Owen asked.

Mark was looking down at the floor. He looked up at Father Owen. He wondered how he knew, but figured it was just a lucky guess. After all he did work in a hospital where you would expect to find a lot of nurses.

"Yes. She's a Navy nurse."

"Well then what's the problem? I'm sure she, of all people, would understand why you didn't keep your date."

"I do understand," Barbara said softly as she came up behind him.

Mark jumped up off the stool and turned around. He just stood there looking at her. It was so good to see her that he didn't know just what to do. He wanted to throw his arms around her and hold on to her.

"Would you like a cup of coffee sailor?" she asked with a big grin.

It was difficult for her not to just throw her arms around him and kiss him. Even though she had missed him and worried about him, she was still aware of where she was, in the emergency room with several corpsmen and another nurse watching them.

"I see the doctor coming. Why don't you two find a place to have that coffee," Father Owen suggested.

Mark looked over toward the nurse's station. He saw a doctor getting briefed on the condition of Father Owen's arm.

"I'll be back in a few minutes to see how things are going."

"Okay, but take your time."

Barbara walked over to the staff lounge with Mark close behind her. Mark closed the door behind them. As she turned around, she threw her arms around him and planted a kiss on his lips he could feel all the way to his toes. He wrapped his arms around her and held her tightly against him. Their kiss was long, deep and passionate. Her body felt so good pressed tightly against him that he did not want to ever let go of her.

She leaned back a little, just to look at him. It was hard for her to even see him as her eyes were filled with tears of joy.

He smiled down at her and then reached out to wipe a smudge of soot off the end of her nose.

"You look real cute with soot on your nose."

A tear slowly rolled down her cheek. She was so happy that he was safe with her that she did not care about the soot.

"I need to get cleaned up," he said in a whisper.

"Are you hungry?"

"Yes."

"We can stop at the barracks so you can get some clean clothes. You can clean up at my place while I fix you something to eat," she suggested.

Barbara had him back and did not want him out of her sight. She knew it was late and he was tired, but she needed to be with him, all night.

"Sounds good to me. I need to see how Father Owen is doing before we leave."

She smiled up at him as she reluctantly let go of him and stepped back. Mark noticed he had gotten the front of her uniform dirty.

"I'm sorry about that," he said as he pointed at the smudges of dirt and soot on the front of her white uniform.

"I'm not. I'm just glad your back."

Mark reached up and touched her cheek. She reached up and put her hand over his as he leaned forward and kissed her lightly on the lips. After their kiss, he held her for a minute before he let go of her.

He left the staff lounge and went out to the treatment table where Father Owen was lying. The duty nurse had just finished putting a clean dressing on Father Owen's arm.

"How you doing?" Mark asked.

"I'm fine. They are going to admit me for the night. I've been told the nurse on the ward will fix up this dressing so I can take a shower before I go to bed. A shower sounds real good right about now. What about you?"

"I'm going to get a shower, something to eat and some sleep, too. I'll stop in tomorrow and see you."

"Okay. Mark?"

"Yeah."

"She's a nice looking girl. I can tell she thinks a lot of you. Treat her well."

"I will," Mark replied with a smile.

"See you tomorrow," Father Owen said as he put out his hand to Mark.

Mark shook his hand and nodded, then turned and started for the door where Barbara was waiting for him. They went out into the parking lot side by side.

"I forgot. I don't have my car here. I came with Carol."

"We can get mine. It's at the barracks."

They walked to the men's barracks hand in hand. Barbara waited beside Mark's car as he went inside for a change of clothes and his shaving kit.

When Mark returned, he unsnapped the tonneau cover and tucked it down behind the seats. He opened the door on the driver's side and held it for Barbara.

"Would you mind driving?" Mark asked holding out the keys.

"No," she replied as she took the keys from him.

Barbara got in the car and waited for him to get in. Once he was seated, she leaned toward him. He met her halfway and they kissed. After a soft gentle kiss, she started the car and drove out the main gate and down onto the freeway.

Mark tipped his head back against the headrest. The steady purr of the car's engine and the fact he was so tired helped him to fall asleep quickly.

BARBARA PULLED INTO the driveway of her home and shut off the engine. She looked over at Mark. He was still sleeping. She did not really want to wake him, but she did not think it was a good idea for him to sleep in the car all night. She reached over and touched him lightly on the shoulder.

"We're here," she whispered softly.

He opened his eyes and looked around. He then looked at her and smiled.

"I'm sorry."

"That's okay. A warm shower and something to eat will make you feel better."

After Mark snapped down the tonneau cover, he followed Barbara to the door. He took her keys, unlocked the door, and then followed her into the house, shutting and locking the door behind them.

"You can take a shower in my bathroom, if you would like. I'll fix you something to eat."

Mark reached over and gave her a kiss on the cheek, then went to her bedroom. He passed through her bedroom and went directly into the bathroom. He stripped out of his dirty clothes and put them into his ditty bag. He turned on the shower and stepped in.

The warm water flowing over him felt good. He scrubbed the dirt and the soot off his body. After he was clean, he just stood there and let the warm water run over him.

As soon as Barbara got Mark's dinner started, she went into the extra bathroom and washed the soot off her face. She went to her bedroom and removed her soiled uniform, throwing it into the hamper. She could hear the shower running in the bathroom. She thought about going in and taking a shower with him. Maybe, asking him if he would like her to wash his back for him. Instead, she decided to let him have the time to relax and refresh himself. She opened the door, reached around the door and took her beach robe off the hook, then closed the door and laid the robe on the bed while she took off the rest of her clothes. Slipping into her robe, she tied it closed and left the bedroom to go back to the kitchen.

The meal she had prepared for Mark was ready when Mark came into the kitchen. She turned to look at him as he approached her. He was wearing just a pair of slacks, no shoes or shirt.

"Can I get service here without shoes, sox or a shirt?"

"You can get service here anytime, in anything, or in nothing at all," she grinned.

Mark walked up to her. He reached out, put his hands on her waist and looked into her eyes. She reached up and put her hands on his shoulders.

"I'm sorry the party had to be called off."

"That's all right. We can have the party tomorrow night."

He looked over her shoulder at the pan on the stove. He had not had a hot meal all day. The little they had to eat on the carrier had not been enough and he was hungry.

"What's cooking?"

"Oh, I'm sorry. Sit down and I'll get you a plate. What would you like to drink?"

"Could I have a glass of milk?"

"Sure."

Barbara poured him a large glass of milk and set it on the table in front of him. She then went to the stove and served up a plate of stew she had made from leftover pot roast. It was much like the stew his mother used to make and the kind of stew she liked very much.

"This is good," he said after his first bite.

"I'm glad you like it. Eat up, there's plenty."

"Aren't you going to eat?"

"I'm not hungry. We got good hot meals while we were on duty."

She sat next to him and watched him eat. Occasionally he would put a little piece of meat or a carrot on his fork and offer it to her. She would take it, mostly to please him.

When he was finished, she began clearing the table and putting things away.

Mark stood up, took the milk over to the refrigerator and put it away, then handed Barbara his plate. As she put the plate in the dishwasher, he sensed she was a little nervous. He wanted to stay the night with her, but not unless she wanted him to stay.

Mark decided he would give her the chance to back out, hopefully, without hurting her feelings. He went up behind her and wrapped his arms around her. Mark leaned down and kissed her on the neck. She reached back, putting a hand behind his head and putting her other hand over his hands.

"Would you be more comfortable if I went back to the base to sleep?" he asked softly.

He could feel a slight change in the tension of her body. The only real problem he had at the moment was to figure out what the change meant. Did she want him to stay, or not?

Barbara let go of him and turned around in his arms to face him. She looked up at him, her hands on his bare chest.

"Please stay with me," she said softly.

He pulled her up against him, leaned down and kissed her. She wrapped her arms around his neck and pressed her body against him. It was a long passionate kiss, full of their love for each other.

Mark let go of her, put his arm around behind her and walked with her to the bedroom.

"I'll be back in a few minutes," she said as she took her arm from around him. "I need a shower, too."

Mark smiled at her and took his arm from behind her. He watched her as she went into the bathroom. As soon as the door shut, he moved to the side of the bed and took off his pants and shorts and crawled under the covers. After pulling the covers up to his waist, he laid back on the large pillow. The last sound he heard before he fell asleep was the water running in the bathroom shower.

Barbara stepped into the shower. The warm water running over her body felt good. The smooth lather of the soap felt good against her skin. She rinsed off, stepped out of the shower and dried herself off. She no longer had any reservations about being in bed with Mark. She wanted him to hold her, touch her and make love to her.

As she slipped back into her robe, she remembered how natural it had felt for her to be naked with him. She went into the bedroom where she found him asleep. He looked so peaceful. It struck her as a little strange, but she felt he belonged in her bed. It would not seem right if he was not there.

Moving around to the side of the bed, she untied the belt of her robe. She opened her robe, slid it off her shoulders and let it fall to the floor. She stood there in the darkness, completely naked as she looked at him. Reaching down, she lifted the covers and crawled in beside him, then pulled the covers up as she rolled over against him.

"You feel good," Mark said in a whisper.

"I'm sorry. I didn't mean to wake you."

"I don't mind."

Mark slipped his arms around her and pulled her up against his side. She folded a leg across him as she let her hand brush lightly over his chest. She noticed a sparkle of light reflect off her engagement ring as she slid her hand over his chest. She smiled as a feeling of contentment filled her.

"I love you," he whispered.

"I love you, too," she sighed.

Wrapped in each other's arms, they fell into a deep peaceful sleep. But, before Barbara fell asleep, she thought of them. She knew that everything was going to be all right and that they would be very happy growing old together.